# WHEN THE FIRST CONKER FALLS

S.L.DAVIS

For Tim, Bobby and Topper, and all who grew up in the 1960s, or love someone that did.

"For what happens to the children of man and what happens to the beasts is the same; as one dies, so dies the other. They all have the same breath, and man has no advantage over the beasts, for all is vanity. All go to one place. All are from the dust, and to dust all return. Who knows whether the spirit of man goes upward and the spirit of the beast goes down into the earth?"

*Ecclesiastes 3:18-21*

"We can judge the heart of a man by his treatment of animals."

*Immanuel Kant*

# PROLOGUE

## November 1952

Glassy splinters of pain knifed her stomach as she stumbled over tree roots she couldn't see. Fog tricked her young eyes, blanking the beam of the torch, hiding all that was familiar.

She stopped, one hand against the rough bark of a tree, the other on her hip. Arching her back she then slumped forwards, but it didn't help. The pain shot to her spine, and for a few seconds, exploded into agony.

Gulping damp white air, she released it in short puffs that warmed her face, her discomfort subsiding. But she couldn't rest for long. Time was running out. *Hold on little one. Just a few more minutes. Let me get to the barn.*

She staggered on; one hand fisted in the small of her back. She'd meant to call her sister from the phone box, but things had happened too fast. She'd have the baby alone and tell Joyce afterwards – there was nothing else she could do.

Joyce had tried to explain what would happen when the baby came. In a fervent whisper, she'd told of waters breaking, afterbirths and umbilical cords. It's all perfectly natural, her sister had assured her. But it hadn't sounded that way.

She'd collected together the things Joyce told her she'd need and hidden them in the barn. No one would find them — rarely visited in winter, the old place stood alone at the side of the woods.

Panting, she reached the wooden door, shining the torch on the rusted lever latch. Tugging it open she stepped inside, breathing in the welcoming scent of summer hay. *I'm here. It'll be ok.*

Pulling one of the bales apart she scattered hay in the far corner, and fetching the hidden cushion and blanket, made a makeshift bed. She got the towels, bottle of water and scissors, placing them by her side. With her swollen stomach she knelt awkwardly, then lay on her back with a small grunt; the wavering beam of the torch a reassuring warm circle in the darkness.

As the pains grew and rippled her body, she gripped the torch, biting down on the rubber to muffle her cries. Tendrils of hair, beaded with fog and perspiration, lay around her face and amongst the hay like knotty black cotton.

In-between pushes, she counted the cobwebs hanging from the rafters above; delicate silver nets shivering silently in drafts from unseen cracks. But when she reached number eighteen, the light from the torch dimmed, pushing the webs back with the shadows. She sucked at her lips and reached for a drink of water. *I'll get through this. The baby will be ok. Please God.*

The contractions came fast and hard now; heavy punches to her groin, each one leaving her panting for breath. The wind picked up outside, creaking the barn timbers and trees, muffling the sound of her moans. Eventually the birth of her baby brought relief and she pulled it to her chest, the child's face screwed and puckered, sticky with blood. She kissed it gently and smiled to herself in the semi-darkness. *Hello. I'm so sorry I can't keep you. But I know you'll be just fine. I love you.*

Reaching for the cold hardness of the scissors, she cut the umbilical cord and tied a knot before laying back, the baby against the warmth of her breast. A boy. She wondered what his new parents would call him.

She'd started to doze when another shooting pain ripped through her body, making her cry out. Again, she had to push, with no time to wonder what was happening. The beam of the torch blinked and gave up; the second baby arriving with a whimper in the darkness. Half crying, half laughing, she brought this baby to the first, kissing them both. She couldn't believe it. Not for one moment had she thought there might be two.

Why hadn't she put new batteries in the torch? She cut the umbilical cord carefully by touch and tied a knot. Rocking her babies gently back and forth in the pitch black, she savoured the warmth of their skin; this precious time alone with them.

While both babies slept, she wrapped each in a blanket. She lay one down in the corner, scooping hay around it. 'Stay warm little one,' she whispered, 'I won't be long.' She'd take one baby with her to phone her sister, then come back for the other. She couldn't risk carrying both at once in the dark.

With the fog dispersed by the wind and the moon hanging low, she quickly got back to the village. She gave her sister the pre-arranged three rings from the phone box and within ten minutes, Joyce was there, jumping out of her old car, running towards her and the baby.

'Kathy! You've already had it! Are you alright?' She hugged her sister and the baby at the same time, her eyes glistening. 'You are alright, aren't you?' Joyce frowned with concern. 'Did the baby come suddenly?'

'Yes, but – ' Kathy hesitated, doubt creeping in. Would her sister's friend want twins?

'What's wrong? Christ Kathy, what is it?'

'There's two. Two babies.' Joyce took a step back, swaying slightly. She caught her sister's arms.

'Oh my god! Is the other one alright?' The baby Kathy held began to whimper.

'Take this one,' said Kathy, holding the bundle out to her sister. 'The other baby is fine; I just couldn't carry both at once. I'll go back and get it now.'

'Wait! I'll come with you.'

'No, you stay here with this one and keep warm in the car. I'll be quicker on my own.'

'Ok, but be careful! And don't worry, Elsie and Reg will want both of them. They'll love them as their own.'

'I know,' Kathy called over her shoulder, relieved.

Running back the way she'd come, she went as fast as she could, only stopping once to catch her breath. It was unnaturally quiet through the woods and fields now, no hooting owls or screaming vixens, no wind. She stopped at the barn door, breathing heavily. Stepping inside, she reached for the upright beams, making her way to the far corner. She knelt in the hay, her chest tightening as she felt around her in ever increasing circles. *Where are you?* She sobbed as she scrabbled everywhere with shaking hands, bitter dust flying in her mouth, irritating her eyes. Feeling faint as the realisation came, bile rose in her throat. Dropping her head to her knees, she screamed; a raw, desolate wail that seared the night.

Her baby had gone.

# Chapter 1

## October 1966

The bell had gone a few minutes earlier, but Jonesey always made the class wait before letting them go home. Billy thought the man enjoyed these brief moments of power, although he wasn't too bad, as teachers go. Once, he'd patiently explained long-division to Billy, as if he was the only boy in the class. When it had finally clicked, Jonesey had patted him on the back. 'That's a boy,' he'd said, and smiled. Billy felt proud he'd learned something and that old Jonesey was pleased. Although he couldn't imagine when or why he'd ever need to use any of it.

'Get off home then,' said Jonesy, clearing his desk. The class streamed out into the autumn sunshine, scattering and re-grouping for their journeys home. Billy, alone as usual, headed for Budds Lane. He briefly wondered what was for tea as he kicked the thin layer of fallen leaves, looking for conkers. He soon spotted one, a rich mahogany brown, glossy as his sister's hair. He huffed on it, softly rubbing it on his shorts, checking it was strong and perfect before slipping it into his pocket.

Several others joined the first in the same way, until his pocket bulged at the seams. He thought about getting them ready for the fights that would take place next week, piercing and stringing the burnished copper balls after they'd been soaked in vinegar and gently baked in the oven to toughen up. He wished it was as easy to toughen himself up.

He reached his favourite tree, an old horse chestnut, strong and easy to climb. He often hid in the V of the upper branches, but today he noticed large black ants scurrying on the bark. There were hundreds of them. He sighed and with his back to the trunk, slid down until he sat on the thick moss between the warped, snarled roots. Pulling out and loading his imaginary gun, he shot big chief Tomahawk right between the eyes.

'Well, just looky who we 'ave here.'

Billy squinted into the sun to see three older boys in front of him. The biggest one who'd spoken had some grubby rope in his pocket, one end dangling at his knee. An involuntary shiver dropped down Billy's spine, his blood coursing loudly in his ears.

'What's yer name?' spat the bigger boy.

'B-B-Billy.'

'Wanna see this, B-B-Billy boy?' The two other boys sniggered. Billy could feel his face burning.

'C'mon, B-B-Billy. Look at what I've got here,' said the boy, as he pushed his closed hands into Billy's face.

'Show 'im, Joe!' shouted one of the boys behind.

Joe opened his hands slightly, enough that Billy could see he held a massive stag beetle; the biggest he'd ever seen. But Billy wasn't scared of the beetle, only of Joe. Or what he might do.

'Nice, ain't he?' said Joe. Billy noticed a gap where one of his front teeth should have been.

'Y-Y-Yeah. He's n-n-nice.' stuttered Billy as the others sniggered again.

'T-T- Trouble gettin' your words out, B-B-Billy?' mocked Joe, smirking.

Looking for an escape route, Billy glanced furtively from left to right, but his eyes gave him away. Joe and the two other boys moved forward, surrounding him, backing him into the tree. His fringe damp with sweat, he wished for the hundredth time he didn't stutter. And that he had a big brother.

Joe stepped back and Billy's heart slowed a little. But he saw something dark cloud Joe's eyes and his heart picked up pace again.

'What's up, B-B-Billy boy? Don't you want to watch me pull its legs off?'

'No!' It came out loud and clear and surprised even him. Now, he felt something much stronger than fear. Anger. Raging red anger that this bully could do what he wanted to a helpless living thing. No matter it was a stag beetle. It had as much right to life as anything else. That this boy could torment, maim or kill, just because he chose to, made Billy's fury explode. He barged into Joe and knocked the stag beetle out of his hand, which flew away out of harm's reach. Taking advantage of the other boys' surprise, Billy legged it, his rucksack banging furiously against his spine, his tie flying over his shoulder, his legs pumping like pistons.

He'd nearly reached the end of Budds Lane before Joe and the two boys even began to give chase. As Billy neared the monkey puzzle tree on the corner, he slowed and risked a quick look over his shoulder. There was no one behind him, but he shuddered to an abrupt halt and fell to the ground. He'd slammed into another boy.

'Whoa! Watch where you're going!' shouted the boy as he reached down to help Billy up.

Knees grazed and stinging, Billy's anger dissipated. He felt like crying. 'S-S-S-' he stammered.

The other boy waited.

'S-Sorry.' Billy finally managed to get out.

A guttural yell came from down the road. 'Wait there you little shit!' Joe and one of his henchmen emerged from Budds lane, running in their direction. The other boy grabbed Billy's arm. 'Come on, quick!' he hissed. Slightly bigger and older than Billy, he yanked him towards Jackdaw Woods. As they sprinted, they became surrounded by beech, birch and oak trees. They'd increased their lead, but the bigger boy continued to half-pull, half-shove Billy down a narrow track through the dry, russet bracken. They stumbled over the uneven ground but were now out of sight of their pursuers, hidden by gorse and saplings as the track widened to a clearing in the trees.

On the other side, a black rusty Austin A30 crouched, its wheels long gone, its windows broken, tiny squares of shattered glass still lying amongst the heather.

The seats were just a tangle of rusted springs with the odd withered scrap of maroon leather caught between them. Its two doors gaped wide like broken wings, and the only comfortable spot was on the passenger seat where the springs were still covered by a wad of horsehair matting. The bigger boy glanced around the clearing, but Billy could see no sign of Joe or the others. It seemed they'd shaken them off. The other boy climbed on the passenger seat of the old car. Billy joined him, panting and looking down at his knees whilst the bigger boy kept a look-out.

'So, what was that about then?' he asked Billy, concern in his voice. Billy was close to crying and his knees were covered in blood.

'H-H-He had a beetle and w-was going to p-pull its legs off. Th-That's cruel. I knocked it out of his h-hand and ran.'

'Was the beetle ok?'

'Yeah. It f-flew off.'

The older boy nodded imperceptibly but Billy saw and felt his approval. His breathing began to slow and he wiped his eyes with his arm. He was feeling better.

'You were brave,' said the boy.

Pride warmed Billy's insides like a mug of chicken soup. This boy had saved him. His opinion mattered.

'What's your n-name?' asked Billy.

'Tom.'

'I'm Billy.'

They smiled at one another.

'You like animals… creatures,' stated Tom.

'Yeah. S-some are better than people. M-most animals are nice.' He hesitated, looking at the bigger boy beside him. 'M-most people aren't.'

Tom grinned at him. 'Yeah, I know what you mean. Do you want to make a pact with me?'

Billy didn't know what a pact was, but he nodded anyway. He thought he'd do anything with this boy.

'You and me, we'll save animals from bad people. Like Batman and Robin rescue people, we'll do it for animals.'

'Y-Yeah, that will be great! We'll be like brothers – s-saving animals from nasty people.'

'Blood brothers,' said Tom. Taking out his penknife he made a nick in his palm. He took Billy's hand and made a nick in his, pressing the two palms together, cut to cut.

'B-Blood brothers,' repeated Billy, smiling as he heard Tom's stomach rumble.

'I'm starving,' said Tom, 'C'mon. It's teatime.'

The two boys jumped from the old Austin and started back across the clearing. Three Jackdaws flew from the wood opposite cawing jauntily and Tom stopped, scouring the trunks and shadows. Billy froze beside him as a figure emerged from the woods.

It was Joe.

* * *

Billy slammed into the ground, a grunt escaping his thudding chest, heather poking his nose and pricking his eyes. He lifted his head to take a breath.

'Keep down,' hissed Tom who was lying beside him, his head on his hands, staring at Joe. Luckily, they were a fair distance from where Joe had come out of the woods, and Billy could see he wasn't looking in their direction. Tom had pulled him to the ground just in time. There was scant cover, but the bushy mounds of purple and the odd fallen tree trunk concealed them for now. Feeling a sneeze coming on, Billy clamped his hand over his nose and squeezed his eyes and mouth shut to suppress it.

'We should face him,' said Tom, 'not be cowards hiding away.'

'No point f-fighting if we don't h-h-have to,' replied Billy, rubbing his nose with the back of his hand. He was relieved he hadn't made a noise and that Joe hadn't seen them. He wasn't worried about being a coward; he just wanted to live. Without getting hurt.

The two boys lay low and still, their eyes fixed on Joe. He skirted around the clearing with a hand above his eyes, shielding them from the bright rays of the sun, low in the sky.

'Joe!' The shout came from another boy who'd just run from the woods. 'Your Ma wants yer!'

Joe took a final look around, then followed the other boy back into the trees.

Billy let out a sigh so long it seemed he'd been holding his breath for hours. 'B-b-blimey, that was close.' He looked at his new friend beside him. Tom's jaw muscles were working; his face pale.

'I should've stood up to him; not hidden like a coward. I swear I'll never hide from him again,' said Tom. 'C'mon.'

They headed home in silence, Tom's eyes on the ground, kicking stones as he walked, Billy trying desperately to think of something to say. He glanced sideways at Tom.

'You d-did the b-best thing. The other two boys h-he was with b-before, they could've been h-hiding in the woods. You're not a coward Tom, you h-helped me.'

Tom looked at Billy's earnest face and smiled. 'Yeah. Maybe.' He shook his shoulders to loosen them up. 'C'mon, I'm really hungry now. Race you to the monkey puzzle tree.'

They ran, the taller boy easily taking the lead. But as they turned the corner and the tree was in sight, Tom slowed and they reached it together. Leaning on the rough trunk they panted heavily. Then remembering the conkers he'd collected earlier; Billy patted his pockets.

'Oh n-no!' he wailed.

'What's up?'

'I've l-lost most of my c-conkers!' Billy pulled out the remaining conkers from his pockets. He held three in each hand.

'But the ones you've got look great,' said Tom. 'They'll all be champs. I reckon you've only lost the losers.'

'Y-yeah.' Billy looked up at him and grinned. He put the conkers back in his pockets.

'All ch-champs. Bound to be.'

# Chapter 2

## September 1967

The rusty ratchet cry of a pheasant jerked through the warm air as Tom headed towards the old Nissen huts to meet Billy. Nature had rapidly taken hold of the huts and with their peeling green paint, clinging ivy and flaking rust, they fitted unobtrusively into the pine woods as if they'd always been. The ground, spongy with old pine needles and strewn with scraggy bits of torn corrugated iron, gave up a sweet scent so familiar Tom hardly noticed it.

Interesting things hid under the old iron. Slow-worms and field mice, sometimes shrews; tiny and easily missed. Grass snakes were the most coveted – as pets for a week or two before being released again, or as a surprise for Mrs Taylor in her desk at school. She was one of the nicer teachers, but her horrified reaction to a grass snake was always so funny. The class took advantage of course, continuing the bedlam for as long as they could, pretending to try and catch the bewildered snake but in reality, prolonging its freedom. It could delay algebra for a good half an hour.

Tom walked through Jackdaw Woods kicking crisp burnished leaves in hues of gold and orange; beauty that lay over rutted darkness beneath.

It wasn't Billy that Tom saw first, but Wilbur; who always appeared from nowhere, like Doctor Who's TARDIS. Tom wondered, not for the first time, exactly how he did it.

'Hello, Tom lad,' said Wilbur.

'Hi Wilbur,' said Tom, 'you ok?' He was the only adult Tom ever addressed by his first name. But thinking about it, he realised he didn't know his surname, anyway.

'Aye. I'm alright lad, but I know a fox that ain't. Just buried him at the graves.'

Tom knew where he meant, but thought only kids used it, not grown-ups like Wilbur. The graves were at a small clearing in the wood, not far from where they were now. Surrounded by fallen trees and banks of brambles, they were tucked away, only visited by children burying their pets. A few rough wooden crosses, fashioned from sticks tied with old string, or inexpertly nailed, stood haphazardly in the ground between ferns and tree stumps. Some graves were only marked by a large stone or upended log, some by nothing.

Tom had buried Tiz there last winter. The ground had been so hard he'd borrowed his dad's trowel but it still took him ages to dig a hole big enough for the small rabbit, chopping through musty soil veined with tree roots. It'd been dusk when he'd finished and he was late for tea, which was good because his grief had dulled his appetite.

Wilbur must have dug a big hole for a fox. Tom looked at the man's strong calloused hands, the fingers ingrained with dirt – and decided it probably hadn't taken him too long.

'How did he die?' asked Tom.

Wilbur seemed not to hear him. They walked on together for some way before he replied.

'Run over by the looks of it, at the side of the road just past Watties. Maybe he was after food from the bins.'

Tom glanced at the man who rarely put so many words together at once. His dark eyes glistened.

'Died in my arms,' Wilbur said, so quietly that Tom strained to hear.

After a while Tom broke the silence. 'Have you done him a cross?'

Wilbur raised his arm and wiped his nose across his coat sleeve, adding to the lines of snot already there, glinting in the light like snail trails. 'Not yet. But I will. No reason why he shouldn't have one.'

'I'll make it if you like,' said Tom.

The man came to a stop and looked at the boy beside him. 'You'd make it for me?'

'Yeah. Well, for the fox. Only if you want me to,' Tom said, hesitating, not knowing if he should say any more. But then Wilbur smiled, and although quite a few of his teeth were missing, it crinkled his eyes and warmed his walnut face. He looked almost handsome.

'Aye lad,' he nodded. 'Aye.'

Walking on towards the Nissen huts, Tom squinted into the mellow sun looking for Billy, whilst Wilbur seemed lost in thought. It wasn't unusual for Billy to hide and jump out on people as a joke. Once he'd jumped on Tom from the old oak tree and they had both fallen to the ground laughing, but Tom had remembered it for some weeks afterwards, his shoulder stiff and sore. As they passed below the oak now, Tom glanced up, but no boy hid among its branches.

Wilbur slowed his pace, his jaw working in concentration, his eyes scanning the woods. Facing Tom, he looked at him intently.

'I've something to tell you lad. A secret.'

Tom could now smell – almost taste – the sweet tang of the pine warmed by the sun. But there was something else; an undertone of dank earth and decaying leaves, churned by the breeze.

The boy and the old man stood still. Tom felt his heart quicken. Wilbur was worth listening to, even if he didn't always make sense. But today, he was in no hurry to tell.

Finally, Wilbur spoke. 'The graves, the special pets buried there, the ones that were – ' he broke off, glancing at Tom. 'Can you keep a secret, lad?'

Tom nodded. 'Course. I won't tell anyone if you don't want me to.'

'Some – well, some – '

19

Billy rushed from behind the tree like a whirligig, pulling Tom to the ground in a play fight. Billy and his lousy timing, thought Tom, but joined in for a couple of minutes before pinning his friend to the ground, forcing him to surrender. Picking himself up, he looked around for Wilbur. There was no sign of him. Tom shielded his eyes from the sun as he scoured the huts and trees. Nothing. The old man of the woods had gone as quickly as he'd arrived. Tom wondered if he'd really been there at all.

\* \* \*

In his dad's shed, Tom looked for two pieces of wood. The sun fading, he didn't want to miss Robin Hood on the telly. He needed to get on and make the cross. *Mum won't come looking.* She was busy cooking tea in the kitchen, windows steamy from bubbling saucepans. It smelt like neck of lamb stew – tasty, but full of raggedy bones with splinters that hid beneath the gravy. She always served it with proper mash made from real potatoes, not that dried stuff that the little laughing aliens advertised on the telly. Dad was still at work and his little sister Lisa was doing her homework.

Tom looked amongst the odds and sods in the far corner. As if placed there ready and waiting, two pieces of dark wood lay side by side, perfect to make a good strong cross. He carried them to the work bench and with his penknife whittled them smooth, softly whistling as he worked. The light from the window diming already, he saw the hand drill by the hammer. A small drill head was already in, so he put the drill to work, turning the handle as he put his weight behind it. He drilled the upright and started the cross, then found a screw and driver. The screw went in, holding the two pieces together firmly, but Tom still bound the pieces with string in a figure of eight. Biting his lip in concentration, he carved "Fox. R.I.P."

He had nearly tidied up when Lisa rushed in.

'Tea's ready,' she said, then noticing the cross, 'what's that for?'

The last rays of light cut thickly through the grime on the window, highlighting the spun silk spider webs with their layer of dust and wood shavings. He didn't want a long conversation with his sister now. He was hungry. 'Just for school,' he said, 'some woodwork.'

She looked up at him through her fringe. 'Like homework?'

'Yeah, like homework,' he smiled.

'Come on, hurry up.' She grabbed his hand, tugging gently. 'It's stew.'

They left the shed, Tom slipping the cross out of sight behind the workbench. Lisa skipped in front, pretending she was a pony. If she wasn't pretending to be one, she was pretending to ride one. He smiled as she whinnied and shook her head. As they neared the back door she stopped suddenly and Tom nearly fell into her.

'I need to ask you something,' she said, 'on our own. After tea, can you come up to my bedroom?'

Puzzled, Tom didn't answer straight away.

'It's important,' she said, her face earnest.

'Yeah, ok'. He saw a glint of thanks in her eyes as they walked into the steamy kitchen and sat at the table for tea. They both ate quickly, mopping up the gravy with thick slices of bread and butter, then went to Lisa's room. Newly decorated with flowery wallpaper and a lacy bedspread, it smelt of talcum powder. Sitting on the bed, Lisa reached for something on the chest of drawers, below the poster of a horse.

'I've got the school trip to Dutch next week,' she said. Tom detected a waiver in her voice. It would be her first time away from home alone. Was she worried? Perhaps she didn't want to go?

'It's not Dutch you're going to,' he smiled, 'it's Holland. It's the people that live there who are Dutch.'

'Oh.' She hesitated, then said in a small voice, 'Will you look after my hedgehog while I'm away? Please? Will you?'

Tom looked at her. 'I didn't know you had a hedgehog. Is it in the garden?' He had visions of having to let it go, it would need to feed and hibernate soon. *How will I break it to her? Pretend it escaped?*

'No, he's here,' said Lisa, slowly opening her hands to reveal a matchbox. 'He's called spikey.'

Tom took the matchbox and opened it slowly not knowing what to expect. There, nestled in a small piece of moss, was half a prickly shell from a sweet chestnut tree. 'Lisa – ' he was going to say: don't be so silly, it's not a hedgehog, just a pretend one that didn't need looking after – but stopped himself. He closed the matchbox gently and put it down on the bed.

'Course I will.'

'Really? Oh, thanks Tom,' Lisa beamed at him, 'I'll leave it on the chest of drawers.'

For a fleeting moment he felt warmth, maybe even love, for his little sister who was generally a pain in the neck and constantly asking to come snake hunting with him.

'Don't forget to leave a gap in the matchbox so he can breathe,' Tom said, playing along with her.

Lisa started giggling. 'Don't be silly Tom,' she said, 'it's not a *real* hedgehog.'

\* \* \*

Long after his sister had gone to bed, Tom piled some clothes under his blankets, put the Beano he had been reading under his bed and turned his torch off before shoving it in his pocket. *If Mum or Dad pop their head round the door they'll think I'm asleep.*

He crept downstairs, counting under his breath to avoid the fifth and eighth stair which creaked if you stepped in the middle of them. Hoping the blare of the television in the sitting room would keep his parents' attention, he crept past into the kitchen and slipped out the backdoor. Hurrying to the shed, he kept the beam from the torch low. Closing the door behind him, he flashed the light behind the bench to get the cross. He studied his handiwork, satisfied it was sturdy enough. His father's wooden mallet was on the bench and he picked that up too before leaving the shed and heading for the graves.

It was dark in the woods; he could hardly see beyond the light from his torch. But a movement snagged his eyes; a jaunty fox crossing his path. Unperturbed by Tom, it stopped momentarily, casually glancing at him before disappearing into the undergrowth. Dry scattered twigs snapped under Tom's bumper boots as he picked his way over the fallen branches and through nettles. He reached the clearing and immediately saw the recently dug grave; a dark hump of soil looming in the shadows showing him the resting place of Wilbur's fox. With the moon behind heavy clouds and the beam of his torch failing, Tom wished he'd got Billy to come with him. He kept thinking of Wilbur's words about pets buried here and wondered what the hell he'd meant to say. The stillness of the night unnerving, he suddenly wanted to get back home.

Holding the upright of the cross steady, he hammered it with the mallet, quickening his blows as a swirling white mist rose from the ground. Finally, the cross stood proud at the end of the grave. Tom's arms ached as he reached for the torch. The beam went out, flickered on again, then died. Damn.

'Thanks lad.'

Wilbur's voice. Tom spun round but couldn't see him; it was darker than under his bedcovers without a torch.

'Wilbur? Where are you?'

'Over here.'

Tom still couldn't see him. 'What were you going to say earlier about the pets buried here?'

'Another time, I've got to go. You get off home.'

Tom didn't need telling twice. He turned to head back the way he'd come. He hadn't seen Wilbur, but thought he'd caught the musty, earthy smell of him for a second. Cold now, but job done, Tom hurried back in the dark. *Is Wilbur a little crazy, hanging around in the woods at night, burying foxes he finds at the side of the road?*

Glad to see the light from his house in the distance, Tom broke into a run.

# Chapter 3

## October 1967

Excitement had been brewing all week at school. Not only was it the last day before half term, but the fair was coming to Tyneford that night. Nobody in the village under the age of twenty wanted to miss it.

The two boys were already taking off their ties as they walked out of school. Billy mentioned the fair first. They were both thinking of whirling switchback rides lit up in the dark; a ghost train and the dodgems; blaring pop music. They could almost smell the warm sweet candy floss mixed with diesel fumes; see the girls squealing with exhilaration, their hair streaming behind them, eyes wild and shiny.

'I really want to go, but Mum says I can't. She says it's a waste of money and d-d-dangerous.' Billy sighed and pushed his hands further into his pockets. Unusually, they were empty, apart from his trusty penknife and some fluff.

They'd walked fifty yards and climbed up the conker tree before Tom replied. 'We could slip out,' he said, casually swinging his legs over the side of a branch. 'You know, pretend we'd gone to bed, put clothes under the blankets in case they look in. My mum and dad usually have the telly on with the front room door closed. I can easily slip out.'

'Y-Y-Yeah! I can climb out my w-window. Oh wow, let's d-do it!' The thrill Billy felt showed on his face. 'I've t-t-two weeks pocket money saved up; we can s-spend that.'

'I've got two bob,' grinned Tom. 'We'll have plenty enough for rides. I'll come to yours, flick a stone at your window and wait for you at the monkey puzzle tree.' He took out a small hunk of wood from one pocket which he was carving into a new catapult, and fished in his other pocket for his penknife. The plan made, the two boys surveyed their kingdom from the branches of the horse chestnut, satisfied they were alone. Then Tom concentrated on his carving, whilst Billy kept lookout, simmering with anticipation.

\* \* \*

The moon, a translucent bone-china plate, shone through the thin curtains at Billy's bedroom window. When the stone came, even though he'd been waiting for it, the ping on the glass made him start. Jumping out of bed fully clothed, he looked down at his friend, dark and silent on the lawn. Tom sloped off, merging with the shadows.

Billy climbed through the window and grabbed the down pipe, slipping and sliding then jumping to the ground. He jarred his left leg but hardly noticed as he half skipped, half ran to the monkey puzzle tree. Tom leaned against the trunk, tossing a two-bob bit in his hands, grinning. 'Come on, let's go and have a good time.'

The fair was in the field near the school, so they took the short-cut across the common. The silver sand that laced the tracks made them easy to follow, even in the dark. Thin bunches of silver-birch saplings appeared ghostly in the moonlight. Halfway across, on the horizon to their left was the old barn, usually quiet and abandoned; but tonight, ablaze with light and noise, a mixture of horses, carts and vans nearby. Surrounded by a small copse, the track to the barn was muddy and rutted; not normally used. They could hear dogs growling and yelping, men shouting and jeering.

'What the hell's going on over there?' said Tom, as he and Billy stared in the direction of the barn.

'D-Dunno,' replied his friend, 'I've n-never seen anyone there before.'

'We'd better have a look. C'mon,' said Tom, jogging towards the barn.

Billy followed, his heart sinking as it crossed his mind they might not get to the fair after all.

As they neared the barn, Tom crouched down behind a clump of bushes, pulling Billy down with him. They could taste danger in the air, clear and sharp as a shard of glass.

The men were loud and raucous. 'I th-think they might be from the fair,' whispered Billy, a quiver in his voice.

They crawled to the side of the barn, and squinting through gaps in the decaying wood, saw about twenty men standing around a rigged-up square in the centre, made from bales of straw and a couple of tea-chests. Oil and battery lamps lit up the inside. Most of the men drank from chipped mugs as money changed hands. Three empty Party-Seven beer cans lolled on their sides next to full ones in a corner. The air was hazy with cigarette smoke, but they could see two dogs being goaded and prodded with sticks in the centre of the square. They strained at the ropes holding them, their teeth barred, growling and ready to fight.

Billy tugged at Tom's sleeve, worried he'd try to rescue the dogs. 'There's n-n-nothing we can do,' he whispered. 'There's too m-many of them. They'd k-kill us.'

As the two boys watched, the rope nooses around each dog's neck were taken off. The men, jeering and cursing, pushed forward to see the action. The dogs flew at each other, biting and ripping, blood and saliva flaying wildly.

Feeling sick, Billy turned away and threw up on the grass.

'C'mon,' Tom whispered. 'We'll call the police from the phone box.' Adrenaline pumping through their veins, they raced across the common to the village green. Both squeezing into the red telephone box, Tom lifted the receiver and dialled 999. Breathlessly, he told them what they'd seen and the location of the barn.

'You stay away son, don't get involved. We'll send a car out just as soon as we can,' said the reassuring voice on the line. But the two boys ran back, crouching behind one of the carts, hearts thumping. The fair forgotten, they wanted to see the dogs rescued and the men arrested.

They waited in silence for ages as their hearts slowed and their legs turned numb. The noise from the barn gradually abated; the dogs whimpering instead of growling, the men quieter. It seemed the fight was over, the bets won or lost.

'Why haven't the p-police come?' whispered Billy, his voice raw.

Tom didn't answer. Standing up, he peered over the side of the cart.

A small puppy cowered in the corner. The whites of its eyes showed, its body shivering. It wasn't like the dogs in the barn – not a fighting dog. It looked shaggy and thin, the colour of dry autumn bracken. The pup had a noose of rope round its neck, tied to a rusted iron ring fixed in the side of the cart. 'I thought I'd heard something,' said Tom.

Billy joined his friend to see what he was looking at. 'Poor little thing, b-belonging to this lot.'

'Not any more,' replied Tom. Taking out his penknife and slicing through the rope, he gently lifted the pup and held it under one arm. Without any hesitation, the two boys ran hell for leather back across the common.

Joe Cooper, staggering from the barn to take a piss, saw the boys running away. It was a couple of minutes before his beer addled brain noticed the pup had gone.

'I'll have yous!' he spat in the direction of the departing figures, a large gob of phlegm flying from his mouth.

'I'll feckin' 'ave yous!' he shouted again.

But the boys had disappeared into the night.

* * *

Tom ran in front. He didn't stop until they reached the shelter, although he'd looked over his shoulder a few times to make sure no one was following them. He knew instinctively this was the best place to come – an abandoned underground air-raid shelter that Wilbur had shown him a while ago. Tom remembered what the old man had said: 'If you come again Tom, make sure no one sees or follows you. It's a secret place that nobody knows about 'cept me. And you, now,' he'd chuckled. 'I look after sick or injured animals here, so they're safe.' There had been a small badger in there when Wilbur took him inside, its leg tied with a wooden splint and bandages.

'He'll soon be right as rain,' Wilbur had continued. Tom was fascinated by the small animal, its stripes looking perfectly painted. 'Found the poor bugger near a trap with 'is leg broken. Bloody bastards.' Fire flashed in the old man's eyes. 'Gillingham from the farm sets traps to kill foxes. But traps don't care what they trap or what they injure or kill. I nearly always get to the traps before Gillingham and release the animals if they're ok; or bring them here if they're not. There's been a fawn as well as foxes, badgers and rabbits. Sometimes you just find a leg in the trap – where the terrified animal has bitten through it just to get away.'

Tom had felt sick. Why did people do such horrible things? He decided – if there came a time when Wilbur couldn't look out for the trapped animals – that he'd do it himself. Even if it meant getting up really, really early.

The pup in Tom's arms whimpered quietly and licked his chin. Tom knew Wilbur wouldn't mind him keeping the pup here for a while. He hoped he wouldn't mind Billy knowing about the place, either.

At the edge of the woods, all they could see in the moonlight were a few scattered branches, thick and twisted brambles rambling over them with clumps of nettles poking through. 'W-where are we?' asked Billy.

Tom looked around again making sure they hadn't been followed. He stroked the little pup's head who responded by licking between his fingers. Tom grinned in the darkness.

'Under there,' Tom pointed to the tangled brambles, 'is a wooden cover, which leads down to an air-raid shelter.'

Billy had recently learned about World War Two in history. 'Wow! R-really?'

'Sshhh!' hissed Tom, looking around again. 'It's a secret place. You mustn't tell anyone, or bring anybody else here.'

'I won't, I p-promise.'

'OK,' Tom knew he'd be true to his word. 'Help me move these branches aside and find the cover.' He put the pup down in a grassy spot close by. The pup immediately rolled on its back, exposing a soft pale belly. 'Stay there, little fella,' whispered Tom as he briefly rubbed its warm tummy.

The boys moved some branches and kicked around in the undergrowth until Tom's bumper boot hit the hard edge of the cover. 'Here,' he called quietly, 'it's under here.'

Together they lifted two heavy branches to expose the cover, merging with the ground. Tom levered it up with a stick left nearby for the purpose. A thick, earthy smell rose up to greet them, musty and permeating.

Billy screwed his face up. 'S-stinks a bit,' he coughed. Tom didn't think so. He breathed in the hoary, primeval air until it filled his lungs and filtered through his veins. To him, it smelled of Wilbur and ancient wisdom.

Billy peered down the dark hole. 'Are there s-steps?'

'There's a ladder fixed to the side.'

Feeling around the top with his foot, Billy found the first rung and lowered himself down. Tom picked up the pup and followed him, pulling the wooden cover back over as best he could.

'B-blimey!' There was a soft thump.

'Sorry Billy, forgot to tell you the bottom two rungs are rusted out.' Tom grinned to himself in the darkness.

Billy felt the wall beside him. Battens and posts shored up the earth.

'Hold on,' said Tom, putting the pup down on the soft dirt floor. He reached in his pocket for his torch. The batteries were low, but it still gave a weak beam. They could see an upturned tea-chest and two logs at the far end which appeared to serve as a table and chairs. On the chest sat two fat used candles and a small box wrapped in newspaper. Tom took off the paper to reveal a box of Swan Vesta matches. He lit the candles, which guttered into life and shadows danced around them.

Sitting down on one of the logs and rubbing his ankle, Billy let out a long, low whistle. 'F-f-fantastic d-den,' he finally got out, looking around. Tom noticed how large his pupils were in the semi-darkness. 'You could h-hide away here for ages!' Billy continued in awe.

Tom reached down for an old tin pan in the corner. 'We need to fill this with water from the stream.' Billy knew where he meant; it wasn't far. Tom continued. 'We can bring food to him each day. He'll be safe here for a while.' The pup was sitting by Tom's feet. 'I'll talk to Mum and Dad soon, see if they'll let me keep him at home.' His friend nodded, and they both bent to stroke the puppy, who had started to shiver. Tom pulled his jumper over his head and wrapped it round the little dog, who settled down and promptly fell asleep.

Billy looked at Tom. 'W-what are you going to c-call 'im?'

The candles flickered and a small cascade of dry soil fell from the ceiling, pitter-pattering on the tea-chest. Both boys held their breath and looked upwards, realising someone was walking above the shelter. Billy, his face white in the candlelight, leaned into Tom to whisper in his ear. 'I-I think it was J-Joe who saw us run off with the puppy. He m-might have followed us.'

A rasping noise came from above. Someone was coming down the ladder. The boys strained to see in the semi-darkness. Tom felt his jaw tighten as he stood up silently, his hands making fists, finger nails digging into his palms. The pup stirred slightly and whimpered, dreaming.

'That you, young Tom?'

Billy released his breath in a whoosh and Tom felt his heart beat slow.

Wilbur's voice.

Tom's words tumbled out. 'Hi Wilbur. This is my friend Billy. He won't tell anyone about this place, he's promised.'

'What're you doing here?' asked Wilbur, before spotting the puppy asleep in the jumper.

'We passed the old barn, there was a dog fight there – '

'Aye,' interrupted Wilbur, 'I came past as they were packing up. Cruel bastards.'

'We – I took the puppy from one of the carts.' Tom looked down at the small bundle at his feet. 'To save it from being used in a fight.'

'You did good, lad. He'd have been used as bait — practice for the fighting dogs, to give 'em the taste of blood.' Wilbur bent down and rubbed the pup's ears. 'You going to keep 'im?'

Tom looked at Billy. 'We're hoping to look after him here for a while, until the fair's left town. Then I'll ask my mum and dad if I can keep him — I think they'll let me, as long as I look after him.'

'That's a good plan.' Wilbur turned his attention to the other boy. 'You going to help 'im, Billy?'

Billy swallowed. 'Oh y-yeah. Yes sir. I l-l-love animals.'

'Well in that case, you're welcome here. But call me Wilbur.'

'Y-yes sir — I mean W-Wilbur.'

Wilbur chuckled, a sound like stones plonking in deep water, and the two boys grinned. Tom looked at the old man's smiling face and his body relaxed. Everything was going to be alright.

# Chapter 4

## February 1911

The boy, awkward in his Sunday best, looked up to his father beside him. Wearing a top hat and tails, his pallid face stark and lined, the boy could have thought him a stranger.

They walked behind the cart that carried the boy's mother. Drawn by two shires, their dark coats gleamed in the weak February sun. The boy had groomed them for hours the day before, the horses enjoying the attention and the rest from ploughing. As he'd brushed them he'd talked in a gentle voice, stopping now and again to wipe the tears from his face.

They rounded the bend and the sandstone chapel came into view. A dozen or more people stood stiffly around the entrance and amongst the grave stones, watching the horses pulling the cart towards them. One or two doffed their caps to his father, even though he walked with his head bowed and wouldn't see them.

Wilbur looked in the cart at the plinth his father had made from the chestnut that had fallen last winter. The polished coffin sat on top, partially draped in linen. Someone had placed a posy of snowdrops on the lid; their lime green leaves standing out against the wood, their flowers pure and delicate. Like his mother.

Rooks cawed from the yew tree; in their permanent funeral attire they acknowledged the arrival of death once again. As the cart drew to a stop, Wilbur looked over to Aunt Agnes, his mother's younger sister. She grasped a handkerchief in one hand, her face red and unsettled. When she saw him looking she managed a smile that moved her lips but not her eyes. He tried to smile back but his face wouldn't obey him. Pain pulsed inside his head.

His father moved to the side of the cart and three other men joined him. Together, they slid the coffin from the plinth and raised it to their shoulders. They carried Wilbur's mother into the cold shadows of the church. He followed behind, fighting to hold back the tears.

* * *

Most of the mourners had left the wake when his father finally sat in front of the fire, a jug of half-drunk ale by his side. His body crumpled and his face strained, he still didn't look like his father, despite having changed into his usual clothes.

The fire warmed the parlour; but not Wilbur. He shivered.

'Are you cold son? Come closer to the fire.' His father took a sip of ale and stared into the flames again.

'Pa? Was it having the baby that killed her?'

His father turned his head to look at him. 'The Doc said your Ma had a weak heart. Maybe the shock of the baby being dead – '

Aunt Agnes walked into the room. She perched on the wooden arm of Wilbur's chair, laying one hand on his shoulder. 'We don't know if the grief or the shock of giving birth to the dead baby killed her. We'll probably never know. But don't go blaming that poor little mite that never lived. God willing, their souls will rest together in heaven.' She squeezed his shoulder with her soft chubby fingers, looking across to his father. 'I've tidied the scullery John. Are you sure you don't want me to move in and look after you and the boy for a while? Just 'til you're back on your feet and the ploughing's done?'

The question hung in the air. Wilbur hoped she'd move in. She looked like his Ma and cooked a great rabbit pie just like she did. *Had.*

Finally, his father replied. 'I don't want to put you out none, Agnes.'

Soot fell in the grate and the fire hissed. A frantic tweeting and flapping echoed in the chimney. Wilbur's father jumped from his chair, running to the kitchen and filling a pot with water. He doused the fire just before the exhausted bird fell in the wet ashes. He picked it up tenderly, holding its wings by its side, murmuring to the tiny form in his hand as he took it outside. Wilbur followed him, watching as his father placed the bird on the ground. It rested for a couple of minutes before flying off.

'There's been enough death for one week,' muttered his father as he returned to the house. Wilbur followed him to the parlour and heard his aunt's voice.

'You won't be putting me out none, John.'

His father smiled for the first time in ages. 'I'll bring the cart round tomorrow then, and pick up your cases.'

* * *

When his aunt moved into the back bedroom, Wilbur had already ploughed three rows in the field. The day had dawned dry, dictating the ploughing continue. He'd been glad; it would keep his mind from dwelling on the death of his mother. But dark clouds, heavy with rain, hovered on the horizon. The mare pulling the plough was unusually skittish.

'Calm down, Daisy,' whispered Wilbur. 'If the storm comes, I'll take you back to the barn.'

The shire shook her great head, the blinkers flapping against her face. Wilbur clicked his tongue and the horse's bunched muscles pulled the plough through the soil again, the sods breaking and parting to blackness. When they neared the small copse at the top of the field, the mare stopped. 'Walk on, Daisy,' said Wilbur, gently letting the reins fall on her broad back. But she didn't move. He was puzzled. This mare was a grafter, she always worked willingly.

'What is it, girl?' he asked, just before the flash of lightening hit one of the trees on the edge of the small wood. Wilbur heard the loud crack, then the thud as it fell, the leafless canopy shaking on the ground less than a yard before them. Breathing hard, he jumped from the plough and went to the horse's head, stroking her neck.

'Thanks, Daisy,' he whispered. 'You saved my life.'

# Chapter 5

## November 1967

For the next two weeks Wilbur, Billy and Tom fed and watered the pup in the air-raid shelter. Wilbur went in the early morning mist and last thing at night under the glow of the moon. The two boys rushed there after school and stayed as late as they dared. At weekends they played with the pup all day and took him for walks in Jackdaw Woods.

Tom bought a tin of Chappie from Watties each morning using his school dinner money which his mum gave him on a Monday. He could only afford a packet of crisps at lunchtime, so got up early for a good breakfast and finished his evening meal in record time. His mum noticed.

'Tom! Anyone would think you were starving. Can't you eat a bit slower?'

'Leave him be Elsie,' said his dad. 'He's a growing lad. He needs his food.'

Tom smiled ruefully at his dad, who winked back at him. Tom was glad he was deflecting his mum's attention. At least she hadn't noticed the blanket missing from his bed that he'd taken for the pup. He'd have to speak to them soon, tell them about the little dog. But there was no hurry. The pup, who he still hadn't named, was safe where he was while the fair was still in town.

The dog gained confidence in his saviours and every time they came, he cried with excitement, tail wagging furiously. He'd jump on Tom and Billy, licking their faces until they were in fits of giggles, whilst Wilbur, in his soft, calm voice, talked to the pup for hours. By the end of the second week the puppy sat, lay down and kept quiet on command. He was eager to please and quick to learn. His amber-flecked warm brown eyes watched Tom with a gentle, age-old intelligence; as if he knew this boy had saved his life.

The following week, Wilbur joined them one afternoon and brought the news Tom had been waiting for.

'Fair's left town. They packed up and went in the night.'

Tom grinned. 'Good. I'll talk to Mum and Dad about bringing the pup home.'

'You'd better think of a name for him then, lad,' Wilbur smiled. 'How about Digger? That's the second hole he's dug today.' The pup's front legs were throwing up dirt furiously from the corner of the shelter.

Billy flashed the torch over there. He saw something glint in the beam of light, and went over and picked it up. 'It's a sixpence,' he said, wiping the coin on his jumper and studying it in the light from the torch. 'Blimey, it's d-dated nineteen thirty-five.'

'Probably dropped here in the war,' said Wilbur.

'Why did they have a sh-shelter h-here, miles from anywhere? Who would've used it?'

'When the war started,' Wilbur began, 'there was a hospital here. This shelter was built in the grounds for the patients and staff. You can still see some of the hospital foundations under the brambles. It got bombed to the ground during the war. I think it was in nineteen forty-three. The bricks and debris were eventually cleared away and the brambles and nettles took over. This shelter probably saved a few lives.'

'H-how did the ill people g-get down here?' asked Billy.

'They weren't ill in their body,' said Wilbur. 'It was a mental hospital. I think the nurses or doctors would have led them down here.'

Tom, who'd been quiet, shouted out excitedly. 'Tanner! That's what I'll call him! He dug one up, so I'll call him Tanner!' The little dog stopped digging, trotted over to Tom and licked his hand.

'Seems he already knew his name,' said Wilbur. 'He was just waitin' for you to figure it out.'

* * *

44

On the way home, Billy offered the silver coin to Tom. 'You k-keep it Tom. Go on, you can put it with the money to buy d-dog food.'

'Thanks.' Tom slipped it in his pocket.

'You going to t-talk to your folks tonight,' Billy asked, 'about taking T-Tanner home?'

'Yeah, maybe. If they're in a good mood.' Tom grinned.

They reached Tom's house on the outskirts of the village. It was down an unmade lane leading to the woods. Billy's house was a quarter mile further on near the pub and off-licence, where they took their empty Tizer bottles. Tuppence deposit per bottle was paid back when the empties were returned. At the end of the week the pub and off- licence put the empties in the back yard for collection. It wasn't unknown for the boys to scale the yard wall and put a few bottles in a sack tied with a long piece of string. They'd then lower the sack gently over the wall, take the bottles out and present them at the front a second time round. This added to their pocket money quite substantially. They didn't do it often; but it was considered fair game, like scrumping apples from the Bannon's orchard.

'Bye,' said Billy. 'G-good luck.'

'See you tomorrow,' Tom said over his shoulder as he walked round to the back door.

The kitchen was steamy and smelt of beef stew and dumplings. Little rivulets raced down the window against the black night. A saucepan stood on the stove.

Tom went over to smell it; a skin had started to form on the gravy.

His mum walked into the kitchen. She sighed. 'There you are, Tom. It's late, we've been worried about you.'

'Sorry Mum,' Tom mumbled.

Her blue eyes sought his. 'Is something going on? Only you've been staying out quite a lot,' she said quietly.

Tom's dad came in from the front room. 'Alright son? You must be starving. Me and your mum couldn't wait any longer, we've had our tea.'

'Where's Lisa?' asked Tom, sensing his sister wasn't at home. She nearly always ran to see him.

'She's at her friend's,' said his mum, re-heating his stew.

It occurred to Tom that tonight would be a good time to tell them about Tanner. With his sister not here, he could explain things properly and tell them about the dog fight. Tom knew they'd been worried about him being late home all the time. Hopefully they'd understand. But his hunger demanded he eat first. His mum placed a plate of stew in front of him and he devoured it in less than two minutes.

His dad smiled. 'Isn't too much wrong with you, Tom, is there?' he said, winking at his wife. But she didn't smile back like she normally did.

Tom mopped up the gravy with a hunk of bread and butter. 'Mum, you asked if there's anything going on,' he started.

His mum turned from the sink to face him. 'I've been concerned, Tom.'

'Sorry but, it's just that – well – I've found a dog.'

His mum's face softened. 'Oh?'

'I should've told you before, but I thought you might be cross.'

'Why would we be?' asked his dad.

'Well, it was more that, well, I took the dog. Stole him, really. It was the night the fair first came to town. I slipped out and met up with Billy after dark to go there.' His mum's eyes widened. They looked at him but didn't interrupt. 'Go on,' said his dad.

Tom told them about the dog fight, taking the pup from the cart and looking after it with Billy's help. He didn't mention the air-raid shelter or Wilbur. 'The thing is,' said Tom, 'I know I shouldn't have taken him,' he hesitated, 'but they didn't deserve to have animals,' his voice cracked. 'I want to keep him. He's called Tanner.'

'Oh Tom,' sighed his mum, smiling at him. 'You should have told us earlier. Of course we're not cross you took the puppy; you've probably saved him from a life of misery.' Tom could hear the relief in her voice. 'But,' she went on, putting on a firm voice, 'you shouldn't have sneaked out that night.'

'You can bring him home Tom, as long as you look after him,' said his dad. 'We both like dogs. You're old enough now to take on the responsibility.'

'That's great! Thanks Dad. Can I bring him home tomorrow after school?'

'Yes, that's fine,' said his dad, who then looked at his wife and raised his eyebrows. Imperceptibly, she nodded. 'As it happens, Tom, we've something to tell you, too. Something we should've told you earlier.'

Tom wasn't paying attention. He was wondering if they'd let Tanner sleep with him in his bedroom. 'Please Release Me' played on the radio. His mum switched it off. The sudden silence made him listen.

'You took that pup because you knew it was the right thing to do?' continued his dad.

'Uh huh,' mumbled Tom.

'And you love and care for him like he's yours?'

'Yeah, of course.'

'Well, your mum and me, we're sorry if this comes as a shock, Tom. But we, well, we did the same with you. We're not your real parents. What I mean is that I didn't father you, and your mum didn't give birth to you. But we love and care for you like our real son. Which you are, as far as we're concerned.'

Blood drained from Tom's face. He felt dizzy. How could they not be his parents? He looked from one to the other, his gaze unsettled.

His mum continued in a soft voice. 'The woman, or rather the girl, who gave birth to you – she was still at school. She wasn't old enough to look after you or provide for you. We, your dad and me, we wanted to do that because she wasn't able to.' Tom studied the brown and orange pattern on the tablecloth, his body slumped into the chair. 'We have always, and always will, love and care for you as our own son, Tom.'

The floor under Tom's chair crumbled. Everything he knew, all he took for granted, wasn't real. He wrapped his arms around himself, rocking backwards and forwards. His mum rushed to his him, kneeling by his side, throwing her arms around him. 'Nothing's changed Tom, nothing is different.' She stroked his hair. 'Everything's the same as it's always been and always will be. We love you as our son. Your mum loved you too. It was just that she couldn't look after you; not that she didn't want to.'

Time seemed to have stopped, but Tom could hear the starburst clock on the wall ticking along to the hum of the fridge.

'Did you adopt me?' he finally asked. He'd developed a tic below his right eye.

'Not officially. Your mum, her name was Kathy, didn't want anyone knowing. She, well, it wasn't considered right for her to have a child when she was young and unmarried. She wasn't much older than you are now.'

'Where is she?' asked Tom, his voice rising. Why didn't he know her?

'She died, Tom,' said his dad. 'When you were five. She had a serious illness.'

Silent tears slid down Tom's face. This room, that had always been so homely, seemed strange; hostile. 'What about my dad?'

'We don't know, Tom. Kathy didn't tell anybody who your dad was; not even her sister, your aunty Joyce.'

'Aunty Joyce is my real mum's sister?'

'Yes. She's your real aunty.'

'I want to talk to her,' said Tom, wiping his face on his arm.

'Of course you do, but not – ' The shrill bell of the phone cut through from the hallway. His mum went to answer it. His dad walked over to him, putting his hand on his shoulder. Tom brushed it off.

The big man pushed his hands deep into his pockets. Shaking his head slightly, he stared at the floor. 'We should have told you. Before. When your mum died.' His voice was so quiet, Tom strained to hear. He couldn't look at this man, this pretend dad. Tom had always looked up to him, admired him; but now he felt betrayed. Who was he really? Just a liar named Reg.

'But you,' his dad continued, 'you were just a boy, Tom. Too young to understand. Me and Elsie – we wanted you to have a happy childhood.'

Elsie returned to the kitchen. 'That was Lisa. She wants to stay the night at Sally's. I've said it's ok.'

'What about Lisa?' Tom's voice was hard. 'Is she adopted too?'

Elsie looked at him. 'No, she's our real daughter. We didn't think we could have our own children – but then Lisa just came along.' Her husband put his arm around her. Tom didn't see the tears brimming in his eyes as he spoke. 'As far as we're concerned, Tom, there's no difference. You're our son and Lisa's our daughter. We love you both the same.'

Tom jumped up quickly, the chair he'd been sitting on teetered on its back legs, then clattered to the floor.

He didn't stop to pick it up. Striding to the back door, he yanked it open, slamming it hard behind him. A draft of night air blew in; but it didn't disperse the cloud of accusations smouldering in the air. Reg opened the door and shouted Tom's name, but he'd already vanished into the night. The big man turned and wrapped his arms around his wife. Her body sagged against him as her anguished sobs began.

# Chapter 6

## November 1967

Outside, Tom started to run towards the air-raid shelter. More than anything, he wanted to hold Tanner; bury his face in the dog's soft fur, breathe in his smell. It would give him time to think. But after two hundred yards, Tom slowed to a walk. He realised Wilbur would likely be there. He couldn't face explaining anything to anyone at the moment; not even Wilbur. There were too many unanswered questions racing around his head.

Unsure and confused, Tom turned around. His aunt Joyce lived a half-hour walk away, but she was the only one who could give him some answers. It gave him a purpose; somewhere to head for. He'd felt sick, but the steady rhythm of walking helped calm him as he breathed in the cool night air. A light drizzle began to fall and, further on, the damp pavement shimmered orange under the street lights. As Tom walked beneath them his shadow lengthened, then disappeared; reclaimed again by the night. He wished his thoughts could disappear as easily; but they rattled and bumped in his head, making it ache. How could life change so suddenly?

He reached the street where his aunt lived. Lights blazed from the house. The front door was wide open; Joyce a silhouette on the doorstep. She shouted his name and ran towards him, arms out-stretched. Hugging him tightly, she whispered in his ear. 'They phoned me, Tom. They're so worried. They hoped you'd come here.' Tom nodded. He didn't trust his voice. 'Don't blame them for not telling you before,' his aunt continued, 'they wanted to, but couldn't find the right time.'

His aunt led him into the front room, gently guiding him back onto the sofa. 'John's making us a cup of tea.' Tom could hear his uncle in the kitchen; the kettle boiling, the clink of metal on china. Everyday sounds that seemed so incongruous.

'Your mum Kathy loved you dearly, Tom,' his aunt continued. 'She would've kept you if she could.'

Tom picked at the skin around his nails. 'Did she ever come to see me? I mean… when she was alive?'

'Yes, oh yes! Many times. But she knew you were secure and settled… happy. She didn't want to upset your world. You were only four when she became ill. She died less than a year later.'

Tom didn't know what to feel. He thought he should be sad for her, this girl-woman who'd given birth to him. He should be upset she died so young. But how could he be when he'd never known her?

'What was she like?'

'You look so much like her, Tom. Dark. Handsome. You've got her blue eyes.' His aunt swallowed. 'She was a lovely person. Strong. Kind-hearted. Even when,' Joyce rubbed her eyes, 'even when she was told she'd die, she never thought herself unlucky. As long as you were safe and happy, that's all that mattered to her.'

John came in with two mugs of tea and set them down on the Formica-topped coffee table. He smiled at Tom, but Tom didn't notice; his eyes were fixed on the steam rising from the mug in front of him. Joyce looked at her husband and flicked her glance to the door. He nodded once and left the room.

The woman and boy sat in silence for several minutes. Joyce nursed her tea whilst Tom had shifted his gaze to the lava lamp on the sideboard, it's gaudy pink and green glow reflecting in his eyes. The amoeba lumps of softened wax rose and fell hypnotically.

'Try your tea, Tom, it might help. I think you're in shock.' He reached for the mug and took a sip. It didn't help so he placed it back on the table.

'Did... did they tell you about your twin?' his aunt asked, putting her mug down with a clatter.

'Twin?' Tom focused on her. 'No – what twin?'

Joyce sighed. 'I think it's best you know everything now.' She picked up her mug again. It was luke-warm. She put it back down. 'When Kathy gave birth to you, she actually had two babies.'

Tom stared at her. 'I've a brother or sister? Where?'

'Your mum gave birth alone in a barn. She couldn't carry both babies at once. She was bringing them to me

54

– to give to Reg and Elsie. She brought the first baby –
you – to me, then ran back to the barn for the other one.
But when she got back there, the baby had gone.'

Tom searched his aunt's face for answers. 'But
how? How had the baby gone? Where is... ' Tom's voice
trailed off.

His aunt glanced at the floor. 'We don't know, Tom.
We're not sure what happened. We think that somebody
– a person – must have taken the baby. Perhaps your
twin is out there somewhere, being brought up by
someone. We... well, I hope so.' Joyce cleared her
throat. 'Kathy didn't want the police to know, she didn't
think they'd find out anything. Before she got ill, she
searched everywhere for that baby. She checked all the
new borns in the village and would ask everybody she
met if they knew anyone with a baby. Every week she
searched the woods and the common and returned to
the barn. She never gave up hope, Tom. Until the day
she died, she clung to the thought the baby was safe
somewhere.'

Tom began to understand how it must have been
for his birth mum. She'd loved him; done what she
thought best. And he knew he had a mum and dad who
loved him now. But his twin, thought Tom, might not
have been so lucky.

'The other baby, was it a boy or girl?'

'We don't know. Kathy had it in the dark.'

'Did she – ever tell her own mum and dad – your
mum and dad – about me?' Tom asked, his thoughts
solidifying, settling.

'No, she never told them. She was ashamed about being pregnant and unmarried. She made me promise not to tell them either. But I'm sure they would love to know about you Tom. They'd love a grandson.' Joyce paused. 'When Kathy died, they were heart-broken.'

Tom ran his hand through his hair. Joyce noticed the dark circles beneath his eyes. 'You look all in, Tom. Do you want to stay here tonight? I can make up the spare bed.'

'No,' he smiled for the first time that night. 'No thanks.' He stood up from the couch and stretched out his arms to hug her. 'I want to go home.'

* * *

The following afternoon, Billy's teacher looked around the class of boys, disappointment on his face. Five pupils had failed to produce homework due in and the results of the English test set last week were abysmal. The bell for home-time had rung five minutes ago.

Billy looked out the window, wishing Jonesey would let them go. He wanted to see Tom and Tanner; not sit in a stuffy old classroom. He smelt the chalk just before the board rubber hit his right ear. A puff of white dust filled his mouth. Jonesey was always a good shot. 'What's your excuse, boy?' the teacher asked, staring at Billy, who could feel himself going red. Rubbing his ear, he swallowed as his heart began to hammer.

'I-I-I… ' Billy took a breath. He heard Mark Dunn snigger behind him. 'I-I… ' More sniggers. He gave up and hung his head.

'Get out, the lot of you,' shouted Jonesey, 'and if anyone forgets homework next week, they'll find themselves doing five hundred lines.' All the chairs scraped back at once and the class surged towards the door. As Billy passed him, the teacher grabbed his arm. When the others had left the room, he closed the door behind them. 'Sit back down, Billy.' Jonesey faced him, sitting with the chair-back between his knees. 'I'm sorry I singled you out. That wasn't fair of me. But you should have done your homework.'

Billy nodded, but couldn't look at the teacher. Instead, he studied the wooden desk top, with its yellowed varnish patterned by gouged compass lines and splodges of ink. His fingers picked at the old lumps of chewing gum stuck underneath.

'I've noticed your stutter a bit more just lately, Billy. You'll probably grow out of it, but I could refer you to someone who might be able to help in the meantime. Would you like to see someone about it?'

It was in school, Billy thought, that he stuttered the most. So how could school help him? It just made things worse. He thought of Tom, who'd be waiting for him at the conker tree. Without raising his eyes, he shook his head. Jonesey sighed. 'Alright, but if you change your mind, come and see me. Go on lad. Get off home.'

'Y-yes sir,' replied Billy, grabbing his rucksack and sprinting out the door. He didn't stop running until he reached the old tree. Tom sat on a bare-leaved branch. Heavy clouds hovered above; it was nearly dusk.

'We can take Tanner back to mine tonight,' grinned Tom.

'Th-that's great!' Billy thumped the air, school forgotten.

Tom half-climbed, half-slid from the tree. They walked through the woods to the air-raid shelter.

'Your mum and d-dad ok with you h-having him then?' Billy had half-hoped he could keep the pup if Tom couldn't.

'Yeah.'

Walking side by side, they kicked up the leaves. Tom glanced at Billy.

'I'm adopted,' he blurted out.

'Oh?' replied Billy, not sure what it meant.

'My mum and dad – they're not my real mum and dad,' Tom continued, 'and I've got a twin. But no one knows where it is.'

'H-how come?' asked Billy, interested now.

'We were born in a barn. My real mum took me to her sister, but when she went back to get my twin, the baby wasn't there.'

'H-how come?' Billy said again. 'D-did somebody take it?'

'Yeah. Maybe. No one knows.'

Billy thought about this for a while. Who would want to steal a baby? He wondered who Tom's twin was; where he could be. It was strange, Tom being born in a barn. Billy's dad was always telling Billy he was born in a barn.

'I c-could be your twin, Tom! My dad's always saying I must have b-been born in a b-barn!'

Tom stood still, then threw back his head and laughed so hard that hot tears sprang to his eyes. Falling to his knees, he rolled on his back in the dry brown bracken, holding his stomach and gasping for air. Billy laughed with him, pleased he'd said something funny. Eventually, Tom sat up. Wiping the back of his hand across his eyes, he grinned at his friend.

'How can you be my twin, Billy? You're two years younger than me!' Tom snorted with laughter again, his shoulders shaking.

'Oh y-yeah,' grinned Billy.

'And as for being born in a barn – your dad says that, because you never close the door behind you!'

'I know th-that,' said Billy, who didn't.

'Besides,' continued Tom, hiccupping, 'we don't look anything alike. You've got girl's hair.'

Billy jumped on him and they rolled around play-fighting. But Billy knew he was right. Tom was taller than him with thick, dark hair. His own hair, much to his disgust, was blond and wavy. Even he thought of it as girl's hair.

They continued on their way, Tom sniggering now and again, Billy play-thumping his arm each time he did. Reaching the air-raid shelter, they looked around before lifting the cover and climbing down. Tanner whimpered with delight, jumping on Tom's shoes and peeing with excitement. The boy scooped him up, the little dog licking the dried tears of laughter from his face. 'Hello,' whispered Tom, breathing in the dog's familiar warm scent. 'I need to teach you to pee in the garden,' he said softly, ''cos you're coming home with me.'

The two boys left the shelter, carefully concealing the entrance, and walked back towards the woods. Tanner followed behind, sniffing and wagging his tail, never letting them get too far ahead. Dark now, he used his sense of smell.

'I need to find Wilbur,' said Tom, 'to let him know I'm taking Tanner home.' Billy thought Wilbur would guess that, when he found the dog wasn't down the air-raid shelter. But he was quite happy to look for Wilbur with his friend, so he didn't say anything.

The Nissen huts loomed from the darkness ahead. The boys walked around them. Billy saw Tom's face, high-lighted by the moon passing between the clouds.

'You know, T-Tom, I've just thought who you d-d-do look like,' said Billy.

'Yeah?' Tom looked over his shoulder to check Tanner was still following them. 'Who's that, then?'

'Th-that Joe. You know, the b-bully from the fair.'

Billy saw red anger flare in Tom's cheeks. 'No I'm not! I'm not like him at all!' He walked on quickly, leaving Billy lagging behind.

'I-I don't m-mean you're l-like him,' said Billy, running to catch up. 'B-but you do look a bit like him.'

'Well, he's no twin of mine,' spat Tom.

'N-no. 'Course not.' Billy wished he'd kept quiet.

They reached the abandoned old Austin. Neither boy could see Wilbur. Tom stooped down to pick up Tanner. Billy knew it was because of he didn't want the dog to cut a paw on the broken glass lying around.

'What's this about a twin, Tom?' Both boys jumped and spun round. Wilbur was right behind them. He reached out to stroke Tanner, and the dog licked his hand. Wilbur chuckled. 'Made you lads jump, didn't I?'

'Y-yeah,' said Billy, as Tom sighed quietly.

'Tom's got a t-twin,' blurted Billy, 'they w-were both born in a barn. But the other b-baby got taken.'

The puppy wriggled in Tom's arms, trying to get to Wilbur. The old man took him. 'That right, Tom?' he asked.

'Yeah,' said Tom. 'No one knows what happened to the baby.' He climbed into the car and pushed his hands inside his jacket. It was getting cold. Billy scrambled up behind him. 'I'm taking Tanner home,' said Tom.

Wilbur didn't reply. Tom looked over his shoulder. Tanner was sitting on the ground – but Wilbur was nowhere to be seen.

'I wish he wouldn't disappear like that,' said Tom. 'It's freaky.'

'Yeah,' drawled Billy. 'It's f-far out, man!'

The boys burst out laughing again, and the old car rocked and creaked. Billy wrapped his arms around himself, trying to ease the pain of the laughter-stitch in his side.

\* \* \*

61

They got to Tom's house.

'You coming in, Billy?' Tom hoped he would.

'N-no. I better g-get home.'

'See you tomorrow then,' said Tom, slipping round the side of the house with Tanner trotting behind. He shoved his left hand in his trouser pocket, crossing the first two fingers. Opening the back door, he saw Mum, Dad and Lisa sitting at the table eating pudding. It smelt like butterscotch flavoured Angel Delight, his favourite. There was an expectant hush in the room; then Tanner ran in, tail wagging, slipping and sliding on the quarry tile floor.

'Hello little fella,' said Tom's mum softly, reaching out her arm for Tanner to sniff. The pup's tongue darted in and out, licking and tickling her hand. She laughed. 'He's lovely, Tom.'

Lisa jumped down from the table and ran to the dog, bending down on one knee to hug and kiss him. 'Oh, I love him Tom!' she squealed, as Tanner licked her face.

'He'd better have the welcome treat we saved for him,' said Tom's dad, reaching for a plate of scraps on the side and handing it to Tom. Putting it down in front of Tanner, Tom's shoulders relaxed and his stomach settled. Tanner wolfed everything down, his tail wagging constantly. 'What a grand little dog,' said his dad, as he rubbed Tanner's ears.

Later, Tom gave Tanner his first bath and dried him with an old towel his mum gave him. Now clean, the little dog's coat was a soft, warm apricot colour. Tom put a bowl of water in the kitchen for him and took him outside in the garden several times.

When he headed up to bed, Tanner followed him. Tom thought his parents might not let the dog upstairs; but they never said anything. He opened his bedroom door to find a new collar and lead on the bed and a soft, flat cushion on the floor in the corner. Tanner seemed to know the cushion was for him; he bounced onto it, curled up and promptly fell asleep.

Placing the collar and lead carefully on the bedside table, Tom lay in the darkness thinking of all the things he would do with his dog; the tricks he would teach him, the exploring they would do. His toes reached out for the lip of the rubber hot-water bottle his mum had placed in the bed. When he squinted his eyes, he could make out Tanner's silhouette. He was now lying on his back, belly up. As he watched, the little dog's legs twitched, and a sigh escaped him.

Tom turned the pillow once more, the cold side against his cheek, and closed his eyes. A silver moth flittered against the windowpane; having lost interest in the light bulb, it was entranced by the light from the moon. Tom's thoughts of being adopted and having a twin had almost faded to nothingness; tucked in a cranny at the back of his mind. And that is where they stayed – until more than a year later, when the fair came back to town.

# Chapter 7

## September 1911

Wilbur sat with his back against the hay bales, glad the harvesting was almost over. Two more days should do it and it looked like the weather would hold fair. He closed his eyes against the late afternoon sun, still warm on his face.

'Are you asleep?' Amy's soft giggle drifted into his thoughts, then his reality. He opened his eyes. She stood before him, her white dress lit from behind, her figure discernible beneath. His heart quickened.

'No, just resting.' He smiled up at her. She lived in the village and they'd grown up together. But where he was still a gangling youth, somehow she'd left him behind and become a young woman. During the harvesting she'd visited him in the fields most days. She said she liked helping with the horses; but he dared to hope she came to see him as well.

'Have you finished for the day? I can help you take the horses back.'

The sun was low in the sky now. He looked across to the farmhouse.

'Pretty much. I expect Aunt Agnes has the dinner on the stove.'

Amy sat beside him. She smelt of roses. 'Has she moved in for good?'

'I'm not sure. It's been seven months since Ma… ' Wilbur swallowed.

Amy reached for his hand. 'They seem to get along well.'

'She's a lot like Ma. Like Ma was, I mean.'

She squeezed his hand gently. 'That's good.'

He looked away, unable to answer.

'You're still angry, aren't you? About your Ma dying.'

A shiver crept up Wilbur's spine. How did she know? He thought he'd managed to hide the turmoil inside him.

'I'm not angry at Ma. Or the baby that died. I'm angry at… God. For taking them away.' He could feel tension build behind his eyes. Amy wouldn't understand. Her family was God-fearing; her father a priest. She attended church every Sunday. To Amy, God could do no wrong. Wilbur heard her suck in a breath, but it was a while before she spoke.

'Maybe God didn't take them. Perhaps people die from disease, or accident, or by another person's hands. Maybe God doesn't decide who dies; or how or when.'

Wilbur let his eyes drop from her face, scanning the field and darkening copse. The only sound came from the shire horses, chomping the oats in their nose bags.

His voice was cold; edged with steel. 'If I can't be angry with God, who can I be angry with?'

'You can be angry with God. He understands. But I think you're angry with yourself, Wilbur. There was nothing you could have done to save your Ma. It's not your fault she died. You have to let it go. I think God probably sent your Aunt Agnes to live with you and your Pa. To help you both.'

Wilbur looked at her again. If only he could believe in a God that did all of the good things and none of the bad. And he wished he could feel grateful that Aunt Agnes was looking after them. But he couldn't admit to himself that she was good for him and Pa. If he admitted that, he'd be a traitor to his Ma; to her memory. But Amy was right – he needed to let go of the anger.

Smiling, he put his arm around her shoulders. 'I don't know how you do it lass, but you always make me feel better.'

She smiled shyly at him. 'You've lots of things to feel better about. No more Grammar school. No more arithmetic. No more Latin!'

He laughed, drawing her closer.

Together, they watched the bats skitter in the dusk.

* * *

The following week, Wilbur's father worked in the top field repairing the post and rail fencing, while Wilbur whistled to himself as he cleaned out the shires' stable. He'd clean the harnesses, stays and cart tomorrow, but this afternoon he'd pick the last of the apples. Harvesting was over; everyone was getting ready for the winter, when they only grew turnips. There would be no more barley, oats or rye until they sowed the seeds next spring.

Wilbur put the old wooden ladder in the back of the cart and talked to Daisy as he harnessed her up. She was his favourite; so gentle, hard-working and intelligent. He ran his hand across her strong shoulder, breathing in her horsey scent. Nothing smelled nicer – well, except for Amy.

There were already sacks and slatted boxes in the cart; Wilbur added a bale of straw to wrap the apples in as he packed them. He'd take them carefully from the tree, making sure they didn't bruise. These apples they'd keep for themselves; packed well, they'd last until spring.

Wilbur jumped on the cart and took the reins. 'C'mon girl,' he said to Daisy's rump, 'Let's get those apples in.' The horse's great hooves plodded down the rutted track as they headed towards the apple trees at the side of the copse. It was a small orchard; five apples, two pears and two quince. He'd taken the early apples to the mill at Sloebridge two weeks ago. As well as making bread at the mill, old Mr Cuthbert and his wife had a small side-line in cider. Wilbur thought they drank most of it themselves, judging by their ruddy faces.

'Whoa, Daisy.' Wilbur stopped the cart under the first tree and reached up for one of the apples. He took a bite and savoured its juicy sweetness before jumping down from the cart and giving the rest to Daisy, who crunched and swallowed it in seconds, swishing her luxurious black tail. His father had refused to have any of his horses' tails docked as most farmers did. Needless and cruel he'd called it. 'Horses need their tails son, to keep away the flies. What right do people have to cause them pain and deprive them of it?' Wilbur agreed, admiring his father for his kindness.

His pa didn't farm animals, either; only crops. Couldn't bring himself to kill them, he said, or take them to slaughter. They were probably poorer because of it, but supplied several towns with wheat, barley and oats. Some of it was taken a long way away by train. Delivering their crops kept him and his pa busy for most of autumn. Wilbur enjoyed the trips to the mills with the horses; sometimes he'd even see Amy.

He'd nearly finished picking and packing the remaining apples when he saw the dog. It limped towards him, tail between its legs, then cowered in the dust ten yards away. The colour of wheat with clear hazel eyes, he was skinny as a whippet, his fur straggly and matted.

'Hello boy,' Wilbur said softly. 'Where have you come from?' The dog wagged the tip of his tail, rolling on his back and exposing his belly. Slowly, Wilbur walked towards him, murmuring. Squatting down, he rubbed the dog's tummy, the fur here soft and downy.

'You're not very old, are you?' he whispered as the dog licked his hand.

Looking at the paw the dog had been limping on, Wilbur immediately saw the problem. One of his nails was hanging on by a thin shred of skin, the pads cut and torn.

'You need a cleaning and patching up fella. You'll have to come back with me and Daisy.'

Wilbur scooped him up gently, placing him on an empty sack in the back of the cart. The dog lay quietly, resting his head on his front paws, the injured hind leg stretched out behind him. When they got back to the farm house, Wilbur carried him inside.

'What have you there, Wil?' asked his aunt Agnes, walking from the scullery, wiping her hands on a rag. 'Is he hurt?'

'I think he's a stray – I haven't seen him before. He's hurt his back paw.'

Agnes bent forward and looked at the dog's hind leg. She could see the blood. 'I'll get the carbolic soap and some water.' She returned with a pot of water and a piece of cloth. The dog watched her with wide eyes as she gently dabbed his paw, wiping away the blood and grime. She tore long strips of clean rag, wrapping them around his paw. As she tied the last knot she smiled. 'There you are, boy. All done.' The dog licked her hand. 'Keep 'im inside tonight, Wil, give the paw chance to heal. He looks like he could do with feeding – there's some left-over scraps in the kitchen you can give him. An' put 'im down a pot of water, case he's thirsty.'

'Do you think Pa will let me keep him?' Wilbur asked.

'Well, there's a question,' Agnes teased, looking serious.

Wilbur's face dropped. Agnes laughed. 'Of course he will!'

Wilbur chuckled as he ruffled the dog's fur.

# Chapter 8

## March 1969

Billy was sitting on one of the higher branches, swinging his legs and waiting for Tom, their routine now well established. They'd meet at the conker tree after school – go to Billy's, on to Tom's to collect Tanner, then to the woods or common. At each boy's house, they'd pick up anything they needed, change out of school uniform and grab a drink. Most nights, if they could get away with it, they'd have a sugar or strawberry-jam sandwich to keep them going until teatime. Now the evenings were getting lighter, they'd started to meet up again after tea as well, staying out until dark. If someone asked Billy 'What do you and Tom get up to?' he wouldn't have a proper answer. 'This and t-that,' he'd say. But it was always the best part of the day.

When Tom got to the tree, Billy was already half-way down, having spotted him turning into Budds Lane. They went to Billy's, then on to Tom's. It was warm for late March, and they heard the soft drone of a lawnmower as they walked past the last of the houses. The sweet smell of cut grass made it feel like summer.

Tanner, now fully grown, waited patiently for them at Tom's front gate, as he did every afternoon. When the two boys rounded the corner, he ran to them, tail twirling like a windmill. Jumping up, he licked their hands, and each boy gave him a bear hug.

Billy waited in the kitchen as Tom went upstairs to get changed. Hearing the stairs creaking, Lisa came out of her bedroom. 'Hi Tom. Mum's gone out to see Aunty Joyce. Tea's at six o'clock, she said don't be late.'

'Okey-dokey.' He ran downstairs just in time to catch Billy stuffing a squashed-fly garibaldi biscuit in his mouth.

'Help yourself, why don't you?' Tom laughed. 'Good job Mum's not in.'

'I g-got one for you as well,' Billy grinned sheepishly, proffering the biscuit.

They walked towards the woods, Tanner trotting behind. Reaching the first of the trees, they spotted two boys about Billy's age near the top of a large, knarled beech. A couple of blackbirds were flying around them, squawking with alarm. Billy looked up and raised his hand to shield his eyes from the sun. 'That's a hard tree to c-climb.' The lowest branch could only be reached by standing on someone's shoulders, and the next branch was high up too.

'Look!' said Tom, pointing to a bird's nest set on a bark ridge in one of the branches at the top. The first boy was just below it. 'They're after the flipping bird's eggs!' Tom ran to the tree. 'Oiy!' he shouted, 'leave the eggs alone!'

The boy reaching his hand into the Blackbird's nest looked down at Tom. 'Why? You want 'em?' He threw one of the blue speckled eggs down at Tom. It broke and splattered on his shoulder. The two boys up the tree laughed. 'Want another one?' the same boy goaded, reaching into the nest again.

'No!' shouted Billy, hating them hurting the birds; hurting his friend. 'L-leave them alone!'

'They're only pissin' bird's eggs,' sneered the other boy. 'Clear off and mind your own business!'

Tanner, with his front paws on the tree trunk, started barking furiously. 'An' shut your bloody dog up, or I'll shut 'im up for yer!' the boy shouted.

Tom pulled Billy's arm. 'C'mon,' he said, 'let's go.'

Billy looked at him, puzzled. His friend wouldn't walk away and let them destroy the bird's eggs – would he? Maybe he was worried for Tanner.

Tom saw Billy hesitating and threw him a wink. They stopped forty feet away, when Tom ducked behind an oak tree. 'You can't reason with that sort,' he said. 'We'll go up this tree. You got your catapult?'

'Yeah,' Billy grinned, as they filled their pockets with stones.

'Tanner – stay here boy.' The dog sat down and watched as Tom scooted up the tree with Billy close behind him. When Tom was level with the boys in the beech tree, he shouted out again. 'Oiy! What are you going to do with the eggs? Blow them out? Let them gather dust in your skanky bedroom? Why can't you leave them alone?'

The boy looked over at Tom. Billy recognised him. It was Mark Dunn from school.

'Piss off!' Dunn shouted back, continuing to put the eggs in his pocket.

Pulling out his catapult, Tom whispered, 'Load up, Billy, aim for his chest.' Billy nodded, concentration on his face as he placed a stone in the rubber sling. 'Take aim.' Both boys pulled back on the strong elastic. 'Fire!' Letting go at the same time, the target practice they'd done during the winter paid off. The stones hit Dunn in the centre of his chest. Stunned by the sudden sharp pain, he snatched his hand back from the nest, reaching out to steady himself. He looked like he might start to cry.

'Put the eggs back!' hollered Tom.

The other boy up the tree with Dunn hadn't seen the catapults – nor the stones hitting Dunn.

'You 'eard us before!' he shouted. 'Ain't none of your business!'

'Let him have it too,' said Tom, and they loaded their catapults again. 'Take aim – fire!'

When the stones hit, the boy squealed in pain. He waivered on the branch and losing his balance, fell sideways. He managed to grab the branch, but now hung from the underside, his legs swinging, unable to move up or climb down. It was a long drop to the ground.

'Help!' he shouted, 'Mark! I'm gonna fall!'

Mark Dunn edged away from the nest, but not towards his friend.

'Put the eggs back!' Tom shouted again. Dunn reached in his pocket and Tom saw him return the eggs to the nest, before starting to climb down.

'C'mon,' Tom looked at Billy. 'We'd better catch the other one before he breaks a leg. I don't think his mate is going to help him.' Dunn had already reached the ground and was running away towards the village. Billy grinned at the sight of his retreating back.

Climbing down as quickly as they could, they ran to the beech tree. Standing beneath the boy still clinging to the branch, Tom shouted up at him. 'Let go! We'll catch you!'

'No you won't!' the boy shouted back, but his arms were aching, his hands red and numb, his knuckles bone white.

'We will,' said Tom, 'just let go.'

He couldn't hold on any longer. As he dropped from the tree, Tom and Billy threw their arms around him and all three fell to the ground. They'd broken his fall – he was alright. Tanner jumped on them, licking all their faces. They got up, the other boy snivelling.

'I'm telling my dad of you,' he whined before running towards the village.

'If you hurry up,' Tom shouted after him, 'you might be able to catch up with your mate!'

Tom and Billy grinned at each other. 'N-nice one!' laughed Billy. 'You were b-brill!'

They walked on towards the woods. 'We'd better go to the Nissen huts,' said Tom. On the side of one of the huts, hanging from a rusty nail, was a picture of Harold Wilson that Tom had torn from the newspaper and glued to a cornflakes box. It was what they used as a target.

'Why g-go to the huts?' asked Billy.

'Your aim was terrible,' laughed Tom, 'you need more practice!'

'N-no it wasn't!' Billy rugby tackled Tom's legs and they collapsed on the ground again, laughing. Tanner joined in, bouncing around them.

After a while, when they'd calmed down, Billy spoke. 'D-do you think that those two will tell? Will we get into t-trouble?'

'Nah,' said Tom.

Billy wasn't so sure; but it turned out Tom was right.

\* \* \*

Twenty miles away – as Tom and Billy went home for tea – Topps Fair was packing up to move on. Five big lorries lined up, with an assortment of vans behind. The big rides – the dodgems, ghost train and switchback – were on individual trailers. Eight caravans, pulled by battered Cortinas, Hillmans and Vauxhalls, came behind the vans. Bringing up the rear were five carts, four of which had horses harnessed to them – two skewbald and two piebald. The heavily built cobs waited patiently. The fifth horse, a black mare with a white blaze down her nose, was fine-boned and more refined. She was tethered to the fifth cart but not yet harnessed. The cart contained an assortment of dogs; lurchers and rottweilers among them. Last year, the dogs had run behind the carts, but the police had put a stop to that.

Joe Cooper sauntered across the worn and trodden field, heading towards the mare. Seeing him coming, the horse laid its ears back flat. Nostrils distending, the mare danced on her front legs; hooves pounding up dirt, her head tugging on the rope.

Keziah watched from her mother's caravan window as Joe moved closer to the horse. She could see the whites of the mare's eyes; feel its distress. She remembered the last time Joe Cooper had ridden it. He'd returned with the horse in a sorry state, it's flanks bruised and cut, its mouth bloodied and foaming. Keziah overheard him tell his mother the mare had bolted; that the horse wouldn't stop no matter how hard he pulled on the bit; that it'd cut its own flanks by running through gorse. Keziah wasn't sure whether Joe's mother believed his lies – but she didn't.

That night, unable to sleep, Keziah had gone out to the mare. She'd washed the horse's wounds as she murmured to it gently, dabbing the cuts carefully with diluted Dettol, stroking its silken neck until the moon disappeared and the birds began to sing.

Watching Joe now, her throat was dry; her body coiled. She heard him shout at the mare. 'Keep feckin' still, will yer!' Lashing the harness on the horse, he notched up the leather as far as it would go. The mare stepped back, snorting. 'I told yer to keep still!' Raising his arm, he brought his fist down hard on the mare's nose. The horse whinnied, rearing up a little, sweat glistening on its neck.

Feeling sick, Keziah ran from the caravan, pushing herself in front of the mare to protect it from any more blows. 'Leave her be, Joe!' She meant it to be an angry command; but it came out high-pitched and strangled.

'Get out my way, I'm harnessin' her up.' Joe's voice was low; menacing.

'Don't ill-treat her then! You've got the harness far too tight!' She drew courage from her anger.

'It's jus' a feckin' horse, here to do my bidding,' spat Joe.

'But animals can feel pain – they have feelings!'

'Yer feckin' soft in the 'ead! Jus' get out my way afore I make yer.'

Keziah stepped back, but kept watching Joe as he finished harnessing the horse. He was rough, but at least he didn't hit the mare again.

The fair set off with the sun low on the horizon, the lorries bumping from the field onto the road. The convoy held up the evening traffic and the horses, trotting behind with their carts, struggled to keep up. The pretty black mare was frightened by tooting horns and cars over-taking, but she trotted on, her black mane streaming in the wind. Joe Cooper, driving the mare alone, grinned every time a car hooted or cut up close.

Whether the mare skittered or not; he flogged her hard on the spine.

* * *

After tea, Tom and Billy met up again, walking Tanner to the Nissen huts. They lifted bits of corrugated iron left rusting on top of the pine needles. Looking underneath for snakes or mice, they only found ants. Some carried a white egg in their mandibles, a few carried a leaf. All scurried in their ordered little tunnels and mounds.

'H-how do you reckon each one knows w-what to do?' asked Billy as he watched.

Tom shrugged. 'I dunno.' He started chortling. 'Perhaps they have a meeting every Monday morning and thrash it all out. Or maybe Queenie Ant writes a list out for each – '

Billy jumped on him and they rolled around, their laughter echoing around the huts.

After a while they did some target practice; Tom with his catapult, Billy with his new spud gun.

'D-did you hear about the fair c-coming back?' Billy asked.

Tom looked over at him, then at Tanner, who sniffed in the undergrowth at the side of the huts. 'Yeah, I heard.' Chewing a stalk of grass, Tom spat it out. 'They're coming this weekend, aren't they?'

'T-tomorrow, I think.'

'We knew it'd happen sooner or later. Do you think Joe would recognise Tanner if he saw him now?'

'I d-don't think so. He's not a puppy any m-more. He's grown a lot.'

They headed towards home, walking in silence.

'Take him to the air-raid shelter.' Tom spun round at the sound of Wilbur's voice. The old man stood behind them. 'You don't want Tanner to get taken by that lot.'

'No,' replied Tom, 'but Tanner wouldn't understand being taken back to the air-raid shelter now. He'd fret without me down there. He might even bark.'

'Well, don't bring him out from your house then, not 'til the fair's gone.'

'No. No I won't,' replied Tom.

Billy looked at Wilbur, with his dirt ingrained skin and his torn, filthy coat. 'D-do you think he'll be ok?'

The man stared into the distance. 'I ain't got no crystal ball, lad. But if he's kept indoors, it's not likely they'll find him.'

Tom looked around for Tanner, who wasn't by his side. About ten yards back, the dog had dropped to his stomach, ears flicking backwards and forwards. 'C'mon boy,' called Tom, but Tanner didn't move. A rumbling, threatening growl came from deep inside the dog and Tom stepped back in surprise. He'd never heard Tanner growl like that before. 'What's up, boy?' said Tom, looking around the clearing. He saw nothing. Tanner sniffed the air, his ears back low, a line of fur from his neck to his tail standing up on end.

'Can't s-s-see nothing,' said Billy, glancing around. 'Let's g-get back. I'm feelin' the heebie-jeebies.'

Tom knelt down by his dog. 'C'mon boy,' he said again, reaching for the dog's collar. For a second, Tanner looked at Tom as if he was a stranger. But then he got up and wagged his tail, licking Tom's hand.

'That was strange,' said Tom, unnerved by Tanner's behaviour.

'J-jus' smelt somethin' I suppose,' replied Billy, looking around and realising Wilbur had gone. 'Or h-heard somethin' maybe.'

Tom, who'd seen the look in Tanner's eyes, knew it was more than that.

# Chapter 9

## March 1969

Late the following evening, Topps Fair was fully set up, ready to open the next day. Joe Cooper, bored with putting up rides and stalls for the last ten hours, called to a couple of the others who'd just finished erecting the ghost train. 'Wanna go rabbit jumpin'?'

They both grinned. 'Yeah,' replied Jake, a year older than Joe. 'There's farm land down Minsley Road. There'll be loads of rabbits there. I'll harness one of the nags.'

The horses were roped up, grazing behind the caravans. Untying one of the skewbalds, he walked it back. Passing Keziah's caravan, he caught sight of her in the window, her raven-black hair glossy in the glow from the light, tumbling past her shoulders and framing her delicate face, pale and beautiful. Sometimes he'd imagine what she'd look like without her clothes; what he'd like to do to her. He knew it would never happen – but if he was lucky, he might dream of it tonight.

He harnessed the horse to the cart belonging to Joe's mother, and the three young men set off with two lurchers in the back. They didn't care it was dark; the odd car blasting its horn because the cart had no lights. One or other of them would raise their fingers in a v sign. None of the cars stopped.

Pulling the cart into a tree-lined layby opposite the first field on Minsley Road, they tied the horse to a branch. Grabbing the lurchers, they crossed the road and climbed through the barbed wire into the field, dragging the dogs beneath. Thin and hungry, they caught the scent of a rabbit and disappeared into the darkness. Joe Cooper, carrying a large flash light, snapped it on. The doe, fat with unborn kittens, twisted, turned, and jumped for her life; but she didn't stand a chance. The first lurcher clamped its jaw around her neck, the second dog snatched her hind quarters. The rabbit squealed once before the dogs tore it apart, each ripping at their piece of flesh.

Joe Cooper and his two mates laughed as the dogs finished their meal. 'Told you mine'd get it first!' shouted Joe, bubbling with adrenalin. He took a roll-up from his pocket, lighting it with a match. For the next two hours, they bet on which dog would catch each rabbit first, and which would catch the most. The lurchers ate the first two rabbits. The next four were strung together to be taken back for food. Another six were killed for the fun of it, thrown bloodied and broken to the side of the field. Some of them had given the dogs a run for their money

– one lurcher, its muzzle dark red in the flash light, lay down panting.

'C'mon,' said Joe, 'I need a beer.' They started to walk back to the cart, Joe whistling for the other dog on the far side of the field.

'What the hell's he doin' over there?' Joe mumbled.

'There's houses over that side. Maybe he's fed up with rabbit and found somethin' else to eat out a bin,' laughed Jake.

'Bloody animal,' Joe muttered when the dog didn't come. But he wouldn't leave it – the best rabbiter he'd ever had, it had won him over four pounds tonight. 'Won't be long,' he said. As he sauntered across the field, a mist began to rise.

* * *

Dusk fell as Tom arrived home that evening. Lisa ran into the kitchen, dropping to her knees to hug Tanner. She giggled as the dog licked her nose. *Does she know I'm not her real brother? Have Mum and Dad told her?* But he dismissed the thought. It didn't matter. To him she was still his little sister.

'Lis – ' he hesitated, searching for the right words. 'You know I told you about when I took Tanner from someone that worked at the fair?'

'Yeah. You took him from a cart.'

'That's right. Well, the fair's coming back for a while. I don't want anyone from there seeing Tanner, in case – well, in case they try to take him back... '

'They can't do that, he's ours! We love him!'

'Yeah, but they might try. I think we should keep him out of sight while they're in town, then they won't know he's here.'

'Oh, ok. I won't take him out anywhere. How long will the fair be here for?'

'Two, maybe three weeks. I'll tell Mum and Dad later.'

'Ok,' said Lisa, starting to get up. They both jumped when the phone rang in the hallway. Their mum answered it on the third ring.

'Tyneford 5633... ' she said, then stayed quiet, listening. Tom realised how late it was getting; that his dad wasn't home yet.

'Thank God for that... you're sure?' said his mum. She listened again for a couple of minutes, then said 'I'll wait up. I love you too.' She put the phone down.

Both Tom and Lisa stood by her. 'What's up, is it Dad?' Tom asked.

'Yes. He's fine, so don't worry – but he's been involved in an accident. No one's hurt, but the car needs towing to the garage, then someone from the garage will bring him home. He's waiting for the tow truck to arrive.' She turned to face her daughter. 'Up to bed Lisa, it's late. Dad won't be back for quite a while.'

Rubbing her eyes, Lisa headed for the stairs without argument. 'Night-night,' she said.

'I'll be up in a minute,' her mum replied.

'What happened?' Tom asked when Lisa was out of sight.

'As your dad drove round a bend, a motorbike came towards him in the middle of the road. He swerved to miss the bike and ended up hitting a tree on the verge. He's a bit shaken up, but he's not hurt.'

'What about the person on the motorbike?'

'Didn't even stop. Your dad said it's possible he may not have seen the accident.'

'What'll happen about our car?'

'I expect the garage will be able to repair it. If not, we might get a replacement.'

Tom hoped it'd be replaced. 'When will Dad get home?'

'He's not sure, but it'll be at least another couple of hours.' She smiled at her son. 'He won't be bringing your normal Friday night treat I'm afraid.' His dad always got him and Lisa a bottle of Tizer and some sweets from the off-licence on Fridays.

'That doesn't matter,' said Tom, yawning.

'I'll wait up for him, Tom. Get off to bed, you're tired.'

'Ok.' He took Tanner outside in the garden to have a pee, waiting while he sniffed about for a few minutes. Then he went back indoors, kissed his mum goodnight on the cheek and padded upstairs, Tanner close on his heels. He'd tell Mum and Dad about the fair tomorrow. He drifted off to sleep with Tanner's head resting on his legs. The dog had abandoned his cushion in the corner months ago.

\* \* \*

It was close to midnight when Tom's dad got home. His wife hugged him. 'Are you sure you're alright?' she whispered, after kissing him.

'I'm fine, love. Really.'

'There's some supper for you in the fridge if you're hungry.'

'Thanks, I am.' He noticed dark smudges under her eyes. 'You look as tired as I feel. Go on up, I'll bring you a cocoa after I've eaten. We'll talk in bed.' Elsie smiled gratefully and turned to climb the stairs.

Going into the kitchen, Reg put the kettle on and pulled out the plate covered in foil from the fridge. He wolfed down the homemade pie and vegetables without heating them up. Making a mug of cocoa, he poured a small whiskey for himself. As he reached the bottom of the stairs, Tanner rushed down.

'Hello boy, what's up? Want a pee?' Tanner wagged his tail a little, but trotted straight to the back door. Normally he'd have made a fuss of Reg, but tonight he stood waiting to go out, quietly growling. Reg opened the door and Tanner slipped into the night. Wondering if something was in the garden, Reg went to get the torch, but remembered it was in the car – which was at the garage. He went outside with only the faint light from the kitchen window holding back the gloom. He heard Tanner growling at the far side of the lawn by the back hedge. Reg looked around the garden and into the field at the rear. He couldn't see anything other than a silver mist rising silently in the darkness.

'Come on boy, there's nothing there,' he called softly, but he couldn't even see the dog now. Reg sighed. Tanner wasn't normally a problem. Perhaps he'd got the scent of a fox or badger. Reg called the dog's name again, but he still didn't come. Walking to the shed, he wedged the door open. An old rolled-up carpet stood in one corner. Reg unrolled it onto the floor. Tanner would have to sleep in there tonight. Reg turned and went back to the house. Tiredness washing over him, he locked the back door and went up to bed. His wife was already asleep, and two minutes later he'd joined her.

* * *

Tom woke as the dawn chorus began. Something wasn't right. The weight and warmth of Tanner's body was missing from his legs.

Getting out of bed, he looked around the room. There was no sign of him. He thought back to last night – yes, Tanner had definitely joined him on the bed as normal.

Tom went out onto the landing, looking through the narrow gap in the door to Lisa's room. Tanner hadn't pushed his way in there. The door to his mum and dad's room was closed. A heavy, slow churning started in his stomach. Quietly, he called the dog's name, but the house was silent. *Where is he?*

Running downstairs, Tom checked the front room, then the kitchen. The back door was locked. Tearing back upstairs, Joe Cooper's sneering face – like an image after a camera flash – scorched in front of his eyes. Bubbling, burning panic rose in the back of his throat. Bursting into his mum and dad's room, he shook Reg awake. 'Dad! Where's Tanner? He's not in the house!'

His dad stretched his arms out slowly, then brought them to his face, pushing the hair from his eyes. 'Calm down Tom! He's probably in the shed. He went into the garden last night and wouldn't come in. I left the door to the shed open so he could sleep on the carpet I rolled out for him.'

In great leaps and bounds Tom jumped down the stairs. Blood pounded in his ears like waves in a storm. Grabbing the key from the side, his hands shook violently as he struggled to unlock the back door. He wrenched it open as the lock finally slid free, the door banging as he raced across the lawn. Another image of a laughing Joe Cooper flashed unbidden before him. Reaching the open shed, he grabbed for the door frame as his legs gave way.

Tanner wasn't there.

# Chapter 10

Hearing Tom's guttural cry, Reg pushed his feet into his slippers and hurried downstairs. He found his son slumped in the shed doorway; his face ashen.

'He's not there then? Don't worry, he'll soon be back. The car is at the garage, but I can borrow Aunty Joyce's car, we can – '

'You don't understand!' screamed Tom. 'The fair's back, they've taken him!' For all the world, Tom wanted his dad to say 'don't be silly, Tanner's in the kitchen, come indoors and get your breakfast.' But he didn't – couldn't. His dad wasn't able to make things right, not this time. A burning anger brewed inside Tom – not towards his dad, but himself. Why hadn't he protected his faithful friend? The dog who slept with him, played with him, loved him and followed him like a shadow? He knew Tanner would have protected *him*.

He didn't exactly blame his dad, but the feeling he had about him was like on his last birthday – when he'd really hoped for a record player; but had been given a game of Kerplunk instead.

Reg looked at Tom, reaching out his hand to help him up. 'I'm sorry son,' he said quietly, 'but I didn't know the fair was back. If I had... ' his voice trailed off. Tom took his hand and his dad pulled him up.

'They wouldn't have known Tanner was here, though, would they?' his dad went on. 'They don't know your address – or even that it was you who took him. I'm sure he just went off after a fox or something and got lost.'

'Tanner wouldn't go away without me, you know that! If Joe Cooper saw him – stole him – he might be dead by now!' His dad flinched at the force of his words. Tom fought to get air in his lungs. It felt like they'd collapsed inside him.

'I'm sure he's ok, Tom. He'll turn up soon or someone will find him,' said his mum, who'd appeared behind his father's shoulder. Tom remembered how she'd given Tanner some pie last night, laughing as he'd licked her fingers clean, his fluffy tail wagging.

Tom ran back to the house to get dressed. *Find him.* His mind grasped his mum's words like a thirsty man grasped a glass of water. *Find him. No matter what, I'll find him.*

And he knew where to look.

* * *

Shoving his penknife and catapult in his back pocket, he tore downstairs to the back door. 'Where are you going?'

his mum shouted, but Tom didn't stop or reply. They'd try to stop him, or worse still, follow him. Minutes later he banged hard on Billy's door.

'Bit early aren't you, Tom?' asked Billy's mum as she opened the door to him wearing her purple housecoat and curlers. 'Up to something special today?'

'Hello Mrs Heath, can you call Billy?'

'Go on up and get him out of bed.'

'Thanks,' Tom rushed past her up to Billy's room. He shook his friend's shoulder. 'Billy, wake up! Tanner's gone; they've taken him!'

Bleary-eyed, Billy suddenly sprung from the bed. 'N-no!'

'Get some clothes on,' said Tom. 'We're going to find him.'

Billy had never dressed so fast in his life. Running downstairs, the two boys slammed out of the back door, through the hole in the fence at the end of the garden and into the woods. When Billy's mum got to the door and shouted after them, they were already out of earshot.

Coming to the clearing, they ran past the old car and on through the common. As they reached the main road a milk float, still laden with crates of full bottles, struggled up the hill. Panting heavily and bent double, the boys caught their breath. Tom wanted to run into the fairground, get Tanner, then take him home. Billy tugged on his sleeve. As if he could read Tom's mind, he said 'We can't just r-rush in there. There'll b-be loads of them to stop us finding Tanner.' They looked across the road into the field. Everything was set up. They could see the switchback and dodgems and lots of stalls standing behind. The lorries were parked at the left of the field. And although they couldn't see them, Tom and Billy knew the caravans would be at the back. That's where they always were.

The fair seemed strange in the early morning light – eerily quiet; desolate. The rides were hulking monsters; the garish bright colours and painted hoardings gawdy, chipped and dirty. Without the people, the lights and the music, the fair held no magic at all.

'You don't have to come with me if you don't want to,' said Tom. 'You can wait here.'

Billy snorted. 'Of course I'm c-coming! I just think we should stay out of s-sight. Find Tanner and leave before they know we've been here.'

'Ok,' replied Tom, 'we'll use the rides and stalls as cover. With any luck, they'll still be asleep. Stay close behind me.'

'I will,' said Billy.

The two boys crossed the road.

\* \* \*

With Tom leading the way, they ran to the dodgems, squatting out of sight. They couldn't see the caravans, but Tom didn't want to take any chances. Any of the fairground workers could be wandering about. Using the rides and stalls as cover, they sprinted from one to the next, heading towards the back of the field. When they reached the last line of stalls, they could see the caravans. They were positioned in a rough semi-circle, the horses and carts on the left. Tom and Billy hid behind the candy floss stall, its bleached-out canvas roof billowing slightly in the breeze, the pink and white stripes echoing the colours in the sky.

'Stay here and cover me,' whispered Tom. 'I'm going to check the carts. If anyone comes out, shoot at the caravan sides to make a noise and distract them so we've time to get away.'

Billy nodded. He was a cowboy in the wild west, his catapult his gun. Taking it from his pocket, he hunted in the grass for stones.

Bending forward, Tom crept silently to the first cart. The horses grazed close by, tied on long ropes to a tree at the edge of the field. A pretty black mare startled as he approached, letting out a snort and soft whinny. Suddenly the cart came alive with dogs jumping up from inside, straining against the ropes that held them, barking and growling. Tanner's familiar golden coat wasn't among them. The cacophony of aggression rattled the air, ricocheting around the stalls. With no time to think, Tom ducked under the cart, crouching behind a wheel.

Seconds later the door of the nearest caravan flew open. A bare-chested man, thick-set with tattooed arms, filled the entire doorway. He was at the wrong angle to see Billy; and too high up to see Tom. Billy raised the catapult to his eyeline, pulling back on the elastic. Tom caught sight of him and held his breath, closing his eyes for a second. *Don't shoot Billy, for God's sake don't shoot.*

The man looked around but didn't move from the doorway. Eventually he turned and faced the dogs. 'Shaddup!' he shouted. The dogs quietened a little, and the man stepped back inside, slamming the caravan door. As Billy lowered his catapult, Tom breathed again.

Crawling from under the cart, Tom stood up and peered over the side, checking Tanner wasn't lying injured. He checked the other carts, but there was no sign of him. Relief touched him momentarily, but he had no doubt that Joe Cooper had done something to Tanner. Going back to Billy, he crouched down beside him. The dogs growled menacingly.

'He's not there,' whispered Tom.

'W-what next?' asked Billy.

'I dunno,' admitted Tom, shrugging. 'Maybe go and find Wilbur. Start searching everywhere.'

'Y-yeah. Wilbur will know where to look.' The dogs were still watching them. Tom could sense Billy wanted to get away – the whole place felt edgy; danger lacing the breeze.

'We'll have to be quick,' said Tom. 'When we start running, the dogs will kick up a racket again.'

'Y-yeah.' They tensed their muscles, preparing for the fastest run of their life.

'Ready – go!' Tom set off like a champion sprinter from the blocks. He'd reached the other side of the stall and was tearing towards the ghost train before Billy had even taken stock. The dogs howled and barked. Billy jerked into action; his eyes fixed on Tom's back. He heard someone holler behind him. He ran faster.

Closing the gap between him and his friend, Billy didn't see the coiled steel cable lying in the grass. Catching his foot, he catapulted headlong onto the ground. He didn't know what'd happened, but panic gripped him. As he scrambled to get on his knees, the figure of a man shadowed over him. Planting his boot in the middle of Billy's back, the man forced him into the dirt, pinning him to the ground.

'Oh no yer don't,' he spat.

* * *

One by one, the other caravan doors opened. Half a dozen men came over to them, forming a rough circle around Billy.

'What's going on Jed?' said one of the men, looking at the man with his boot on Billy's back.

'Ask this little shit,' he said. Taking his boot off Billy, he nudged him in the side. 'What were you doin'? Stealing summat?'

'N-no!' shouted Billy, sitting up and looking around wildly for Tom.

'So, what then?' asked the other man, who seemed to Billy to be the oldest. He was bald; but a mass of tight, curly grey hair poked through the gaps in his shirt.

Billy wiped his forearm across his face. He had grit in his eye. His mind was blank apart from one thought. *Don't say anything about Tom.*

'Well boy? Lost yer tongue?'

'I-I'm looking for my dog,' Billy finally managed to say.

'Yeah? 'Ave you found 'im?' The older man laughed, showing more gaps than teeth. The other men grinned. 'Don't look like he's 'ere, does it?' He swept his arm theatrically wide, a thin-lipped sneer amongst the stubble on his face. 'Those dogs in the cart yappin' – all of them be ours.'

Tom, who'd reached the road before realising Billy wasn't behind him, turned and ran back. 'Leave him alone!' he shouted, seeing Billy on the ground in the circle of men, his face covered in dirt. Billy shot Tom a shaky smile.

'An' who are you?' asked the older man. 'What you doin' 'ere?'

Tom faced him. 'I'm looking for my dog.'

'Are yer now. A lot of dogs go missin' in these parts then?' The men around Billy snorted with laughter. 'I told yer mate 'ere, and now I'll tell you. The dogs in the cart be ours. There ain't no other dogs. You oughtn't be snoopin' around.'

'Where's Joe Cooper?' asked Tom, his sure, unwavering voice belying the sickness he felt inside.

'How d'you know Joe?' asked one of the younger men.

'He took my dog.'

'He ain't got yer dog! His huntin' dog's in the cart. He's had 'im for years. He ain't got no other dog. You'd better clear off, afore he wakes up.'

'I'm not going anywhere,' said Tom, his heart thudding. 'Not until I've found my dog.'

The man stepped close in front of him. 'Seems to me,' he hissed, 'that you need a good thumpin'.'

Billy jumped up, pushing through the men to stand beside Tom. 'You'll have to thump b-both of us then!'

The men laughed again as one of them shouted, 'Bet you're cackin' yer pants, eh Jake?' They started jostling for position. Each wanted a good view of the fight.

'Nah,' interrupted the older man, holding out his arm as a barrier to Jake. 'We don't want to 'ave to move on already now, do we? We've only just bloody got 'ere! Go an' wake Joe an' get him 'ere.'

Jake turned and walked towards the far caravan, muttering under his breath. Banging on the door, he opened it and stuck his head inside. 'Joe! There's a boy 'ere, says you've got his dog. Nobby wants yer outside.'

Joe Cooper yanked the door wide, pushing past Jake. Jumping over the two metal steps to the ground he strode over to the small crowd. Looking at Billy and Tom, he stood still for a few seconds before he spoke. 'I ain't taken no dog.' He spat on the ground in front of Tom's feet, then stared at him, smirking. Tom returned his stare, as Cooper's face reflected a shade of blue, returned to a swarthy tan, then reflected blue again.

A shout went up. 'The bloody pigs are 'ere!' The men looked past Tom and Billy, who turned around to see two police cars. They'd pulled round the side of the ghost train, their blue lights flashing silently. Tom could see the drawn faces of his mum and dad in the back of the second car. Two policemen got out the front and four more joined them from the other vehicle. The dogs in the cart barked furiously and a small group of women and children had gathered in front of the caravans.

The police started walking towards the men. Joe Cooper narrowed his eyes to slits, clenching his jaw. Leaning in to Tom, he dropped his voice low. 'Yer just a feckin' grass – a feckin' piece of settled shit.' He hissed the words like a snake. 'Yer never find yer dog alive.' Cooper's breath, rancid and smoky, was laden with flecks of spit. Wiping his face with the back of his hand, Tom held Cooper's eyes with his own; the same shade of light cobalt blue.

What Tom saw there chilled his soul.

# Chapter 11

The police were all in uniform, but none wore a helmet. The first one to speak was tall with short brown hair. He looked at Tom.

'You and your friend – get in the back of the car.' He pointed to the empty Ford Cortina. Tom's parents still sat in the back of the other panda.

'I want my dog first,' said Tom.

The policeman sighed heavily. He looked at Nobby. 'Is the boy's dog here?' The other policemen stood by and behind him, forming a tight group. A couple of them glanced around the site.

Nobby spat on the ground. 'Takes six coppers to come an' find a dog now, does it?' Some of the men hooted with derisive laughter.

'We don't want any trouble, Nobby. Just answer the question.'

'We've already told 'im. We've only got our own feckin' dogs.'

The policeman looked at Tom. 'Have you seen your dog here?'

Tom looked him in the eye. 'No. Not yet.'

'Why do you think he's here?'

'Because Joe Cooper took him.'

The policeman looked at Joe. Tom realised they knew all the fairground workers' names.

'I 'aven't got his feckin' dog!' shouted Joe. 'I've already told 'im! Wanna come an' look in my van?'

The door to the far caravan was still open, banging in the wind.

'He's taken him somewhere,' said Tom.

'Did you see him take the dog?' asked the policeman, already knowing the answer.

'No,' admitted Tom. 'But I know he has.'

'Yer don't know nothin'!' sneered Joe.

'Alright, alright,' said the policeman. He looked at Tom again. 'There's no evidence your dog's been taken, lad. We'll record him as lost and keep an eye out for him. Now, you and your friend – get in the car.'

Joe Cooper stood there smirking.

Tom looked beyond him to the caravans. The way they lurched there, with their dirty cream paintwork and gaping doors, made Tom want to smash them to smithereens. He saw himself ripping off the doors; jumping on them until they were nothing but battered metal. He felt the glass in the windows give way, cracking under his fists. He'd kick the van sides, over and over, crushing them under his boots. Anything left, he'd burn. He'd pour the petrol and light the match. And warm his hands on the fire.

'Get in the car, son,' the policeman said again.

Tom needed to find Tanner. That had to come first. He turned and walked to the car. As he got in the back, Billy slid in beside him.

The caravans could wait.

**\* \* \***

'We were so worried about you, Tom. We had to call the police.'

Since the police had dropped them all home, his parents hadn't stopped talking.

'We'll help you look for Tanner. The people from the fair – ' his mum's voice trailed off. She glanced at her husband. 'The people from the fair are not – well, they're not – '

'They're not the sort of people to make an enemy of,' finished his dad. 'They live by different morals, Tom – different rules.'

'I won't go back to the fair,' said Tom, looking at the floor. 'But I have to find Tanner.'

'Where will you look?' asked his mum. 'When we get the car back – '

'Me and Billy will find him,' interrupted Tom. 'We'll start looking in the woods and over the common.'

'That's a good idea,' said his dad. 'If he went after a fox – '

'Yeah,' said Tom, jumping up from the chair and opening the back door. 'See you later.'

And for the second time that day, he ran to Billy's.

Billy's mum let him in again. His friend sat at the kitchen table, eating a beef dripping sandwich. The smell of it – normally something Tom loved – made him feel sick.

'Now listen to me Tom,' began Billy's mum. 'I know you're a good friend to our Billy. But I don't want him coming home in a police car again. It'll be the death of me. You know what folk around here are like. They love nothing more than a good gossip. They'll think Billy's got into trouble.' She looked round at him and added 'Oh, and I've told him he's not to go anywhere near that fair – '

'Mum!' shouted Billy, using his sleeve to wipe grease from his mouth.

'I know you're not responsible for him Tom but you are nearly two years older – '

'For g-goodness sake Mum!' Billy stood up from the table. 'Leave Tom alone! He's my friend, not my k-keeper. I'm old enough to make my own decisions.'

Billy's mum didn't look convinced. But she didn't say any more, and left the room. Tom noticed Billy's face was clean again, but there was a purple bruise forming below his left eye.

'Did one of them hit you?' Tom asked.

'Eh?'

'You've a bruise on your face.'

Oh, t-that,' said Billy, raising his hand to it. 'It's where I fell over. It doesn't hurt. I didn't even know it was t-there until Mum made me wash my face. She saw it.'

'It's quite a shiner,' grinned Tom.

Billy pulled his shoulders back and stood up straight. 'Yeah, it is,' he smiled.

'Thanks Billy,' said Tom quietly.

'What for?'

'For being there to cover me. I'm sorry you fell over; that the police got involved.'

'It wasn't your f-fault,' said Billy. 'C'mon. Let's find Tanner.'

\* \* \*

The boys spent the rest of the day searching Jackdaw Woods and Silversand Common. They checked round the clearing, the old Austin, the Nissen huts. They checked the air-raid shelter, Stickleback Brook and the railway tracks for a mile or so each way. They checked the graves and the old barn. They'd called Tanner's name hundreds of times.

Nothing.

The sun was setting as they went back to Tom's, dragging their feet in silence. Neither had talked much all afternoon; both carried heavy lumps in their throat. Tom wondered where Wilbur was – they hadn't seen him all day. He'd know where to look for Tanner – what to do next.

Tom was exhausted, but he didn't think he'd sleep. He glanced over at Billy. The dark rings under his eyes and the purple bruise stood stark against his pale skin.

'You go on home,' said Tom. 'Hopefully we'll find Wilbur tomorrow. He'll be able to help us.'

'What about the field behind your g-garden? Where your d-dad thinks Tanner went?'

'Yeah. I looked over the hedge this morning, but I didn't have a proper look. I was sure he'd be at the fair.'

'L-let's have a look now. Before it's too dark.'

They walked round the side of Tom's house into the back garden. The shed was at the far end on the left, the dense blackthorn and dog-rose hedge behind. Tom had never known Tanner go through it, but he supposed it was possible.

The boys squeezed through to the field beyond, mainly used to graze horses. Other than collecting a ball once or twice, Tom hadn't been in there.

Walking along the edge of the field towards the road, they called Tanner's name and looked in the scrub and undergrowth that bordered the field. About half-way along, they heard some quiet buzzing. It became louder as they walked. Billy thought it was a swarm of bees to begin with, but as they got closer, they saw it was flies. Hovering around a lump in the hedge, they dispersed as the boys approached. The sight turned their stomachs. Looking down, they saw half a dozen rabbits lying dead in the grass, their glazed eyes unseeing; their fur thick with blood.

Both boys sank to their knees and Billy retched some bile.

'He's been here alright,' choked Tom. 'Joe bloody Cooper. I bet he did this to the rabbits with his hunting dog.' Tom's voice had cracked. He began to shake. 'What the hell's he done to Tanner?'

Unable to think of anything to say, Billy threw his arm around his friend's shoulders.

\* \* \*

The next morning, Tom and Billy knocked on doors one after the other. Full milk bottles stood on many of the doorsteps; some of the gold tops had little holes where the bluetits had taken an early morning drink. They'd started at the Bannon's house and worked their way along Sandy Lane then up Daffodil and Daisy Crescent. They did the houses in School Road and Ragtag Lane, then came back down Minsley Road.

Whenever someone answered the door, Tom said what he'd rehearsed. 'Good morning. Sorry to bother you but my dog has gone missing. He is a mongrel with golden-red wavy fur.' Tom then showed them a photo of Tanner taken by his mum about a month ago. 'That's him. Please let me know if you see or hear about him.' He'd then give them a hand-written note which read:

LOST DOG Called Tanner.
Golden-red mongrel with wavy fur and blue collar. If found, please let Tom know at 5 Sandy Lane. Telephone Tyneford 5633. Thank you.

If no one answered the door, they slipped a note through the letterbox. Tom had written about sixty notes the night before – Billy had done about forty. By the middle of the afternoon, they'd run out and had visited every house in the village.

'Can you write some more tonight, Billy? I'll do some too, then we can go to Minsley tomorrow after school and deliver some there.' Minsley was the next village, where Tom's aunty Joyce lived.

'Y-yeah, sure.' Billy didn't mention his hand still ached from the writing he'd done last night. He wanted to find Tanner as much as Tom did.

'Sh-shall we walk to the huts? See if Wilbur's around?'

Tom nodded. They passed the monkey puzzle tree and reached the woods before Tom spoke. 'Where do you reckon Wilbur goes? He doesn't even know Tanner's missing yet.'

'I d-d-dunno. I heard someone call him a t-tramp once. I d-don't think he's got a home – well, not a house, anyway.'

As they neared the Nissen huts it started to rain. Soft and slow at first, the boys didn't notice until it became a deluge. They sprinted to the first hut and through the open doorway, the rain pounding the roof like hundreds of bullets. The sound reminded Billy of his family's annual caravan holiday in Bognor. It always rained.

They'd already looked in the huts the day before; they were the same as always. Spindly brambles snaked in through the gaps and crisp brown ivy clung to the walls. The ground, spongy with old pine needles, smelt faintly of a dusty Christmas.

Tom and Billy's eyes had only just adjusted to the gloom when Wilbur appeared.

'T-Tanner's gone, Wilbur! He's been t-taken!' shouted Billy.

Wilbur's eyes narrowed as he glanced from Billy to Tom. 'That right, Tom? I'd a gut feeling yesterday that something had happened.' He wiped his wet face on his sleeve. 'I checked all the traps last night. Found a fox I let go, but nothin' else.'

'Joe Cooper's taken him,' said Tom, looking intently at Wilbur, daring him to dispute it.

He didn't.

'Y-yeah,' said Billy, 'but he's not at the fair. We checked.'

'You went to the fair? Just the two of you?'

'Yeah,' replied Tom. 'Tanner wasn't there.'

'Don't ever go there again.' Wilbur's voice was low; steely. 'Not without me. There are some dangerous people there.'

'W-why would you c-coming make any difference?' Billy asked.

Wilbur didn't answer straight away. He shifted position slightly, leaning against the frame of the open doorway.

'They're afraid,' whispered Wilbur, holding Billy's eyes. 'Not of me; but of what they know I can do.'

'W-what can you do?' asked Billy, confusion in his voice. He didn't think Joe Cooper would be afraid of anything or anyone – especially not Wilbur.

The old man looked through the doorway into the woods. He seemed to be looking for something. 'Just don't go there again,' he repeated.

'Alright,' replied Tom. They'd no reason to go there at the moment, anyway. 'We've searched the woods and common and put notes around the village. We'll go to Minsley tomorrow and do the same there.' Tom swallowed. 'Can you think of anywhere else we could look? I have to find him Wilbur. What am I going to do if he's… if he's… ' Tom broke off, unable to say the word.

'He ain't dead Tom,' said Wilbur softly. 'I know he ain't dead. Just keep on lookin'. We'll find him.' He turned and walked out of the hut, the tattered tails of his coat swirling behind him. Tom and Billy watched as he disappeared into the rain and pine trees.

'What do you th-think he meant?' asked Billy, his words tumbling out. 'What could Wilbur do that'd f-frighten Joe Cooper? How does he know Tanner's not d-dead?'

'I dunno,' said Tom, shaking his head, still staring at the spot where Wilbur had gone into the woods.

'D-do you think he's a bit – well, a bit – crazy?'

Tom took a deep intake of breath, then let it out slowly. 'I really don't know,' he said.

* * *

Mrs Dawes sat in her favourite armchair, dozing. She jumped at the knock on the door and looked at the clock on the mantlepiece. Who would be knocking at ten in the evening? 'Move over Kitty,' she said, gently pushing the cat off her lap. She picked up her walking stick and shuffled to the front door. Opening it a few inches, she saw a girl on the doorstep. Guessing her to be around fifteen, she pulled the door wide.

'Can I help you?' She peered intently at the young woman who had long dark hair and enchanting eyes. She's a pretty little thing, thought Mrs Dawes, despite her torn, dirty dress. Surely, she's not selling lucky heather at this time of night?

'Hello,' smiled the girl. 'I'm trying to find someone who's lost a dog.'

'Ah.' Like the flicker of a moth's wing, something stirred in Mrs Dawes's memory. She tried to catch it.

'A golden-red mongrel,' continued the girl, trying again. 'Someone in the village has lost one?'

'Wait a moment,' said Mrs Dawes, turning to the telephone table to look for the note she'd had through the letterbox. 'There's a piece of paper here somewhere about a lost dog.' As she looked through the papers on the table, one fluttered to the floor. 'Here we are,' she said, stooping to pick it up. 'Can you read, dear?'

'Yes, thank you,' smiled the girl as Mrs Dawes handed her the note. She looked at it quickly. 'Yes, this is the right dog, I think. Can I keep this for the address?'

'Yes, yes dear, of course.'

'Thank-you,' she said, turning and walking on up the road.

Fifteen minutes later she stood in front of 5 Sandy Lane. A light was on downstairs so she knocked on the door.

'Hello?' said Tom's dad, looking at the young woman standing there.

'Is this Tom's house? It's about his dog.' Her voice was gentle but clear.

'Tanner? Is he ok?'

'I'm not sure, but I think I know where he is. Are you Tom?'

'No, but hold on, I'll go and get him.'

Tom had heard the knock at the door and was already half-way down the stairs.

'Whoa!' exclaimed his dad as Tom nearly hurtled into him. 'There's a girl on the doorstep. Says she might know where Tanner is.'

Tom pulled open the door. He stood mesmerised. It was cold and dark, the moon a slither; yet her beauty shone out like the sun.

From behind strands of raven black hair, her striking eyes met his.

# Chapter 12

'Hello,' she smiled. 'I think I might know where your dog is.'

'Where?' uttered Tom, finding his voice. 'Is he ok?' He noticed she held one of his notes in her hand.

'I'm sorry but I – I don't know anything for certain – ' she paused, trying to find the right words. 'I overheard a group of men talking about a dog. I'm pretty sure it's your dog they were talking about. He's been left tied up at an abandoned railway station a few miles away.'

'Joe Cooper? Joe Cooper took him there?'

The girl looked away. 'I'm not sure. A few of them were talking together at the fair. They've been drinking all night.'

'Do you know if he's alive?' Tom's voice was thick; broken.

'I'm really sorry. I don't know. But I definitely heard them say he'd been tied up in one of the old station buildings, so I think he must have been alive then – when they left him.'

'Did you hear anything else?'

She bit her lip. 'He might be injured.' She looked at the floor. 'It sounded like they might have beaten him when they took him – to stop him growling. When he came back round, they tied a rope to his collar and made him run behind a horse up the old tracks. That's all I know.'

'I need to find him. Which way up the tracks?'

'North. It's quite a way. I can take you by horseback at first light?'

'No,' said Tom. 'I have to go now.'

'Alright. But we won't be able to go as fast in the dark.'

'That's ok. Look, thanks for finding me. Hold on.' Tom ran up to his bedroom. Grabbing his torch, penknife and jacket, he ran back down leaping three stairs at a time. His dad hovered in the kitchen doorway.

'We're going to get Tanner,' Tom said, pulling on his boots by the front door.

'Do you want me to come?'

'No, that's ok. We'll be quicker on our own.'

'Where is he?'

'Up the old railway track, tied up somewhere.'

'I wish I had the car, Tom. Be careful.'

Reg watched as Tom joined the girl on the porch. She began running up the lane to the woods and common. Tom ran right behind her.

They stopped for breath at the same spot he and Billy had the morning before. On the other side of the road, the fair was winding down for the night. Only a handful of people still milled around, reluctant to go home. Tom felt the girl looking at him. 'I live in one of the caravans. No one will bat an eyelid at me taking the horse out. But they mustn't see you. They'll remember you from yesterday.'

'Did you see me yesterday?'

'Yes. Wait here Tom, I'll be back as fast as I can.'

He liked the sound of his name on her lips. She must have remembered it from the note.

He watched as she flew across the road, disappearing into the fairground. He sat on an upturned log near-by, breathing deeply. Staring at the fair entrance, he longed for her to return; he felt uneasy with her out of sight. It added to his worry about Tanner, alone and injured and maybe... *don't*, he thought*, just don't.*

A few minutes later, the girl rode towards him on a black horse with a white flash down its nose. It had a bridle on, but no saddle. Tom wasn't about to mention that he'd never ridden before.

'Get on behind me,' she said, manoeuvring the horse sideways to the log Tom had been sitting on. He stood up, awkwardly throwing his leg over the horse's rump. Half-jumping, half-scrambling, he finally managed to sit behind the girl, his chest touching her back. 'Hold on,' she said as they started off down the road. Tom lurched sideways at the unfamiliar movement, and since there was nothing else to hold onto, he slid his arms quickly around the girl's waist, linking his hands together across her stomach. 'Not too tight,' she laughed, as she guided the mare past the fair and further along the road to another field. Deftly, she unlatched the gate and pushed it open, riding through then turning the horse to close the gate behind them.

They headed diagonally across the cornfield to the old embankment beyond. The girl guided the horse with the lightest of touches on the reigns; sometimes clicking her tongue or murmuring gently, the horse flicking its ears back to listen. Sure-footed and calm, the mare seemed to know there was someone on her back who hadn't ridden before. They reached the top of the embankment and looked down on the old tracks below, grass and weeds growing in the gaps.

'Hold on tight for this bit,' said the girl, talking to Tom over her shoulder. 'Grip Beauty's sides with your legs so you don't push me too far forward. Lean back a little. I'll take her down slowly.' It worked. They got down the steep slope onto the tracks and headed north, the horse walking at a steady pace. Apart from the rhythmic clopping of hooves on metal and the occasional hoot of an owl, the night was peaceful; serene. Tom relaxed a little. The scent of the girl's hair filled his head; like the sweet-peas his mum picked in the summer and placed on the kitchen table. He hadn't stopped worrying about Tanner; but somehow, being with this girl removed the sharp edge of his fear.

As they rounded a bend a couple of miles further on, she spoke. 'I think this might be it.' In the soft moonlight, Tom could make out a ramshackle building ahead on the right. As they got closer, he saw it was an old brick-built waiting shelter on a crumbling platform. The windows and door were boarded up; but brambles and ivy scrambled around them, looking for a way in. Clumps of green, brown-tinged nettles pushed up through the cracks in the concrete before it.

'Whoa, Beauty,' said the girl, as she pulled the horse to a stop. Tom raised his leg over the horse's back and slid clumsily to the ground. The girl jumped off, talking to the horse. 'Good girl, stay here,' she said, patting her shiny neck. The mare put her head down and started nuzzling some clumps of grass between the tracks.

Jumping up on the platform, Tom pulled his torch from his jacket pocket and switched it on. Flashing the beam over the building, he couldn't see a way in. Hearing the girl behind him, he swung round, aiming the torch to light her path.

'Watch the stingers,' said Tom, as she came towards him through the nettles, her skirt gathered up in her hands like a dark-haired Cinderella.

'Have a look round the other side, Tom. The nettles are squashed over there,' she said, pointing to the right-hand wall. Tom followed the trodden-down path to the back of the old waiting room, where he found a wooden door wedged half-open. Mostly rotten, only tangled ivy held the planks of the door together. Thick, thorny brambles stood either side, listing like drunken sentinels.

'Tanner?' Tom called, tearing the skin on his hands as he thrust aside the brambles, forcing his way through the gap. 'Tanner? Where are you boy?' Tom breathed the musty, rank air as he flashed the torch over cobwebs and broken benches.

He made his way to the far end. Stepping over the debris, dust fell in his eyes. 'Tanner?' he shouted again. 'C'mon boy, where are you?'

He heard the faintest of whimpers.

'Tanner? Tanner!' Swinging the torch around, Tom rushed to the corner where Tanner lay listless, a chain through his collar keeping him captive. Falling to his knees, Tom knelt by his side, shining the torch over him. Tanner tried to wag his tail, but only the tip wavered weakly in the torch-light. Tom's stomach churned. His dog's eyes, normally so bright and glossy, were dull and sunken. Matted fur, crusty with congealed blood, lay flat around his face. The pads of his paws were torn and ragged.

Raising his head, Tanner tried to sit up, but lay back down, panting. 'Don't worry boy,' Tom whispered, throwing his arms around his neck. 'It's alright now, we'll get you home.' Tom's vision blurred as Tanner licked his hand, the dog's tongue dry and sticky. He left him here to die, thought Tom. That bastard Cooper just left him here to die.

'He needs water,' said the girl, who stood inside the door. 'The brook isn't far.'

She's one of them, thought Tom, but immediately dismissed it. *She's nothing like Joe Cooper.*

Tom unbuckled the heavy rusting chain from Tanner's collar, quickly freeing him. He lifted the dog to his chest as he stood; cradling him like a baby.

He glanced at the girl. 'Can you bring the torch?'

Nimbly she came to him and picked it up. Walking to the door she shone the beam in front, Tom following behind. She slipped through the gap to the night outside, but Tom kicked out at the door, widening the space for himself and Tanner to get through. Climbing the embankment, they tracked downhill through knee-high grass to the twists of Stickleback Brook.

Shining the torch on the bank, the girl watched as Tom placed Tanner down in the soft grass like a piece of fine china. Cupping his hands in the water, he lifted them to Tanner's mouth. Over and over, Tom refilled his hands until Tanner wanted no more. The dog still lay down, but he was on his stomach instead of his side, and raised his head up to Tom's hand for a stroke, like he used to.

'You're going to be alright, boy,' Tom's voice a raspy whisper. 'You're going to be ok.'

'Do you want to lay him over Beauty's back to get him home?' the girl asked softly.

Running his hands over Tanner's body, Tom couldn't feel anything broken, but wouldn't take the risk.

'No,' he replied, 'I'll walk and carry him. He'll be more comfortable.'

'It's a long way, Tom.'

'I'll be ok.'

He picked up Tanner again and they made their way back to the mare. The girl jumped on the horse's back, aiming the torch beam ahead.

'You walk in front, Tom, I'll shine the torch for you.'

118

'Thanks.' He smiled up at her, the skirt of her dress bunched around her thighs, her hair wild. Trying to avoid jolting Tanner, he carried him along the tracks at a slow but steady pace. The dog's eyes closed and he fell asleep, his body warm against Tom's chest. The mare walked sedately behind, occasionally shaking her head when the moths circling the torchlight got too close.

They walked for three miles and had nearly reached the place where they'd first descended the embankment. Tom stopped. 'I need to stretch my arms for a moment.' He placed Tanner gently on the grass without waking him. The girl on the horse watched in silence as Tom reached his arms to the moon, flexing his muscles and rolling his shoulders to shake off the brittle cramp.

Bending to collect Tanner, he continued walking with the girl close behind. When they finally reached Tom's house, his dad, who'd waited up for him, rushed to the door.

'Thank God you're back and you've found him,' he said, taking Tanner from Tom's arms. He took him into the house, laying him down on the sofa. Fetching an old blanket from the airing cupboard in the hallway, he looked at Tom. 'Do you think he's ok?'

'I don't think anything's broken. There's dried blood on his face and paws, but I didn't see any large cuts. I think he'll be alright.'

'Good.' His dad gently laid the blanket over Tanner, stroking his head. The dog licked his hand, then closed his eyes again. 'He looks dehydrated. Has he had a drink?'

'Yes, at the brook.'

'We'll let him sleep tonight and take him to the vet tomorrow for a check-up.' For the first time, Tom realised just how much his dad cared for Tanner.

'Thanks, Dad. I'm sorry if it seemed like I blamed you when he went. I know it wasn't your fault.'

'Don't worry, son. It was partly my fault for leaving him outside. It won't happen again. He's home now, and hopefully he'll be fine. That's all that matters.'

'Yeah, I guess so.' But Tom wasn't sure he agreed. Other things mattered too. Like justice. Pay-back.

Tom's mum came down in her dressing gown. 'Thank goodness you're home.' She moved to the sofa. 'Poor Tanner. Is he alright?'

Reg put his arm around his wife. 'We think he'll be fine. The vet can check him over in the morning.'

Hearing the horse's hooves outside, Tom rushed to the door. In the moonlight he saw the girl trotting the horse down the road, its tail swinging from side to side. His torch stood on the doorstep.

'Wait!' shouted Tom, sprinting after her, 'I want to thank you! I don't even know your name!'

She slowed and turned to face him, raising her hand in a wave. 'That's ok!' She clicked her tongue for the mare to go on.

'What's your name?' Tom shouted again.

'Keziah,' she called back as she reached the monkey puzzle tree. 'My name's Keziah.'

She turned the corner and disappeared from sight, the sound of the trotting horse fading into the night.

'Keziah,' whispered Tom as he turned to go back indoors. He rolled the name around his tongue; savouring it like his dad did a single malt whiskey. For a few seconds, the scent of sweet-peas filled the porch.

He came in, closing the door behind him. Walking back into the front room, he looked down on Tanner sleeping peacefully.

Finally, relief surged through him like a flood.

# Chapter 13

Tom woke in his bed with Tanner's head resting on his knees. Smiling in the dark, he reached down and stroked the dog's ears, feeling his tail banging against the blankets. Both still tired, they slept on, not waking again until Tom's mum called from the hallway.

'Come down for breakfast Tom. There's something nice for Tanner as well.'

Tom stretched and looked at his alarm clock on the bedside table. It was quarter-past ten. He dashed downstairs, Tanner behind him. 'I'll be really late for school,' he shouted to his mum as he saw the plate of egg, bacon, sausage and tomato on the table, steam spiralling up from the plate. Tanner headed straight for his dish – it was full of chopped sausage, bacon and egg.

'You don't have to go to school today. I phoned them to say you won't be in until tomorrow. You were so late home last night – your dad said you were exhausted. You needed to sleep.'

'Thanks, Mum! Yeah, I guess I did carry Tanner quite a long way.' He smiled. A day off school and the best breakfast ever.

'And I thought you'd want to spend some time with Tanner today and go to the vet with your dad this afternoon. He's gone to the garage to collect the car.'

'Yeah, that's great. This breakfast looks good.' Tom sat down at the table and picked up the knife and fork, suddenly ravenous.

'Lisa was so happy to see him home safe this morning. She said she's going to get him a bone from the butchers on the way home from school.'

Tom grinned. 'He'll like that. Expect he's Hank Marvin like me.'

'Go on – eat your breakfast,' she smiled. Tom dived in as Tanner finished, rattling his empty bowl looking for more. Tom's mum put some dog food in his bowl and another chopped sausage on top. As Tanner ate, Tom could see that he looked better already. His eyes shone and he stood as normal, although the fur on his face and paws was still matted and flat.

As if she could read his mind, Elsie filled an old bowl with hot water from the kettle and added some cold from the tap. She pulled out a bottle of Dettol from the cupboard under the sink and added a capful to the water. Checking the temperature, she reached for a clean rag. 'Hold still, boy, I'm just going to clean you up,' she whispered. Dipping it in the water she knelt beside Tanner, gently cleaning his face. Tom watched as the water in the bowl turned a muddy maroon.

'There's a couple of cuts on the left side of his face, but I don't think they're really bad,' said his mum. 'They might need a stitch or two.'

Tanner licked her ear and she laughed. Filling the bowl with fresh water and more Dettol, she picked up one of his front paws. 'Let's have a look at your feet, boy,' she said, and laughed again when Tanner licked her nose.

'He's cleaning you back,' grinned Tom, stabbing the last piece of sausage with his fork.

When she'd washed all his paws she said, 'They're cut a bit, and the pads look bruised, but he'll be fine, Tom. He just needs some rest and a bit of feeding up. Don't you boy?' She gave Tanner a hug and he wagged his tail. With his mouth open and his tongue out, it looked for all the world as if he was grinning in agreement.

'So, what happened last night? Where did you find him?'

Tom recounted what Keziah had said; what they'd done and where they'd found Tanner. But he didn't tell her he'd ridden behind Keziah on the horse.

'So – it might not have been this… Joe Cooper? It could have been anybody from the fair? Keziah didn't know? What a pretty name that is.'

'She said she didn't.'

'Well, I know it's a horrible thing to have happened, but you can't blame Joe Cooper for taking Tanner if you don't know for sure he did it. Tanner's back, and he'll be ok. Just forget it Tom. The fair will move on soon.'

Yeah, thought Tom. It will. But I've a score to settle first.

* * *

High in the branches of the conker tree, the leaves sticky and lime-green new, Tom sat waiting for his friend. He smiled when he saw Billy coming down Budds Lane, his satchel on his back. He was blowing into half-closed hands practising a hooting owl sound. It reminded Tom of last night.

'Hey Billy! Tanner's home!'

Billy looked up. 'Oh wow! Th-that's great Tom! I was r-really worried when you weren't in school. Is h-he ok? Where was he?' Billy dropped his satchel at the base of the trunk and scrambled up the tree. He sat on a different branch, but level with his friend. Tom told him everything, including the vet putting three stitches in one of the cuts on Tanner's face that afternoon.

'S-so not all the fair people are horrible then. Did K-Ke-Ke, the girl on the horse – say it was Joe Cooper?'

'No. I think she knows it was him but didn't want to say so. She knew I'd want to bash his brains in. I'm going to see her again – go to the fair.'

Billy frowned and looked down the lane. 'W-why?'

Tom hesitated. 'To thank her. And… ask her about who she overheard talking.' He didn't mention the strange longing he had to see her again.

'It w-won't do any g-good Tom. You know what W-Wilbur said.'

'So, we just let Joe Cooper get away with it? He left Tanner to die, Billy! If it hadn't been for Keziah hearing them and coming to find me, Tanner would be dead in a few days!'

'B-but you d-don't know for sure it was him!'

'Yes I bloody well do.'

'You c-could get hurt Tom.'

'Oh, so you wouldn't come with me? I didn't have you down as a coward.' Tom knew he wasn't being fair. But why didn't Billy want revenge for Tanner?

'I'm not a c-coward!' Billy nearly slipped off the branch, but grabbed on with both hands, his face radish-red. 'You know I'd h-help you do anything! But we might never f-find out who did it, n-not for sure. There's s-so many of them, we wouldn't stand a chance without Wilbur.'

'I don't see how Wilbur can help,' said Tom, his expression sullen.

'We c-can talk to him and a-ask.' Billy's voice trembled.

Tom sighed heavily. He felt bad for upsetting Billy. 'I'm sorry. I know you're not a coward. It's just… I'm so angry that he'll get away with it. The police won't do anything.'

'N-no. Not without proof.'

For a few minutes, they both sat in silence, swinging their legs as the birds sang unheard.

'Let's find Wilbur,' said Tom. 'I'll tell him Tanner's back home. And maybe – maybe I'll ask him, or, well – try and find out how he could help if I went to see Cooper at the fair.'

'Y-yeah. But can I come to yours to see Tanner first?' asked Billy. 'I've missed him.'

'Course you can,' smiled Tom. 'He's half yours, anyway. But your half is the smelly bum-end.'

'W-well thanks for n-nothing,' grinned Billy, cuffing Tom round the ear as they slid to the ground, laughing.

\* \* \*

As soon as Tom and Billy walked in the back door, Tanner ran to them. Tail wagging, he wriggled and yelped with excitement. Billy sat down on the floor and threw his arms around his neck, giggling as the dog licked every part of his face.

'I think he's pleased to see you,' grinned Tom.

Lisa burst in the door. 'Tanner!' she squealed, throwing herself on the floor beside Billy. Tanner wriggled and licked all over again, Lisa laughing in delight.

'I'm so glad you found him, Tom. Mum told me this morning before school but said I mustn't disturb you. I looked round your bedroom door, you were both fast asleep.'

'Yeah, I didn't go to school today,' smiled Tom.

'You lucky thing!' said Lisa, then added quietly, 'I've been so worried about him.'

A pang of guilt fizzed in Tom's chest like Alka-Seltzer. Mired in his own anguish, he hadn't given a thought to how Lisa or Billy might be feeling.

'You don't need to worry about him anymore, Lis. The vet's checked him over, and apart from having a couple of stitches in a cut on his face, he's fine. He just needs a rest, that's all.' Tom looked at the brown paper bag by her side on the floor. Something inside was wrapped in foil. 'You got him a bone?'

'Yeah. Mum said he needed feeding up.'

'Thanks Lis, he'll love that.'

'I asked Mr. Parker for the best bone he had.'

Tom winked at her. 'Do you want to give it to him now?'

'Not yet,' said his mum, walking in from the hallway. 'He's just had another big dish of food. He'll explode if we're not careful!'

Lisa laughed. 'Or get fat!' She looked at Tom. 'Did you find out who took him?'

Elsie shot her son a warning glance. 'No Lis,' he said, 'maybe he just wandered off and got lost.'

Lisa buried her face in Tanner's fur. 'Now, don't run away again you naughty boy!' she said in a mock-stern voice, and they all laughed. 'Can I play with him tonight?'

'Course you can,' said Tom. 'He won't be coming out with me and Billy for a while, and we need to pop out for a bit.'

Elsie turned to the sink, pulling on her yellow marigold gloves. 'Don't be late back. Tea will be ready at six.'

Tom looked at the kitchen clock. They had less than two hours to find Wilbur.

* * *

They'd checked nearly all the woods and common and hadn't seen any sign of Wilbur, except for a small pile of black-charred wood on white ashes near the graves, where he'd probably had a fire the night before.

'Does it s-seem to you like he's n-never around when you look for him?' asked Billy.

'Yeah,' replied Tom. 'Look for him and you can't find him anywhere. Don't look for him and he appears from nowhere when you least expect it, scaring the hell out of you.'

'Let's head back and not look for him,' grinned Billy. 'He might just turn up.'

But he didn't. They got back to Tom's as his mum was dishing up mashed potato, mince and peas. 'Are you staying for tea, Billy?' she asked.

'Uh – oh n-no thanks. Mum's expecting me b-back.'

Tom walked with Billy to the gate. 'I'm really sorry about earlier. I know you'd stand by me – that you're just looking out for me.'

'It-it's alright.' Billy gave him a lop-sided grin.

'See you tomorrow,' said Tom.

'Ok. I-I'm so glad Tanner's back,' replied Billy.

'Yeah,' said Tom. 'Me too.'

\* \* \*

Tom went to bed early, but although he felt tired, he couldn't sleep. Slipping out of bed he dressed and picked up his torch. He whispered to Tanner. 'You've got to stay here boy. Be quiet, I won't be long.' Tanner thumped his tail twice in reply then closed his eyes again, curling up with his nose under one of his back legs.

Putting a bundle of clothes under the covers, Tom pushed down on the handle of his bedroom door and opened it soundlessly. He crept downstairs avoiding the fifth and eighth stair, and tip-toed past the front-room door. Leaving the house, he jogged to Budds Lane and walked down to the road. Crossing over, he went through the school grounds to the back playing-fields which ran alongside the fair.

Taking off his jacket and throwing it on the ground, Tom settled down behind the hedgerow. He watched the caravans through a gap in the bushes. Some looked cosy with warm, yellow lights shining through paisley curtains. The black mare he'd ridden the night before and four other horses were tied to a tree close by. They nibbled the grass, swishing their tails at the flies.

He wasn't sure how long he sat there in the dark, the fair just a stone's throw away. Smoky-sweet air carried the sirens and screams from the ghost-train, jumbling them with echoing laughter and distorted pop-songs. Bright flashing lights from the stalls shaped strange-coloured shadows, that flickered in the depths of the hedge.

The door of the caravan furthest away swung open and a woman stepped out. Tom thought it was the one Joe Cooper had come out of the last time he was here. Maybe the woman was his mum, he thought. She quickly disappeared into the fairground, the caravan she'd left now in darkness.

As Tom was about to give up and go back home, the door of one of the middle caravans opened. It was Keziah. She stepped out and immediately went round the side away from Tom.

'Damn,' he hissed under his breath, but the next minute she was walking towards him, a large bundle of hay in her arms. She came close to the tree where the horses were tied, shaking the hay on the ground.

'Psssst! Keziah!' whispered Tom, standing up. Keziah saw him over the hedge, her face breaking into a wide smile, her dark hair in a loose bun, tendrils around her face.

Tom could hardly breathe.

'Tom.' She came towards him. 'How's Tanner?'

'Fine, thanks to you. I wanted to thank you again and let you know he's ok. I can't tell you how glad I am that he's back home.'

'So am I, Tom. I love animals, I can't bear to see any hurt.'

'No, neither can I.' He glanced beyond her to the caravans.

'Joe's not here. He went out with his mates this afternoon. I haven't seen them since.'

'Can we chat? Will you come round the back of the school with me? It'll be quieter.'

'Yes, sure. I'll just get a drink for the horses first.'

Tom watched as she walked behind the caravans and came back carrying a bucket of water in each hand.

She placed them on the ground by the base of the tree. The black mare and one of the skewbald cobs walked towards the buckets, their heads low. He could scarcely believe that last night he'd ridden bareback for several miles with his arms around this girl. He reached out his hand to her and she took it as they scrambled through the small gap in the hedge. He led her to the back of the school, a tingling charge passing between them. They sat on a bench which faced the playing fields, but only looked at each other. They could still hear the noise and the music of the fair, but it was quieter; no longer a part of their world. A cool breeze lifted Keziah's fringe from her eyes.

'I'm really glad you found me and took me to Tanner,' began Tom. 'Where did you get the note?'

'I started knocking on a couple of doors down there,' she pointed in the direction of Minsley Road. 'I hoped to find someone in the village who knew about a missing dog. The first door I knocked on, nobody answered, but at the second house, the lady gave me your note.'

'Who was it that you overheard talking about Tanner?'

'They were round the other side of the firing-range stall – I didn't see them. But I recognised their voices. Joe Cooper was one of them. The other two are his mates. Three of them usually go around together. But I couldn't tell you who actually took Tanner – or hit him and chained him up. It could've been any one of them, or they might have done it together. You can't talk to them or reason with them, Tom. They carry knives and fight dirty. They're not even scared of the police.'

'But Joe Cooper's the ring leader?'

Almost imperceptibly, she nodded. 'They — well, they're all cruel to animals,' said Keziah. 'It upsets me. I'm ashamed they're part of the fair.'

'I'm sorry you have to put up with them,' said Tom, who thought he'd do anything to make sure she didn't have to. 'You know I'm not like that?'

'Yes. You seem really kind,' she smiled.

'Animals can't protect themselves, can they? I think I'm good with animals; but maybe not so good with people,' he grinned wryly. Billy's red face from earlier that day flashed in his mind.

Keziah laughed. 'Nobody's perfect, Tom.'

He reached up and removed a small wisp of hay caught in her bun. He touched her cheek with the back of his fingers. It felt like silk.

'I think you are,' he murmured, dropping his hand back to his lap.

Keziah picked it up, placing her other hand behind his neck. As the high notes from 'Young Girl' rang out across the field, she gently pulled his face to hers.

# Chapter 14

## April 1913

'But Pa!'

Her father's face was as flinty as when he stood in the pulpit condemning sinners. 'Don't argue with me, Amy. Go to your room.'

She turned and ran up the grand staircase. Slamming her bedroom door behind her, she fell on the bed crying. Why wouldn't he let her go to the farm? Why couldn't she see Wilbur anymore? But although she told herself she didn't understand – in her heart she knew. They didn't want her mixing with a farm-hand. They thought he wasn't good enough.

There was a short tap on the door before her mother stalked in, perching on the edge of the bed. 'Your father has got your best interests at heart, Amy. He can see you've grown into a pretty young woman, and Wilbur – ' she hesitated, 'well, most boys his age – will be interested in you. But it can cause trouble. You could be with child before you know what's happened – before you're even wed.'

Amy sat up. 'Wilbur's not like that. He's a friend!'

Her mother looked across the fields and copse through the mullioned window. Amy knew her Ma couldn't see the farmhouse, but she could guess what was going through her mind. Her Ma had disapproved of Wilbur's Aunt moving in with Wilbur and his father so soon after Wilbur's mother died. She would be wondering about all the ungodly goings on at the farmhouse – that Wilbur, his father and aunt would be sitting eating supper together and wasn't *that* a strange arrangement. She'd be thinking that nothing but trouble could come from her daughter's friendship with such people.

'Don't you realise, Amy,' her mother said, exasperation in her voice, 'that your father – a man of the cloth and guided by God – knows what's best for you?'

'It's because Wilbur's just a tenant farmer's son, isn't it? You don't think he's good enough.'

Her mother stood up, smoothing the creases of her skirt. 'You're not to see him again and that's an end to it.' She strode to the door, closing it behind her with a distinct click. Only the ghost of her words lingered in the room.

Amy hiccupped. Reaching for her lace handkerchief she wiped her eyes and blew her nose, trying to swallow the sick feeling in her chest. An image of Wilbur came to her as she'd seen him last, two days ago. Working on the land bare-chested, she'd watched as the muscles in his arms had bunched and relaxed; sweat trickling between his shoulder blades, his tanned body lithe and strong. He'd kissed her before she'd left – she remembered the gentle touch of his lips and shivered. She shouldn't think of such things; but now she'd admitted her feelings to herself, she felt emboldened. And it wasn't just his body she found attractive. She loved his soul.

**\* \* \***

'Barley, here boy.' Wilbur didn't have to call loudly; the dog hardly left his side. For the last six months, Wilbur had patiently trained him. The dog proved intelligent and quick to learn.

Sitting in front of Wilbur and wagging his tail, the dog awaited instruction. But none came. Instead, Wilbur knelt beside him, putting an arm around him and ruffling his fur. 'Good boy, Barley. You're a good dog.' Wilbur smiled as Barley's hot tongue found his ear.

A fleck of colour and movement across the field made Wilbur focus. Two people were walking towards them. Barley wasn't concerned, so it couldn't be strangers. Then he saw the first figure was Amy and his heart quickened. But who was with her? And why wasn't Amy waving and running as she normally did?

He walked forward to meet them, Barley by his side. Amy's face was set; unsmiling. 'What is it? Are you alright?' He looked at the woman with her. She'd stopped and stood uneasily ten yards behind Amy, her eyes staring like an eagle watching a mouse. 'Why is your mother's housemaid with you?'

Amy spoke in a whisper. 'Mother would only let me come and tell you if I had a chaperon.'

'Tell me what?'

'That I'm not allowed to see you anymore, or come over to the farm.' Her eyes glistened. Wilbur reached for her hand, briefly squeezing it, sensing he could do no more.

'But we're friends. We have been all our lives. Your Ma and Pa know that. Why can't we see each other?'

Amy glanced behind her. The woman still watched. She lowered her voice further. 'They think we're too old now to meet alone. They think – '

'That I might take advantage of you,' Wilbur finished for her. 'I can't not see you Amy.' His voice broke. He hadn't wanted to tell her like this, in these circumstances, but the words came out anyway. 'I love you.'

Tears tracked down Amy's cheek. 'I love you too.' She reached up, running two fingers down the side of his face.

'Come along, Miss Hartington!' called the housemaid, stepping forward. 'We must get back now!'

Thinking quickly, Wilbur whispered fervently. 'I'll get a message to you. We'll meet in secret. Keep an eye out for Barley.'

Amy nodded. Wilbur thought he saw a flicker of a smile touch her eyes before she turned and walked back to her chaperon. He watched as the two figures retreated, the housemaid glancing back at him once or twice. She's making sure I don't follow them, he thought.

When they'd disappeared from sight, Wilbur looked at Barley. 'Come on, boy, we've got work to do. You're going to be a messenger dog.'

* * *

Amy didn't know why she went to the window to look across the graveyard. It had been four  days since she'd told Wilbur she couldn't see him anymore. But she still hoped – no, knew – he would find a way to get in touch. If someone had asked why she chose to look through the window at that moment, she'd probably have said intuition; a sixth sense. Hadn't her mother told her once that her grand-mother, who she'd never known, had professed to have the 'sight'? Perhaps she had inherited it from her. It certainly hadn't come from her mother.

The setting sun turned everything different shades of ochre. All was quiet except for the rooks cawing as they settled in the yew for the night. Amy was used to them; she fancied they were old women huddled in black capes, gossiping about nothing. Her mother wasn't playing the piano downstairs as she normally did at this time, as her father had gone to see Reverend Smith in the next parish.

Amy's eyes were drawn to the newest grave at the far side by the hedgerow. Wilbur's mother.  There was something in front of the headstone. She blinked, then squinted. An ear flicked. Barley!

Her heart pounding, she knew her mother would be in the drawing room downstairs at the front of the vicarage. She'd be able to slip out unnoticed. Picking up her shawl, she threw it around her shoulders over her nightgown. She went down the stairs keeping to one side to avoid the creaks, reaching the rear lobby which opened onto the graveyard. She gently closed the door behind her.

Barley started wagging his tail, but stayed sitting down until Amy got to him. 'Barley,' she whispered, cuddling him. 'Did your master send you?' She looked around for Wilbur, but knew he wouldn't have come, it would have been too risky. But her parents didn't know Barley so wouldn't suspect anything even if they saw him. She ran her hands around the dog's neck and felt a leather pouch strung to his collar. She undid the knot with shaking fingers and removed the piece of paper inside. In the dying rays of the sun, she read: *Meet me Friday evening 7 o'clock at the old barn. Tell your Ma you're collecting decorations for Mayday.*

Tying the pouch back on Barley's collar, she whispered in his ear. 'Good boy. You're a good dog. Go on back now.' The dog licked her nose before picking his way through the churchyard to the field beyond. Amy watched as he headed home, then went back to her room, the note clenched tightly in her hand.

\* \* \*

Sitting with his back to a tree, Wilbur hadn't taken his eyes off the far field since he'd sent Barley on his way more than an hour ago. He sensed rather than saw Barley run through the copse and across the field towards him. Opening his arms wide, Wilbur called to him. 'Good boy Barley!' The bundle of fur jumped on him and they wrestled playfully before Wilbur took the pouch from his collar.

The note had gone. He smiled in the darkness. Barley had done his job.

# Chapter 15

## March 1969

Tom didn't remember walking home that night, but he got back to his bedroom unnoticed by anyone except Tanner. The next morning as soon as he woke up, he was already thinking about Friday, when he'd arranged to see Keziah again.

He met Billy at the conker tree after school. He didn't tell him he'd been to the fair and seen Keziah the night before. He certainly wouldn't tell him he'd kissed her. It was a memory he wanted to savour – to keep to himself.

After a few minutes, they left the tree and started walking down Budds Lane.

'Shall we go out after tea to find Wilbur?' Tom asked.

'If you l-like,' replied his friend.

'It's just that if we go a bit later, we might be able to find him,' Tom added.

'W-will your m-mum and dad be ok with that? With you going out later, I m-mean?' Billy didn't meet his eyes.

Tom wondered if Billy didn't want to find Wilbur. Maybe he was worried that Wilbur would help him sort out Joe Cooper. 'Yeah,' replied Tom, 'I think so. They're starting to loosen up a bit again. As long as we're back before nine I think it'll be ok.'

'Al-alright,' said Billy. 'I'll knock for you after tea.' He opened his back gate, leaving Tom to walk back to his house.

'Billy?' said Tom, just before he headed home, 'are you ok? You're a bit… quiet.'

Billy shrugged. 'I'm f-fine.' But it wasn't his normal voice. Tom had to wait another two hours to find out why.

When Billy came round later, they walked towards the woods in the twilight. The clocks wouldn't be going forward for another week.

Billy was still quiet. 'So, what aren't you telling me?' Tom asked.

It came tumbling out. 'There w-were robberies last night. Down my r-road. Two neighbours were burgled. Not really close to us, but Mum and Dad know them. The p-police came, asking questions at all the h-houses before school this morning.'

'Blimey. Was anyone hurt? What was stolen?'

'I d-don't think anyone was at home in the places that were b-broken into. M-money and jewellery was taken, I think. We heard from one of the other neighbours that one back door was j-jemmied, and the kitchen window smashed at the other house.'

'Did you see or hear anything?'

'W-well. That's the strange thing. I'm n-not sure.'

Tom stopped walking and stared at Billy. 'What do you mean, you're not sure? Either you did or you didn't.'

Billy swallowed. 'When I woke up this morning, I th-thought it'd been a d-dream I remembered. I heard Joe Cooper's v-voice in the dream. But when the p-police came and asked if we'd s-seen or heard anything, I wasn't sure it had been a dream. I might have actually h-heard Joe Cooper last night. I'm not sure, Tom. But the more I think about it, the m-more I think I did hear him.'

'Well, I wouldn't be surprised if it was them. Cooper and his cronies. Did you tell the police you might have heard him?'

'No, b-because I wasn't sure. And, w-well, you won't believe this – '

'What?'

'I'd s-seen the copper that came to the door b-before. He was one of the policemen that came to get us at th-the fair.'

'Yeah? So?'

'I knew I'd seen him before th-that – even before the fair. B-but I couldn't remember where. Then, at school today, I remembered.'

'Where?' asked Tom, 'where had you seen him before?'

'Th-that night when we first found Tanner. At the d-dog fight. He was one of the men in the barn.'

Tom let out a long low whistle. 'Bloody hell. Are you sure?'

'As s-sure as I can be. I remember seeing him take a large bundle of fivers off one of the other men. They all seemed to be b-betting on the fight.'

'Why didn't you tell me earlier? At the conker tree?'

'I d-dunno. I guess I wanted to wait, to be sure in m-my mind. I've been thinking about it all day, wondering whether to tell mum and dad. B-but there's no proof, is there? No p-proof of anything.'

Walking on, they were in the thick of the woods before Tom answered. 'No. I s'pose not. It sounds like Cooper and the others have at least one bent copper in their pocket. Dog-fighting's illegal, as well as cruel and just plain wrong.' He paused. 'I wonder if that's why the police never came out that night? Because they knew that at least one copper was there watching the fight, maybe even more?'

'I d-dunno,' said Billy. 'But I d-don't think there's anything we can do about it.'

Tom hesitated. 'Maybe not. But I've heard my dad say – I think it might have been someone famous said it first – that for there to be evil in the world, it only takes good men to do nothing. Something like that, anyway.'

'But they t-treat us like kids Tom, they d-don't listen! What can we d-do without proof?'

'Let's speak to Wilbur. See what he thinks.'

Billy looked around at the dark clumps of trees. The moon, like Wilbur, was nowhere to be seen.

'Yeah,' he said. 'If we can f-find him.'

* * *

They finally saw Wilbur about half an hour later, walking towards them from the direction of Stickleback Brook, a brown trout in his hands.

'W-Wilbur!' shouted Billy, waving at him.

'Not so loud, son,' said Wilbur, smiling. 'Only you, me and Tom 'ere, you see. Don't want to speak to the whole world, do we?' Wilbur winked at him, and Billy saw the dirt etched in the lines around his eyes.

'We've been l-looking for you.'

'Ave you now. Well, you've found me. Want to help me with my tea?'

'Y-yeah.'

'Collect some wood for a fire, then. I need to cook this fish.'

Plenty of dry wood lay scattered around. It hadn't rained in a while. Tom and Billy filled their arms with branches and returned to Wilbur, who'd already lit kindling on a cleared spot of ground. He'd placed three large logs close to the fire.

'Take a pew, lads,' he said, theatrically bowing and sweeping his arm to indicate the logs. They put the wood in a pile on the ground and sat down. Picking up a few of the smaller sticks, the old man arranged them over the kindling like a wigwam. Orange flames licked and spat; they watched with primeval fascination. As Wilbur added thicker wood, the fire crackled with flares of yellow and blue, blazing and bobbing in the dark. Hot already, Billy pushed his log seat back a bit.

'Burning your toes, eh?' cackled Wilbur, a black smudge across his nose and cheek. Billy grinned at him, noticing how long his beard was now, streaked with grey like a badger.

'Y-yeah, but don't you lean in too close W-Wilbur, your b-beard might just go up in smoke.'

The old man guffawed, coughed, then wheezed. 'Aye lad. I'll move back a bit too, then.' He shuffled his log backwards, and Tom did the same. Reaching inside his coat, Wilbur pulled out an old metal fork and raggedy string. Selecting a thin branch, he tied the fork to the end and speared the trout. Holding it above the flames, the fork glowed gold in the firelight.

'Y-you like fish, then?' said Billy. 'I don't. T-too many bones. Like needles.'

'I gotta eat, lad. I eat vegetables and fruit mainly. Mushrooms in the autumn. But I sometimes have fish, or a pheasant.' He raised the fish slightly higher, so it was in the smoke. He sensed the boy's unasked question. 'I kill them as quickly and painlessly as I can. They've had a good an' free life. They haven't existed jus' for me to eat 'em. Not like the poor buggers in the farms.'

'What happens to farm animals then? Is it cruel?' asked Tom, who hadn't thought about it before. He liked the meat pies and stews his mum made, and loved roast chicken. He hadn't given any consideration to how the animals lived, beyond seeing cows or sheep in a field.

'A lot of it is, lad. Not all; but most. Some animals are pumped full of chemicals to make 'em grow quicker, so they're too fat to move. Some are locked up all their lives, never seein' the light of day. Some have their beaks an' claws cut off, or holes put in 'em.' Wilbur paused, glancing at the boys who listened intently. 'Some get branded with hot irons. Some are bred non-stop with only enough room to turn around. Some don't even get that. I'd say their suffering is terrible, wouldn't you? If that ain't cruel, I don't know what is.'

Tom and Billy, thinking about this for the first time, were silent; their guilt a thick blanket settling around them.

'So, it's wrong to eat meat?' asked Tom.

'No, I don't think it's wrong to eat a little meat if they've had a natural, good, long life. But it's wrong to be cruel and cause suffering; to make them live a life of misery. People are too damn full of their own importance, too damn sure they're better than animals. What gives us the right?'

'I guess,' said Tom, 'people treat them any way they want because they're different, because they're not people.'

'Aye. In law, animals are just possessions, like slaves used to be. But they're living creatures with a will. They have their own wants and desires, just like us. People shouldn't think about how different they are, but how they're the same. Do animals have feelings; memories?

147

Do they play; have a family; look after their young? Can they feel happiness; pain? Do they suffer?' Wilbur took the fish from the fire. 'Of course they bloody well do.'

Tom and Billy watched as Wilbur pulled a flattish piece of wood from the pile and laid the fish on it. Untying the fork from the stick, he used it to pull the fish from the bones.

'One day,' said Wilbur, 'in the future – not in my lifetime – an' maybe not even in yours – but one day, mankind will hang their heads in shame about the way they've treated animals. 'Ere,' he said, picking up a small chunk of fish and handing it to Billy. 'Ain't no bones in that.' Billy put it in his mouth before it burnt his fingers. Wilbur gave Tom a piece. They ate listening to the crackling fire, thinking about what Wilbur had said. Billy remembered how over-joyed Tanner had been to see him the day before. He had no doubt that Tanner had feelings; that he could suffer. Like he'd suffered at the hands of Joe Cooper.

To his surprise, the fish tasted good. Billy thought that providing there were no bones, he might be able to live on it. Which was just as well since he didn't like vegetables. Or mushrooms.

'So,' said Wilbur, throwing the fish remains and wooden plate on the fire, 'Tanner's back then?'

Tom sat up with a start. 'Yes. How did you know?'

'He ok?' asked Wilbur, swallowing the last of the fish.

'Yes. The vet's checked him over. He needed a couple of stitches in his face. How did you know he was back?'

Wilbur licked his lips before wiping his mouth on his sleeve. 'Keziah help you, did she?'

'Yeah. She told you?' asked Tom.

'You found 'im tied up at the old railway station, up the line.' It was a statement, not a question. 'She's a good'un, that Keziah. Ain't many like her at the fair.'

Billy looked from Wilbur to Tom and back to Wilbur again. 'You know K-Keziah then?'

Wilbur stared into the fire. He didn't answer.

'Wilbur?' insisted Tom. The old man looked at him. 'Do you know Keziah?'

'Aye.'

'What did you mean before? When you said we weren't to go to the fair without you?'

'What I said, boy. There's only trouble for you there. You'll not change the likes of Joe Cooper.'

'Maybe a good thumping might make him think,' said Tom.

'They don't fight fair, Tom. Not that lot. And anyway, they wouldn't alter their ways.'

'W-Why would it h-help if you came?' asked Billy. 'W-What can you d-do that they're scared of?'

Flames reflected in the old man's eyes as he spoke. 'There's an old sayin'. It's in Latin.' He pronounced the words succinctly; flamboyantly, like an actor on a stage. ' "Non omnis moriar." '

The two boys looked at him blankly.

149

'You don't do Latin at school anymore?' He shook his head. 'I'll translate. It means "I shall not altogether die."'

'W-What do you m-mean?' asked Billy. There was a tremor of panic in his voice, like when he'd been asked a question by a teacher and didn't know the answer.

'Well, when some animals die – I don't know about – about people... ' His voice drifted off again, glowing light from the fire playing on his face.

'W-What happens? Wilbur! What happens w-when animals die?' He might be odd; but he told of interesting things they'd never hear about from anyone else.

Wilbur smiled. Taking a small silver hip-flask from his pocket, he unscrewed the cap, took a sip and coughed.

'They don't die,' he said, his eyes shining. 'They've got the essence.'

# Chapter 16

Tom sighed. *What on earth is he talking about?*

'W-what's the e-essence?' asked Billy. 'W-why don't they die? I don't understand.'

Wilbur took another sip from his silver flask. 'You ever seen a dead animal? Buried one at the graves?'

'I have,' replied Tom.

Wilbur looked him in the eye. 'When an animal's dead, its body's there, but, well, the essence of 'em ain't there anymore, is it? It's jus' the shell.'

Tom knew what he meant — what he was trying to describe. He'd felt it himself when his rabbit, Tizz, had died.

'The essence of 'em, it doesn't die. It just goes someplace else.'

'L-like a ghost, you m-mean?' asked Billy, leaning forward, his face animated in the orange glow of the fire.

'Some folks call it the soul, or the spirit,' Wilbur went on, 'but you can call it a ghost if you want.'

'H-how do you know?' asked Billy. 'Th-that it doesn't die?'

Wilbur reached over and put another two logs on the fire. 'Because I've seen 'em.'

'W-What do they l-look like?'

Far away in the woods a vixen screamed. Billy jumped.

'Like they do in life. But sometimes they're less solid. A bit see-through.'

Billy's eyes widened. 'Y-you've really seen g-ghosts? Animal ghosts?'

Wilbur nodded. 'An' if I really need to, I can call 'em. An' the fairground people – they know I can.'

'Why does that scare them?' asked Tom.

'Because the essences – if I call 'em – they'll do what I ask. The fairground folk, they know I've a bond with animals. It's only the cruel bastards that have anythin' to fear, you see.'

Tom wasn't sure he did see. Either Wilbur was telling them something astounding – that he could contact dead animals – ghosts – to come and help him when he needed – or he was completely off his head. Tom thought that when he went to confront Cooper, he wouldn't be relying on an old man to help him by conjuring up some ghosts. He'd talk to Keziah on Friday. Ask her what she knew about Wilbur. Whether she thought he was crazy.

Standing up, Tom looked at Billy. 'We'd better be getting back.'

'B-but what about the c-copper? We were g-going to ask – '

'We haven't got time,' interrupted Tom.

Wilbur looked at Billy. 'What about the copper?'

'At the d-dog-fight. W-when we took Tanner. One of the men in the b-barn was a policeman.'

Wilbur sighed. 'I'm not surprised. All sorts of people are dishonest. Corrupt.'

'B-but what can I do if Tom goes to f-fight Joe Cooper? I c-can't call the police to help, can I? Tom might get killed!'

'Don't be stupid, of course I won't,' hissed Tom.

Wilbur narrowed his eyes. 'I've already told you Tom. You can't fight Cooper. Tanner will be ok now. Forget it.'

Fire burned through Tom; hot blood rushed to his head. The image of Tanner chained up lying injured flashed before him. 'Why? Why should I bloody well forget it? What about justice? He should pay for what he did!' Tom's voice was strident; bitter. 'And he upsets Keziah!'

'Calm down, Tom,' said Wilbur. 'Calm down.' The old man surveyed the shadows surrounding them, as if he thought someone might be in the woods listening. Watching. 'Look, I didn't want to tell you this. Seems I've got no choice.' He glanced at Tom. 'There's another reason you can't fight Cooper.'

'What reason?' Tom studied the ground. Why didn't Wilbur and Billy understand? Fed up, he wanted to go home – to see Tanner and think about Keziah.

'That night you were born. You said your twin was left in the barn and got taken?'

'Yeah?'

'I was there fifteen years ago. On the common. I heard a baby crying in the old barn and walked towards it. The fair was in the village.'

Tom and Billy stared at him.

'Just before I got there, I saw a woman go in the barn and come out with the baby. It was still crying. She was rocking it; trying to keep it quiet. She walked towards the fair. I didn't know she wasn't the baby's mother, not then. How could I? It wasn't until you told me about your twin being taken from the barn that I realised.' Wilbur took out his flask again and began unscrewing the cap. 'The baby I saw that night – it must have been your twin.'

The fire hissed and sent out a crack like a shot-gun.

Tom's mouth was dry. 'You saw a woman take my twin? Who was she?'

'Bessie Cooper,' said Wilbur, his voice a whisper. 'Joe Cooper's mother. I'm sorry Tom, but I think Joe Cooper's your twin brother.'

\* \* \*

They walked most of the way home in silence. Tom strode in front, Billy half running to keep up. When they emerged from the woods into Sandy Lane, Billy couldn't keep quiet any longer.

'I s-said you looked like him!'

Tom walked faster; hands deep in his pockets. In a nearby tree, an owl screeched.

'T-Tom – '

'Just shut-up Billy, for God's sake! Wilbur talks a load of flippin' rubbish!'

'B-but he s-said he s-saw – '

'Shut-up and go home! And don't tell anyone what he said. It's not bloody well true!'

Billy watched as Tom walked up the path to his back door and disappeared from sight.

\* \* \*

Tom blinked as he walked in the kitchen, the lights seemed so bright. His mum and dad sat at the table, each with an empty cup in their hands. Tanner ran to him, tail wagging.

'For goodness' sake, Tom!' His mum stood up and faced him. 'Where have you been?'

Tom looked up at the clock on the wall. It was quarter past ten.

'Sorry,' he mumbled, reaching down to scratch Tanner's ears.

His dad's chair scraped back as he stood up. 'Sorry just isn't good enough, Tom! With everything that's happened lately, your mum's been worried sick!' Reg put his arm around his wife, drawing her to him.

Tom pushed past them into the hallway and ran up the stairs, Tanner following behind. His dad's voice rang in his ears. 'We're not having any more of this; you're staying in for the rest of the week. Come straight home after school tomorrow!'

'Stop treating me like a flippin' kid!' Tom slammed his bedroom door and collapsed on his bed. Tanner jumped up and sat next to him. 'Come here, boy,' whispered Tom, holding him in his arms and stroking him. 'Wilbur's a bloody nutcase. Going on about essences. And there's no way on earth that Joe Cooper's my twin. No way.' Tanner thumped his tail on the bed, and catching the faint scent of smoked fish, he licked Tom's chin.

* * *

The next day, Tom heard the rumours at first break. Feeling sick, he ran down to the playing fields to check. They were right; the fair had left. Packed up in the night. Gone before dawn.

Keziah's face came to him, rose-pink lips curved in a smile. Would he ever see her again? His chest tightened as if crushed by a boulder; his breath came and went in raspy gasps. Then Joe Cooper's face replaced Keziah's — sneering; gloating. 'I'm your twin brother!' the image snarled. 'You can't bloody touch me!'

The school bell rang, its sharp metallic clangs setting Tom's teeth on edge. He walked through quick-sand to get back to class; unable to swallow the burning lump in his throat.

After school, when he passed the conker tree, he didn't even look for Billy.

156

'T-Tom!' Billy ran up behind him, panting. 'Y-you d-didn't stop!'

'The fair's gone,' replied Tom, as if that explained everything.

'Yeah. T-that's good, isn't it? Joe Cooper won't be around. We d-don't have to worry about Tanner.'

Walking on, Tom didn't answer. What was the point? Billy wouldn't understand. When they got to Billy's back gate, Tom turned to face him. 'Dad's banned me from going out. Don't call for me anymore.'

Billy stood still and watched his friend walk away until he was out of sight.

It was two weeks before he and Tom spoke again.

And just a few months before their lives changed forever.

# Chapter 17

## April 1969

Lisa sat in her bedroom drawing with the spirograph she'd been given for her twelfth birthday. She loved the geometrically perfect patterns that appeared as she moved one circle inside another. Putting down the red pen, she picked up a green one. All her drawings were bright and multi-coloured. Lisa was so pleased with this one that she wanted to run into her brother's room to show it to him.

But she hesitated. Tom hadn't been himself for the last couple of weeks. Withdrawn and grumpy, he hadn't gone out much apart from school and walking Tanner. He listened to music on his record player in his bedroom with the door shut. She didn't recognise the music he played – it wasn't the Beatles. She'd overheard her mum say to her dad that Tom was "at that funny age", but Lisa didn't think Tom was having much fun. Her mum must've meant funny-strange, not funny-funny. And Tom's friend Billy hadn't called round for ages. She hoped they hadn't fallen out; she liked Billy. Lisa was beginning to realise there was a lot more to growing up than just getting older. Nothing seemed straight-forward any more.

Ringo Starr grinned at her from above the bed. She'd torn the picture from the centre of *Jackie* and sellotaped it to the wall. A year ago, there'd only been pictures of horses. Her friends at school were always talking and giggling about boys now. Susie had told her in a hushed voice at break the other day that she fancied Tom; that he was good-looking and she'd like to go out with him. Lisa wasn't sure what she thought about that. It just felt so *weird*. She imagined Susie kissing her brother and shuddered.

'Lisa!' called her mum from the kitchen. 'Can you come down a minute?'

Lisa left the spirograph picture on the bed. She'd put it up by Ringo later. Padding down the stairs in her pyjamas, she saw her mum putting sausages under the eye-level grill. Elsie turned to face her daughter.

'Sorry love, I've run out of eggs. I was sure I had half-a-dozen in the larder. Would you pop round Whatties and get some for me?'

It was Saturday, the best morning of the week. Mum always cooked sausage, egg and bacon at the weekends. 'Course. I'll just get dressed.' She went back upstairs and changed her pyjamas for jeans and a tie-dyed cheesecloth blouse. Picking up the money her mum had put on the table, she slipped the coins into her back pocket.

'Better take your mac,' said her mum. 'It looks like rain.'

Lisa got to the corner shop in a few minutes. The familiar sweet, sugar-dust smell welcomed her as the bell above the door jangled. She liked wandering around the shop, with its higgledy-piggledy floor and polished wooden shelves with their black, curly brackets. When she was younger, she'd called in every Friday morning on her way to school with her sixpence pocket money. She'd take ages to choose the brightly coloured sweets from the fat glass jars lined up behind the counter. Finally, the brown paper bag would be full of Black-Jacks, Fruit-Salads, Spangles and gob-stoppers; strings of liquorice and tiny Parma Violets. They would last her all week. If Mrs Jones was serving, she'd often drop an extra sweet or two in the bag after weighing them out. But her husband never did. If Mr Jones was serving when Lisa went in, she'd sometimes leave again and come back later when Mrs Jones was there. An extra sweet or two wasn't to be sniffed at.

Lisa looked on the counter. The speckled brown eggs were usually in a large cardboard tray, next to the stacked-up copies of The Mirror. She was surprised to see the tray empty.

'Hello Mrs Jones. Have all the eggs gone?'

'They have Lisa, sorry. I ran out last night. There won't be any more until Monday.'

'Oh. Alright, thanks.' Lisa turned to leave.

'You could try Yeomans Farm,' said Mrs Jones. 'They've usually got eggs for sale.'

'Is that the one up Minsley Road?'

'That's the one, dear,' smiled Mrs Jones.

'Thanks,' called Lisa, as the bell tinkled and another customer stepped in.

* * *

Walking up the pot-holed dirt and gravel drive to the farm, Lisa passed two large barns on her right. When she reached the farmhouse, the porch door was open. A shot-gun leant against the wall inside.

'You come fer eggs?' Lisa turned around to see a woman ambling across the yard towards her. She looked old and wore slippers, despite the mud.

'Yes. Half-a-dozen please,' smiled Lisa, looking around for the chickens. She couldn't see any, although she could certainly smell them.

The woman grunted. 'Surely yer want a dozen?'

'No thanks, half-a-dozen will be fine,' replied Lisa, still looking for the hens.

'Wait 'ere,' said Mrs Yeoman, as she headed towards the nearest barn.

Lisa watched as she went inside. The heavy black clouds that had threatened all morning had gathered together above. Without warning, it poured down. Even holding the mac over her head, Lisa was getting soaked. Not wanting to enter the porch, she ran to the barn and pushed open the door Mrs Yeoman had disappeared through.

Standing inside the doorway, the acrid stench stung her eyes as they adjusted to the semi-darkness. The smell and the sight before her made her gag. The barn was full of small metal cages, stacked in rows one on top of the other. Each one-foot square cage held two or three chickens. There must be hundreds of them, thought Lisa. Semi-lifeless and scrawny with most of their feathers missing, the birds hardly made a sound. Their bead-black eyes peered out from between the bars, fixed and dull. There were no perches, no boxes; no soft hay or straw. Just chicken shit and eggs in the plastic guttering than ran on the outside of the cages. Lisa sensed the hens' lack of hope; felt their utter despair. She rubbed her eyes.

Mrs Yeoman stood at a small rickety table by the door, stacked high with egg boxes. She picked one up and filled it with eggs from the guttering. She handed the box to Lisa. 'You shouldn't be in 'ere,' she said. 'That'll be two bob.'

Lisa took the coins from her pocket and put them in the woman's out-stretched hand. Taking a deep breath, she asked; 'Don't the chickens ever go out?'

Mrs Yeoman let out a humourless cackle. 'They're battery hens. They don't go nowhere. Not 'til they stop layin'. Then they go into my Aga and onto my plate.' She cackled again as Lisa ran through the door out to the yard. 'Want any potatoes?' she shouted after her, but Lisa didn't stop.

'Bleedin' kids,' the woman muttered.

* * *

Lisa carried on running home, even though the rain had stopped. As she turned the corner, she bumped straight into Billy.

'H-hello Lisa. Y-You ok?'

Lisa bent double to catch her breath. Luckily the egg box was still intact. 'Hello Billy. Yeah, I'm alright. Haven't seen you for ages,' she puffed.

'N-no.' Billy kicked at a stone. 'T-Tom said n-not to call for him.'

'Why?'

'I d-dunno.' Billy looked away.

'Did you have a row?'

'N-no. He s-said he wasn't allowed out.'

'That was because he was really late home a while back. He's allowed out now.'

'Oh,' said Billy, looking even sadder.

'But he's not been going out much. I think he's missing you – you two were always together.'

'Y-yeah.' Billy gave Lisa a tremulous smile.

'Why don't you come round now?' she asked.

'Oh, I-I dunno.'

'Come on,' Lisa coaxed, linking her arm through his and walking towards home. 'Mum's doing breakfast. There'll be enough for you as well. Besides,' she continued, 'I bet Tanner will be pleased to see you.'

'I've m-missed him,' said Billy.

'I bet,' continued Lisa. 'And I want to tell you about the poor chickens I've just seen at Yeomans Farm. Do you know they're kept in tiny cages in a barn and never let out? There's two or three jammed in each cage. They've no room to move and hardly any feathers.'

Something stirred in Billy's memory. Something Wilbur had said about not seeing the light of day.

'T-that's cruel,' he said, looking at Lisa. 'M-me and Tom, we m-made a pact to save animals that are badly treated. B-birds, too.'

'Did you? He didn't tell me. Perhaps,' she looked at Billy, 'you can talk to Tom about saving the chickens?'

The spring in Billy's step returned. Lisa had given him a reason to speak to his friend. Something to say that he knew Tom would listen to.

And he couldn't wait to see Tanner. He'd sneak him half his sausage.

* * *

A pan of water simmered on the stove, next to another pan of sizzling bacon. Plump brown sausages and halved tomatoes, blackening at the edges, hissed beneath the grill.

'Just in time!' said Elsie as she heard the back door open. She turned from the cooker to see Lisa, followed by Billy. Tanner, who'd been sitting patiently by the oven waiting for something to fall on the floor, rushed over to them. Yelping with excitement, his tail banged against Lisa's legs as he jumped up, trying to lick Billy's face. Lisa giggled.

'Hello Billy,' smiled Elsie, 'how are you? Would you like some breakfast?'

'Th-thanks, Mrs Grant, b-but only if there's any spare.' Billy cuddled Tanner on the floor.

'There's plenty,' she said, taking the eggs from Lisa. 'I've just got to poach these. Can you pop upstairs Billy and get Tom?'

Billy opened the door to the hallway. Tanner pushed past, bounding up the stairs. Billy hesitated, but Lisa smiled at him, nodding. Trying to think what to say, he followed Tanner up the stairs.

Tanner jumped on Tom's bed. 'Breakfast ready then boy?' said Tom, ruffling his ears.

'Y-yes,' said Billy. 'It smells good.'

Tom looked up, the pleasure at seeing his friend written clearly on his face. They grinned at each other.

'It does,' said Tom. 'Let's get down there quick before Tanner nicks it.'

\* \* \*

Lisa pushed her egg to the side of the plate, unable to eat it; whilst Billy gave all his sausage to Tanner. Tom laughed. 'Didn't even touch the sides.'

After breakfast, the three of them walked towards the woods, Tanner running around them in circles. When they carried on walking, he trotted behind, stopping to sniff now and then.

Lisa told Tom and Billy about the chickens.

'We've g-got to rescue them, Tom,' said Billy, looking earnestly at his friend.

'Yeah.' Tom plucked a stalk of grass to chew. 'We'll have to break in at night.'

Lisa looked at her brother. 'But what will you do? You can't let them out at night. Foxes will get them.'

'Yeah, but we can let them loose in the barn. Make a point about how cruel it is. Paint a message on the walls. It might even get in the Tyneford News.'

Billy's eyes shone. 'Dad's got loads of p-paint in his shed. I can b-bring that.'

Tom nodded. 'Yeah, I'll bring a bru – '

'I want to come,' interrupted Lisa, steel in her voice.

Tom and Billy glanced at each other.

'We'll be more likely to get caught,' said Tom.

Lisa glared at him. 'Why?'

'With three of us. There's more chance of being seen.'

'You f-found out about it,' ventured Billy, 'and told us. Th-that's the important bit.'

'But I want to help,' replied Lisa. 'It's not fair if I can't come.' Tanner trotted up to Lisa's side and licked her hand. 'See! Even Tanner thinks so.'

Tom smiled. 'Ok, fair enough. You and Tanner can be lookouts. But you'll have to stay outside the barn.'

Lisa fizzed inside like sherbet, a big grin on her face. Billy winked at her.

They walked on a few more yards before Tom spoke again.

'We'll go tonight.'

* * *

166

When the stone hit Billy's window, he woke with a start. Lying on top of his bed fully clothed, he quickly remembered. The chickens. He jumped up and flicked back the curtain. Tom, Lisa and Tanner stood in the shadows at the side of the lawn. He reached for the pot of white paint he'd stowed under his bed, his torch and penknife already in his pocket. Creeping downstairs, he let himself out of the back door just as the clock on the mantlepiece struck midnight.

The three of them talked in whispers as they headed towards the farm.

'Y-you got out ok th-then?' asked Billy.

'Yeah. I told Lisa to avoid the fifth and eighth stair,' grinned Tom.

'You've done this before, haven't you?' said Lisa, first looking at Tom, then Billy.

'M-Maybe.' Billy grinned conspiratorially at Tom.

Wearing jeans and dark jumpers, they reached the farm unnoticed. There were no street lights down Minsley Road. The sky was as black as the ink on Billy's fingers.

'I'll put my torch on,' whispered Tom. 'Keep yours off until we're inside the barn.'

'O-Okey d-dokey,' replied Billy.

Lisa giggled.

'Sshhh!' hissed Tom. They'd reached the two barns. 'Which one are the chickens in?'

'That one.' Lisa pointed to the barn nearest the farmhouse.

'You stay here with Tanner, behind this barn away from the house. If you see or hear anything, let us know by knocking on the side of the barn we're in. Then run home with Tanner.'

'Ok,' whispered Lisa, her face serious.

'Don't put yourself in any danger,' added Tom. 'Just run straight home if you have to.' He looked at Tanner. 'Stay here, boy.'

The farmhouse was in darkness; the night quiet. Tanner sniffed the air. Lisa watched as Tom and Billy walked to the second barn, the torch beam wavering over the yard in front of them.

A memory from earlier flashed into her mind. The gun in the porch.

She crossed her fingers.

# Chapter 18

Standing in front of the door Lisa had entered earlier that day, Tom shone the torch on the handle. Pressing down on the latch, the lever came up with a click. Tom put slight pressure on the door, but it didn't open. He leant his shoulder into it but still the door wouldn't budge.

'Damn,' he whispered to Billy. 'It's locked somehow.'

'T-There,' said Billy, pointing to a rusty bolt at the top of the door. There was one at the bottom as well. The top bolt was stiff and Tom had to wiggle it to slide it back. He did the same with the bottom bolt, but it screeched loudly in the darkness. Jarring metal on metal raked a shiver down Tom's spine. Holding his breath, he paused. Watching the farmhouse, his blood pulsed in his ears. But everything remained dark and his heart slowed again. He pushed open the door.

The boys grimaced as the acid-sharp stench stung their nostrils. Tom shone his torch around.

'Bloody hell,' he whispered.

'J-Jesus,' said Billy softly. Even Lisa's description hadn't prepared them for this.

Tom shone the torch on the far side of the barn. 'Paint on that wall over there,' he said. 'I'll start letting the poor buggers out.'

Billy fished in his pocket for his torch. Tom passed him the one-inch paint brush and Billy carried the paint tin over to the other wall. Some of the chickens clucked quietly.

Tom went to the nearest cage and pulled the spring mechanism to open the door. It swung wide but the birds didn't move. They crouched down further on the wire, staring at him. 'Poor bloody things,' whispered Tom, picking up the first bird and placing it gently on the floor.

'W-what shall I write?' called Billy. He'd taken the lid off the tin and held the paintbrush in his right hand, white paint dripping on the ground.

Tom shrugged. 'I dunno. How about… "Let the hens roam free you cruel bastards"?'

Billy chuckled. Propping his torch against an old piece of wood to light-up the wall, he started painting.

Tom lifted the other two birds from the cage and placed them beside the first one, which still hadn't moved. He worked quickly along the rows opening the cage doors and putting the chickens on the floor. He had to watch where he walked as the hens seemed in shock, unable to move out of his path.

Billy put the paint lid back on the can and the brush on top. He picked up his torch and surveyed his handiwork.

LET THE HENS ROME FREE
YOU CRUEL BASTERDS

Tom glanced over and grinned. They'd get the message.

Billy started releasing the birds at the other end of the last row. Just before the boys met in the middle, a dog barked. They froze. The barking continued like a drum, three beats to a bar. It wasn't Tanner. It came from the direction of the farmhouse.

'We'd better hurry,' whispered Tom.

'This h-hen can't move,' said Billy, a desperate note to his voice.

Tom flashed his torch on the bird Billy had just put on the floor. 'Lift her up, I'll look at her feet.'

Shining his torch under the chicken, they could see how the hen's claws had twisted and deformed from endlessly clinging to the thin narrow bars of the cage floor. 'Hold on to that one,' said Tom as he opened the last two cages, lifting the birds inside to the floor. 'One of the first birds I took out didn't move either.' He shone his torch to where he'd started and saw the first hen squatting on the floor in the same place. Tom picked it up.

The dog's barking became furious; punching through the night air.

'C'mon,' said Tom. 'Let's get out of here.'

\* \* \*

171

Fred Yeoman woke with a start. He'd fallen asleep in the chair in front of the fire again, only grey ashes now in the grate. He switched on the standard lamp by his side and shivered. His wife had long since gone upstairs with her mug of cocoa.

*The bloody dog's barking again. Foxes sniffing around the chickens, no doubt.* He wasn't worried. Even if they managed to get in the barn, they couldn't get at the birds in the cages. But it frightened the hens – made them stop laying for a while. *Bloody vermin.*

He got up slowly from the chair, ash from the roll-up he'd smoked earlier falling from his jumper to the floor. *If it's foxes, I'll let the dog off, even though he can't catch a bleedin' cold no more. Too long in the tooth. Should've put a bullet in 'im months ago. All 'es good fer is barkin'.*

He got to the porch and opened the door to the yard. Squinting in the direction of the barn he waited for his eyes to adjust to the darkness. The dog was tied up at the side of the house, straining against the chain that held him. Just as Fred Yeoman was about to yell at him to shut up, he saw a glint of light. Just for a second. There it was again. Something shining through a chink in the wood slats of the barn. *Unless foxes carry bleedin' torches these days, someone's broke into my barn.*

He reached behind him and picked up his shotgun.

*　*　*

172

Tom grabbed for the barn door with his free hand, but both boys jumped back when Lisa barged in.

'Quick!' she hissed. 'There's a light on in the farmhouse. I think someone's coming!'

Tom stepped through the door, looking round the corner of the barn to the house. He heard a door open, although he couldn't see anyone. The dog still barked loudly. 'Run home with Tanner,' he urged his sister. 'Now!'

Lisa sprinted down the drive, but Tanner didn't follow her. She hesitated. 'Go Lisa!' shouted Tom, 'Tanner can come with us!' She disappeared into the night.

'Shit,' Tom said under his breath. A figure strode across the yard towards them. He went back to Billy and spoke quickly. 'Quick! There's someone coming. Put the chicken under your jumper and run as fast as you can to the air-raid shelter. Cross the field to the woods. I'll be right behind you.' Tom pulled his jumper over the chicken he held to his chest and they tumbled out of the barn, half-pulling, half-pushing each other for speed. 'C'mon boy,' Tom called to Tanner as they hurtled towards the field.

'Oiy! Bleedin' thieves!' shouted the man behind them. Billy stalled.

'Keep running!' panted Tom, overtaking him. A shot rang out, ricocheting against the metal water butt next to the second barn.

Billy yelled in surprise, but picked up his pace. He caught up with Tom and they scrambled over the gate, racing across the grass towards the woods.

But Tanner wasn't with them. Facing the man he blocked his path, crouching, ready to pounce. His mouth dripped saliva as he bared his teeth with a menacing, rolling growl.

'Want a bullet between the eyes, dog?'

Tanner stood his ground, snarling; the whites of his eyes showing, the fur along his spine standing on end.

Fred Yeoman sneered as he lifted the gun to his shoulder.

* * *


When Lisa heard the first gunshot she stopped in her tracks. Terrified, she ran back without thinking. As she reached the first barn, she could just make out Tom and Billy running at the far side of the field. She heard growling and, moving to the rear of the barn, saw the man aim the gun at Tanner. She didn't hesitate. She sprinted then sprang as a wild-cat; her momentum slamming the farmer to the ground. He grunted like a pig. The gun soared through the air, going off as it landed in the mud. The bang and smell reminded Lisa of a Jumping-Jack on Guy Fawkes night. Quick on her feet, she grabbed it. 'C'mon boy!' she called to Tanner, and they flew across the field. Before Fred Yeoman even realised what had happened, they were gone.

Just before the trees, Lisa threw the gun in the ditch that ran by the hedge. She didn't stop to look back. Running into the woods, she'd lost sight of Tom and Billy, but kept on along the path. Eventually she stopped, leaning against a tree to catch her breath. She hadn't been scared of the man with the gun; but she was frightened of being alone in the woods. It was darker than Lisa thought possible, the thick canopy of branches blocking any light from the moon. Out of earshot of the farm, she called Tom and Billy's names in a strange, thin voice that didn't seem to belong to her. Tanner stood guard; his legs lost in swirling mist rising from the ground.

After a few minutes, a bobbing light came towards her. Tanner wagged his tail. 'What you doing here Lis? You ok?' Tom's voice. Relief flooded through her. She began sobbing; loud, wracking cries that took her by surprise and shook her body.

'D-don't cry Lisa,' said Billy, moving to her side and putting his free arm around her. 'Sshhh. Everything's ok now.' He stroked her hair with his hand, feeling the warmth of her body as she leant against him.

Tom spoke. 'What happened? Did Tanner go to find you?'

'I heard the… first gunshot.' Lisa hiccupped between sobs. 'I ran back, scared you or Billy had been… shot. But I saw you running across the field. You hadn't noticed Tanner wasn't with you. He was growling at the farmer to stop him from chasing you.' Tom bent down and rubbed Tanner's ears. 'But the man aimed the gun at Tanner. He was going to shoot him, Tom!' Lisa sobbed again. 'I ran at him and pushed him to the ground. He dropped the gun and I grabbed it, running after you. I threw the gun in the ditch as I got to the woods.'

'W-wow! Well done Lisa. You're a hero. Like Emma P-Peel.'

'Thanks Billy.' Lisa managed a lop-sided, shaky smile.

'You didn't get hurt?' asked Tom. 'I heard another gunshot.'

'The gun went off as he fell. But just into the air, I think.'

'You did great Lis. I'm glad I asked you to come,' Tom grinned. Lisa gave him a play punch on the arm. The chicken under his jumper clucked. Billy's chicken clucked back.

Lisa raised her eyebrows. 'Why have you both got a hen?'

'Their feet are bad, they couldn't walk,' replied Tom.

'Are you taking them home?'

'No, we know someone who can make them better.'

'A vet?'

'Well, sort of,' sighed Tom. 'Look, you're exhausted. We'll take you and Tanner home, then me and Billy will sort out the chickens. It won't take us long.'

'Ok,' whispered Lisa. 'But don't go back near that farm.'

'We w-won't,' said Billy, squeezing her hand.

* * *

Billy's shoulder felt sore as he and Tom walked to the woods again. With his free hand he reached inside his jumper to touch it and winced. He looked at his hand in the torch light. It was red with blood. He said nothing, following Tom wearily along the track. As they turned a corner, Wilbur walked towards them.

Tom quickly told him what had happened, and that they were taking the chickens to the air-raid shelter. Wilbur looked at the bird's feet in the light of Tom's torch.

'You lads look done in,' said Wilbur, stroking the head of Tom's chicken with a gnarled finger. 'I'll take the hens to the shelter an' make splints for their claws. They'll be right as rain in a couple of weeks. An' I know a good farm that lets their hens out in the fields every day. When they're better, I'll take 'em there.'

Tom sighed with relief. 'Thanks, Wilbur.' He passed the chicken to him and Wilbur tucked it under one arm. As Billy passed him the other bird, Tom noticed the blood on his friend's hand. 'What's that? Have you cut yourself?'

Billy shoved the bloodied hand in his pocket. 'Y-yeah. C-caught it on the barbed-wire by the g-gate,' he lied.

'Better wash it when you get home,' said Tom.

'If anythin' needs fixin', come an' see me,' Wilbur said. With a hen under each arm, he turned and headed deeper into the woods. Tom and Billy watched as he merged with the trees in the dark. Just before he disappeared, he glanced over his shoulder. 'You did good lads,' he called. 'You an' your sister. You all did bloody good.'

* * *

As Billy slipped in his back door and slowly climbed the stairs, the mantle-clock struck two.

He went into the bathroom, quietly closing the door behind him. Switching on the light, he pulled off his jumper. In the small oval mirror, he studied the ragged stain on his vest. A stark contrast in dark red, it was the size of his fist. He took off the vest, dropping it on the floor as he picked up his flannel. Wetting it under the tap, he patted his shoulder and took a sharp intake of breath. Gently, he cleaned off the blood. He was glad there wasn't a bullet lodged there; he'd dreaded having to fish around with tweezers. It must have just grazed him, but at the time it'd felt much worse. Picking up the small tin of pink Germolene, he gritted his teeth as he smeared some on the wound. It stung like a hundred bees. Reaching for one of the clean rags his mum kept as bandages, he pressed it against his skin; the cream helping to keep it in place as he slipped his vest back on.

Worn out, he went to his bedroom and climbed into bed, trying to relax his shoulder. And when he closed his eyes and thought of Lisa, it didn't even hurt.

# Chapter 19

Sitting in the conker tree a week later, Billy took a piece of paper from his pocket. Dog-eared and crumpled, he unfolded it carefully.

'L-look! See?' Billy's chest puffed with pride as he handed Tom the page he'd torn from the local paper. There was a photograph at the top. It was of the message he'd painted on the inside of the chicken-house at Yeomans Farm. Underneath it, Tom read:

### KIDS RAID HEN-HOUSE

In the early hours of Sunday morning three teenagers broke into Yeomans Farm on Minsley Road. Mr. Yeoman said he was woken by his dog barking and saw a light in the chicken-house. When he went to investigate, two boys ran away but he was attacked by a third. Mr. Yeoman was knocked to the ground and sustained bruising. All of the hens had been released from their cages and Mr. Yeoman believed some had been stolen. Graffiti had been painted on the inside of the barn. Mr Yeoman said: 'My chickens are perfectly happy in cages and lay well. However, I've been intending to build them an outdoor run for some time, and will arrange for this to be done'. The farmer said that from now on, the chickens will be housed loose in the barn at night, and will no longer be caged. If anyone knows who was involved in the raid, please contact Tyneford Police.

Tom looked up at Billy and grinned. 'It worked. We can make a difference. We've shamed him into treating them better. Let's hope he sticks to his word.'

'We c-can go now and have a l-look. See if anything's changed.'

'Yeah. But… hold on… ' Tom was looking at another article on the page. 'Did you see this?' He read it to Billy.

## FUN-FAIR MEN ARRESTED

Police have arrested two men in connection with the theft of property from houses in Daffodil Crescent, which we reported on three weeks ago. Both men arrested work for the funfair which was in the village at the time. The fair has since moved on to Sandham. It is understood the two men are still being questioned and that no charges have yet been made.

'B-blimey. Sh-shame they haven't given their names.'

'They'll get away with it,' replied Tom, 'because unless anyone saw them, the police won't be able to prove anything.' Tom folded up the page and handed it back to Billy. 'You ever heard of Sandham?'

'Y-yeah. That's where my Uncle Jimmy lives.'

'How far is it?'

'I dunno. It t-takes about half-an-hour on the bus. W-why?'

'Just wondered,' mumbled Tom, looking down to the ground. 'C'mon, let's go and look at the farm.'

They scrambled down the tree and headed towards Minsley Road.

'You're n-not thinking of going to Sandham to f-fight Joe Cooper, are you?' asked Billy a few minutes later.

'No, 'course not,' replied Tom as they passed the monkey puzzle tree. 'I'm hoping that Cooper's one of the people the police have arrested.'

'Oh. Y-yeah. That'd be good,' Billy said. 'I'm s-sure he was involved.'

Tom didn't reply. He wasn't thinking of Joe Cooper any longer. He had Keziah on his mind.

Walking down the first part of the drive to the farm, Tom and Billy saw a large, new run. Made of wood and wire netting, it had been fixed to the side of the barn with the door open. The hens were free to come and go and strutted around happily, scratching in the dirt and grass and pecking at scattered seed.

'L-Lisa will be p-pleased,' smiled Billy. It had been worth being shot at, he thought.

'Yeah, it's great,' grinned Tom, 'and all because – '

'The l-lady loves Milk-Tray,' interrupted Billy, chuckling. The advert was always on the telly.

' – All because we did something,' finished Tom. 'C'mon. We'll get Tanner and go to the air-raid shelter and check on the other two.' Lisa had named the two hens with the bad feet 'Hettie' and 'Hattie', but Tom and Billy wouldn't use the names. They were far too girly.

After collecting Tanner, they went to the shelter. Wilbur wasn't there. They checked no one was around before lifting the logs from the wooden cover and removing it, then climbing down the ladder. 'Stay there, boy,' Billy whispered. Tanner laid down by the entrance keeping watch.

Tom felt for the matches in the semi-darkness and lit the candle on the tea-chest. Shadows from the hens loomed large on the dirt walls as they strutted around. They still wore the tiny splints Wilbur had made, but they were both walking well.

'Wilbur said he'd t-take the splints off at the weekend an' they'll be able to go to the other f-farm.'

Tom nodded. Bending down, he picked up one of the hens. Holding it under his arm, he gently rubbed its chest. The hen closed its eyes, making a soft, contented rumbling sound – more a vibration than a noise. He and Billy had popped in to see them every night since they'd been rescued. They'd brought them scraps to peck at and listened to their excited cluck-cluck at a tasty morsel. Tom would miss these little bundles of brown feathers with their funny little personalities. The hens had even laid an egg or two. Maybe he'd keep chickens of his own one day.

'B-better get back for tea,' said Billy, blowing out the candle. They climbed the ladder and covered the entrance, hiding it well with the logs and brambles. Tanner got up and followed them home.

Tom was quiet. Billy looked sideways at him. 'Sh-shall I come over after tea?'

'Er, no, not tonight Billy. I've got homework to do.'

'Oh. Ok. S-see you tomorrow.'

Tom watched until Billy turned the corner. Then he went down the side of his house to the shed. His old bike leant against the far wall between the garden spades and forks. A bit small for him now, he hadn't used it for a while. The front tyre was flat; dusty cobwebs clung to the crossbar and saddle. But it would get him to Sandham.

He looked for the puncture repair kit.

\* \* \*

Keziah washed potatoes at the sink. Later, they'd be wrapped in foil and put in the fire. Her mother sat at the small round table, knitting.

'You dancing tonight, Keziah?' she asked.

'I don't think so, Ma.'

'Why not? You can wear your emerald green dress. You look so beautiful in that.'

Keziah didn't reply. Biting her lip, she looked out of the window at the horses.

'What is it?' asked her mother. 'Is it because of Joe? Or Jake?'

'Both of them, Ma. You know I don't like them leering.'

The clickety-clack of the knitting needles continued. 'Joe's grown into a good-looking lad, though.'

'I don't care what he looks like Ma! He's cruel to Beauty. I'd never go out with him!' Defiant, Keziah flicked her long hair back from her face.

Her mother smiled at her feisty daughter, secretly pleased she didn't like Joe. He was a bad apple. And Jake wasn't much better. 'I haven't seen either of them today. Maybe they'll not be back by tonight.'

'If they're not, then I'll happily dance,' Keziah replied.

'Good. It's time we had some fun. I might even join in. See if I can still shake these old bones.'

'You should, Ma. It's your birthday, after all. And you're still a good dancer,' grinned Keziah. 'And you're not old.' She walked to the door. 'I'm just going to feed the horses.'

'You're a good daughter, Keziah,' said her mother.

'And you're a good Ma.'

As Keziah stepped outside, she gasped at the beauty of the setting sun; the horses silhouetted by blood-red streaks that slashed the twilight sky.

* * *

Tom tapped on Lisa's bedroom door. 'Lis, can I come in?'

'Yeah. 'Course.' Lisa sat on her bed with her back to the wall, a magazine spread open in front of her.

'Billy showed me a page from the local paper today.' Tom lowered his voice. 'They've reported about the night we went to the farm.'

'Really? What did it say?'

'There was a photo of the words Billy painted on the wall. Then it said there had been a raid by three boys –'

'Three boys?' interjected Lisa. 'The farmer couldn't have seen me when I floored him.'

They grinned at each other.

'I expect Billy will show you the paper tomorrow,' Tom went on. 'Anyway, it worked – the farmer said he wouldn't keep them in cages anymore. Me and Billy went past this afternoon to look and the hens were pecking around outside.'

Lisa jumped from the bed and hugged him. 'I'm so glad, Tom! Now they'll have a much better life.'

'Thanks to you,' smiled Tom. 'Lis, I –'

'What?'

'Will you cover for me? Tonight? I wouldn't ask, but, well, it's really important I see someone. I might be back late. I don't want Mum and Dad to stop me going, but I don't want them to worry, either.'

'Who are you going to see?'

Tom hesitated. 'You don't know them, but they helped me find Tanner. When he went missing.'

185

'Oh. Ok. But how do I cover for you?'

Tom sat down heavily on the end of the bed. 'I dunno. But I need to go now, really.'

'I know!' said Lisa excitedly, 'I'll tell them you've gone to help my school friend Ian with his history project about the war. He has to hand it in tomorrow. He was really worried about it when I saw him today.'

'Good idea, Lis. Thanks.'

'But don't be late back, or they might ask for Ian's address. Then we'll both be for the high jump.'

'Ok, I won't be too late. Promise.' For a moment, Tom felt a pang of red-edged guilt. He shouldn't be asking her to lie for him. 'You're a good sister, Lis.'

She looked him in the eye. Softly she said, 'But I'm not really, am I? Not your sister, I mean.'

Tom took a deep breath. 'They told you, then? That I was adopted? And you're not?'

'Yeah. But it doesn't make any difference, Tom, does it? I still think of you as my brother, even though you're not.'

'Yeah. Me too. I mean, I think of you as my sister, not my brother.'

Lisa giggled. 'Nothing's changed, then?'

'No, Lis. Nothing's changed.' He winked at her and turned to leave the room.

'Tom? Are you taking Tanner?'

'No, I wasn't going to. Will you look after him tonight?'

'Course.' She was already cuddling him on the bed. 'You'd better go.'

'Yeah. Thanks, Lis.'

Tom went downstairs. His mum was in the kitchen, so he slipped out the front door, closing it quietly behind him. Walking to the shed, he patted his jacket pocket to check he had his torch and penknife. He checked his other pocket for the page he'd torn from the map he'd found in the bookcase. He realised there were a couple of short-cuts through woods to get to Sandham. It'd take him about three-quarters of an hour. If he wanted a couple of hours with Keziah, he'd have to hurry. Quickly, he checked the tyre he'd repaired on his bike before wheeling it outside, slipping the puncture repair kit into his pocket with the map. Just in case.

With one foot on the pedal, he slung his other leg over the saddle and started pedalling. The sun had already set; only a hovering pink glow remained.

He couldn't wait to see her. The bike began to fly.

# Chapter 20

All the rides and stalls were in darkness; but laughter and music drifted on woodsmoke from the back of the field. A large bonfire burned and spat; a makeshift dancefloor lay on the grass nearby. Painted cream with black diamonds and red hearts around the edge, it reminded Tom of a giant playing card. About twenty people were gathered around, drinking and clapping. Two played guitar; a few of them sang. One man beat the rhythm on two drums strung around his waist; another played a mouth organ. Tom didn't recognise the song, but it was eerily beautiful; the piquant notes gently strumming the night.

Five women danced, but Tom saw only Keziah. Flounces of green dress caught in the fingers of one hand, she swayed and shimmied in time to the tune. Her skin glowed and her hair, held to one side with a silver comb, shone with glints of orange flame. Tom stood mesmerized. Still as a statue, he watched from the dark shadows of an oak.

He could happily watch her dance all night; but he didn't have long. How would he get her attention? He couldn't see all the faces of the crowd. If Joe Cooper was among them, there'd be trouble. He didn't want that, not tonight. Only time with Keziah would ease the aching knot in his chest.

A table, topped with various bottles and jugs of drink, was the nearest thing to him. Glasses lay on the grass underneath. Every now and again someone walked over and refilled their glass or picked up a bottle. All Tom could hope for was that Keziah would want a drink – and come to the table alone.

The song slowed and ended; a different one started up. A few excited children joined the dancers; Keziah took the hands of a young girl and twirled her around, both of them laughing. Tom couldn't take his eyes off her, this beauty in green. Eventually she stopped dancing and went to talk to an older woman at the side of the fire.

Then without warning, she was coming towards the table, an empty glass in each hand. With two other people already standing there, Tom couldn't call to her; he didn't dare step from the shadows. He began to panic – he might never get another chance to see her. He looked on the ground for something to throw to get her notice. There was nothing. Then he remembered the puncture repair kit. He reached in his pocket, feeling for the grip on the tin. Opening it, his fingers scrabbled for the small square of chalk.

It hit Keziah just above the neckline of her dress; she felt the tiny sting and looked up. Tom half-raised his arm in a brief wave. Keziah placed the glasses on the table and walked towards the oak.

'Tom! It is you! I thought for a moment it might be Joe messing about. Thank goodness he's not here. How did you find – '

'Walk with me?' Tom held out his hand.

Keziah took it, and hitching the hem of her dress with the other, she followed him around the back of the oak to a small copse about fifty yards away. Bluebells welcomed them in, and with the laughter and music fading, Tom turned to face her.

'It's good to see you,' he smiled.

She raised her face to his and Tom drew her warm body to him, kissing her tenderly.

'It's good to see you too,' whispered Keziah.

'Let's find somewhere we can talk,' said Tom.

'There's a churchyard just beyond the trees, it has a bench under the yew tree.'

As they walked towards it, Tom pulled his torch from his pocket to light their way. He slipped his other arm around her shoulders. The church spire speared the dark; a slight mist floated amongst the gravestones. 'You're not spooked?' he asked.

'No. Not with you here. And anyway… their spirits aren't here, are they? It's just bones.'

'You sound like Wilbur,' grinned Tom.

'You know Wilbur?'

'Yeah. He – he told me something. I wanted to ask you if you knew anything about it.'

'What's that?'

They sat down on the wooden slats of the bench. Tom turned the torch off and reached for her hand.

'Wilbur thinks Joe Cooper is my twin brother.'

'Really? Why? I don't understand.'

'My folks adopted me. They said my mum gave birth alone in a barn – to me and a twin. My mum couldn't carry both of us at once, so she took me to safety, then went back for my twin. But by the time she got back, the baby had gone. Wilbur told me he saw a baby taken from the barn around the time I was born. The baby was taken by Joe Cooper's mother.'

'Bessie took a baby? That wasn't hers? I don't think she'd do that, Tom. I'm sure Joe is her own son; I've never heard anything to say he isn't.'

'So, why would Wilbur lie?'

'He wouldn't. But maybe he was mistaken? Maybe it wasn't your twin that Bessie had picked up, or maybe it was someone that just looked like Bessie that took the baby.'

'Yeah, maybe.' He wished he could believe that she might be right. But he kept thinking that Wilbur wouldn't have said it unless he'd been certain.

His eyes searched for Keziah's. 'But people have said that me and Joe, well, that we look alike.'

Keziah took Tom's face in her hands. 'A little. You're both good-looking. But you're nothing alike inside! You know that, Tom. I'm sure Joe isn't your brother. He can't be. Wilbur must've got things wrong.'

Tom kissed her. 'I was hoping you'd say that,' he smiled. 'But what sort of person am I, Keziah? I wanted to kill him after what he did to Tanner. Even if I knew for sure he was my brother, I'd still have wanted to kill him, given half a chance. What kind of person wants to kill their own brother?'

Keziah looked into his eyes. She spoke quietly, but firmly. 'You're a good person, Tom. Shouldn't a man be judged by how he treats others weaker than himself? Particularly those that can't defend themselves – like children, or the disabled – or the animals Joe takes pleasure in tormenting and killing? Is the life of a cruel, evil person such as Joe worth more than the life of a true and good animal?' Her blue eyes flashed. 'I suppose some people might think so. But I don't.' Keziah leaned forward and kissed Tom's nose. 'And you're not the only one who's felt like killing him, believe me. Anyway,' she paused, 'you didn't. So, you have nothing to blame yourself for.'

Tom put his arm around her and held her close. *She understands.* They sat silently for a while, watching the bats as they flitted erratically above the gravestones.

Later, he told her about the raid on the chicken house.

She giggled. 'That was brave of your sister! I'm glad Tanner's alright. I'd love to see him again.'

'I can bring him to see you,' smiled Tom. 'I'll bring him next week. Now I know how long it – '

Keziah put a finger to his lips. 'The fair's leaving here tomorrow, Tom. I don't know the name of where we're going, but I know it's a long way. Ma said it'll take us all day to get there.'

Tom looked into the distance. 'So, when will I see you again?' He tried to keep the desperation from his voice; the disappointment from his eyes.

'The fair will come back to Tyneford. I'm not sure exactly when, but it'll be towards the end of the summer. We can see each other then.'

Tom nodded. He didn't trust himself to speak. It was only May.

It seemed Keziah had read his mind. 'I know it seems a long way away, Tom. But the time will soon pass. Then we'll have two weeks together.'

Tom squeezed her hand. 'I'll walk you back. I've got to get going or my folks will send out a search party.' They made their way back to the oak hand in hand. 'Until the end of summer, then,' he said, plucking a bluebell from the base of the tree and putting it behind her ear. 'I'll miss you,' he whispered, before kissing her goodbye.

Keziah watched as he pulled his bike from the tree trunk and with one foot on the pedal, slung his other leg over the saddle. As he rode off into the night, she wiped a hot tear from her cheek.

# Chapter 21

## May 1915

He'd reached the final step to the scullery before Agnes spoke. She fiddled with the fringe on her shawl as she stood side-ways on to the table, not looking at him.

'Your call up papers have come, Wil.'

He sighed, glancing across at his father, his familiar face still and drawn; tinged grey in the early morning light.

'Sorry Pa.' Wilbur wanted to fight for his country – of course he did. Most of the lads from the village had already gone. But who would help his father on the farm? And how long would Amy wait for him?

'We all hoped it'd be over by now, son. Can't say I didn't wish it was. How long before you have to go?'

Wilbur picked up the papers from the table and read the brief message. 'Two days.'

'Don't give you much notice, do they?'

Wilbur's mind raced. He'd have to get a message to Amy. He couldn't leave without seeing her.

'I'll finish the fence at Willow Field today, but I need a few minutes first.' He turned and headed back upstairs.

'I'll start your breakfast,' Agnes called after him. He didn't detect the sob she caught in her throat.

Wilbur wrote quickly. *I've been called up. Have to leave from station at 8 in the morn this Thursday. When can we meet? x.* Folding the paper as he'd done many times before, he placed it in the pouch and tied it to Barley's collar. Taking his dog down to the back of the cottage, he stroked his silken ears before opening the door.

'You know where to go, boy,' Wilbur whispered. Barley wagged his tail and padded off towards the field.

\* \* \*

The dog sat by the gravestone for half an hour before Amy saw him through the window in the kitchen. She finished her breakfast and rushed outside. She wasn't due to see Wilbur until Friday. What was Barley doing here?

'Good boy,' she whispered as she untied the pouch. She hadn't noticed her mother follow her outside.

'Whose dog is that?'

Amy's heart began to hammer. She stuffed the pouch down the front of her dress before turning to face her mother.

'Oh, he's just one of the farm dogs, I think.'

'What's he doing here? I'm sure I've seen him hanging around before.'

Amy thought quicky. She didn't think her mother had seen the pouch or she'd have asked about it. 'Sometimes I give him some scraps from breakfast.'

'For goodness' sake child! We don't want all the waifs and strays coming here. Don't feed him anymore!'

Amy sighed with relief as her mother turned back to the house. But she daren't look in the pouch and read the note yet. 'You'd better get home Barley,' she whispered. 'Good dog.'

\* \* \*

Wilbur's stomach churned when Barley returned without the pouch. Where was it? Why hadn't Amy replied? He wanted to ask her to marry him – to know she would wait for him. Had she got the pouch? But if she had, why hadn't she sent a reply?

Barley, sensing his master's concern, licked his hand, his tail between his legs.

'It's not your fault, boy,' Wilbur ruffled the dog's ears. 'But sometimes I wish you could talk.'

\* \* \*

Amy awoke long before sunrise on Thursday. She'd gone over and over the plan in her head, barely sleeping at all. She'd walk to her friend Jane's house, tack up her horse that she'd arranged to borrow and ride the eight miles to the station to see Wilbur before he left. Her parents wouldn't notice her missing until seven and they wouldn't think to look for her at the station. She'd worry about the consequences later. Seeing Wilbur was the only thing that mattered. So many of the boys that had left the village to fight this war had died in combat. Every time she thought about it she felt sick. She rushed to the wash-stand as bile rose in her throat.

The sun hadn't risen yet, but the moon lit the room with a ghostly silver. She didn't need a light as she quietly dressed in her riding clothes and made her way out of the house. As she walked to Jane's, the sun rose from behind the woods, a pale gold orb, but the moon refused to leave the sky, a translucent half-circle of silver. Gold and silver. Silver and gold. She thought of anything, other than Wilbur going. To war. Not coming back…

Jane's horse was heavy boned but jaunty; dark bay with a thick white blaze down his nose. He stood quietly as she saddled him up. Was he aware of the gravity of his task? She'd ridden Jack a few times before and knew he was sure-footed and fast.

He'd get her to the station in time.

* * *

Wilbur's father drove the cart. Agnes sat in the back on the wooden bench with Wilbur, his holdall between them.

'God willing, you'll be back soon.' His aunt smiled at him. 'Don't worry, me and your Pa will be just fine.'

Wilbur nodded, not trusting his voice. He studied the battered canvas of his holdall, handed down to him from his grand-father. There was a shaving kit inside. Yet he felt like a child with no control over his life. And he hadn't heard from Amy.

Agnes spoke quietly. 'Have you said goodbye to Amy?' she asked, as if she knew what he was thinking. He shook his head. 'She does know you're going, I take it?'

'I'm not sure. I sent her a message. I don't know if she got it.'

Agnes squeezed his arm. 'I'm sure she'll be at the station to see you off.' *God, let her be right.*

When they arrived, Wilbur's father weaved the reins around the black metal railings surrounding the station. The platform was full of men saying their goodbyes to loved ones. They all looked so young, with hope and optimism in their faces and a kitbag slung across one shoulder.

Wilbur stood with his father and aunt beneath a massive horse-chestnut tree. The trunk grew outside the railings; but heavy branches stretched above their heads across the platform, reaching for the tracks before disappearing into the steam from the train.

Wilbur scanned the crowd for Amy, but couldn't see her amongst the men, their folks and sweethearts. He looked up at the passenger footbridge where people had lined up, ready to wave off the train. The steam obscured their faces like rising fog.

A whistle blew. His father looked at him. 'You'd better get on, son.'

Wilbur stepped on the train and had to push for some space. He pulled the carriage door closed and immediately opened the window, leaning through to kiss his aunt.

'I'm sure she's here somewhere, Wilbur. I expect she just can't see us. Take care of yourself, lad. I'll tell her to write.'

His father stepped to the window, briefly reaching up to pat Wilbur's shoulder. 'Goodbye son.'

* * *

Jack stumbled. 'What is it boy?' From his jarring movement, Amy could tell he was limping. 'Whoa.' She jumped off as the horse slowed to a halt and held up his front right hoof slightly, taking the weight off it. Amy bent to pick it up, immediately seeing the sharp stone lodged between the wall of his hoof and the soft frog underneath. She tried to remove the stone with her fingers, but it was stuck fast. She looked around desperately for a stick to lever it out but couldn't find one. She took another flinty stone from the dirt and using some force, pushed it beneath the stuck stone until it eventually popped out.

'There. You should be alright now, boy.'

Amy jumped back on, but the horse continued to limp. 'Your foot must be bruised, Jack' she sighed, jumping back down. There was nothing she could do; she'd have to walk and lead the horse. *What time is it?* Terrified she'd miss Wilbur, she tied Jack to a small birch at the side of the lane. 'Wait here, boy, I'll be back as soon as I can.' Glancing at the sun that had climbed in the sky, Amy started running.

The station platform appeared to shift as bodies surged towards the train; some eager, some reluctant, to step through the doors that would take them from everything they knew.

Amy's heart thudded in rhythm with her feet as she took the stairs two at a time to the passenger bridge; the only place from where she might be able to see Wilbur. She pushed her way to the front to look down on the platform, her eyes searching the men stepping up to take their place in the squash and heat inside the train. There – wasn't that Wilbur's father, reaching through the window of one of the carriages?

'Wilbur!' Amy jumped up and down with her arms in the air. 'Wilbur!'

His father stepped back and Amy saw Wilbur leaning from the window, looking up for her as the whistle blew and the train edged from the station. Steam obscured all but her face.

'Amy! Wait for me!'

'Yes! Of course!' Knowing he wouldn't know the answer, she shouted the question anyway. 'When will you be back?'

As the roof of the train passed beneath the shadow of the horse chestnut tree, it seemed so close she might be able to reach down and touch it. Wilbur's eyes found Amy's through the branches and he grinned at her.

'When the first conker falls!'

He disappeared from view as the train chugged under the bridge and picked up speed. It steamed into the distance, leaving the crowd left behind waving and crying. Amy felt a flutter in her stomach. Protectively, she placed both hands there; the tears falling unhindered from her eyes.

# Chapter 22

## August 1969

As she stood at the Bannon's back door, a rusty key in her hand, Lisa felt grown-up but nervous. Mrs Bannon, who she often chatted to over the fence, had asked her to look after their old dog Woolfy while they were on holiday. But Lisa had always been a little scared of this house and had never been inside on her own before. The oldest one down Sandy Lane, it was black and white and imposingly gothic. Some of the locals reckoned it was haunted.

Half-way through the school summer holidays, the early morning sunshine surrounded her. But as she stood on the old stone step, she shivered. The back door, arched dark oak with black fancy hinges dared her to enter. She had to. Woolfy needed to be let out and fed.

Behind her, the apple, pear and plum trees promised their fruit for autumn, although the grass among them grew long and wild. Bees hummed from one straggly flower to another.

Lisa slipped the key in the lock and the door swung open, creaking. The sound reminded Lisa of a Hammer horror film, that she'd sometimes be allowed to stay up late to watch on a Friday night in the holidays. Tom would always watch too, although he was more likely to laugh than get scared.

Woolfy, asleep in his bed, didn't stir. Dust floated in the large hall, caught in the chink of light that crept round the curtains. Tiny specks of sunshine fell on the parquet floor. The smell was reassuring, like an old library, books lining the walls on wonky shelves. She suspected Mr Bannon was the reader – lots of the book covers had pictures of the war. Here alone, Lisa thought it felt strangely like another time.

She took a deep breath and opened the door on her left to the kitchen. As she bent down to the rickety cupboard next to the sink for Woolfy's food, something soft brushed the back of her leg. Startled, she jumped, then giggled, as Woolfy looked up at her, his tail wagging slowly. Mrs Bannon said he slept most of the day; he was fourteen, an old gentleman, but still had a voracious appetite. 'Hello Woolfy, you've woken up then,' said Lisa, breathing normally again. 'You must know it's breakfast.' He licked her legs in reply.

She spooned the food into his dish and he wolfed it down. Lisa smiled to herself. It was probably where he got his name from. His dish empty, she refilled his water bowl, then let him out in the garden. A bit doddery, he still managed to cock his leg against the nearest apple tree before wandering around the side of the house.

Lisa sat on the step, looking at the orchard and old wood sheds. She didn't want to explore the house, but would've liked to have poked around the garden. It was overgrown and interesting, but with Mrs Bannon not there to ask, she felt it wasn't the right thing to do. She'd let Woolfy wander around for a while, then put him back indoors. She'd pop round again later, after tea. Before it got dark.

She was thinking about Billy when a loud tinny thud and rattle came from the side of the house. She went to look and saw Woolfy had knocked over the empty dustbin that had more rusty holes than metal. He was inside it, just his tail poking out. 'Woolfy! What are you doing?' Reaching in to pull him out by his collar, she could see a few bones from the remains of an old chicken carcass. As she managed to get him out, Woolfy pawed violently at his muzzle, rubbing his head against her. White foam flecked from his lips as he repeatedly opened and closed his mouth. He started running round in circles. 'Woolfy! What's wrong?' Lisa grabbed his collar and tried to calm him but he continued struggling, the whites of his eyes showing. She began to panic. Dad had gone to work; her mum had gone shopping. Tom and Billy were somewhere in Jackdaw Woods.

'I think he's got a bone stuck between his back teeth.' The words came from nowhere. Lisa spun around and looked up. An old man with a white beard and tattered coat stood there. 'Hold him still and I'll pull it out.' Lisa wrapped one arm around Woolfy and held his collar firm. The man gently prised open the dog's mouth with one hand, reaching inside with the other. 'There's the little blighter,' he whispered, pulling out a small chicken bone. It was almost translucent. 'Got stuck in his throat. He'll be alright now.'

Lisa hugged the old dog. He licked her face. 'For goodness sake, Woolfy, you really had me worried! You couldn't have been that hungry, you've only just had breakfast!' She patted him for a while, then looked up to thank the man. But he'd gone.

When she told Tom later that day, and described the man that helped Woolfy, she got the feeling that Tom knew who he was; although he didn't say so. It had been a strange day, Lisa thought. She'd be glad when Mr. and Mrs. Bannon were back.

* * *

The rest of that summer went quickly for Billy and Lisa, slowly for Tom. With Tanner by their side, Tom and Billy spent most of the time in the woods or on the common.

Most days the boys made their way to the Nissen huts where they practised aiming their catapults at the picture of Harold Wilson. The picture became so battered that you could no longer see his face; there was just a hole where his pipe had been. Billy replaced it with a picture of the Kray twins he'd torn from the paper. His dad had said they were evil, so their photo seemed a good one to use as a target. But by August, that needed replacing as well. One of Edward Heath went up.

Wilbur taught the boys how to fish, and after they'd cooked what they'd caught around a fire in the evenings, he'd tell the boys about his time in the first world war.

'Once,' Wilbur said, his face red in the glow from the fire, 'I was ordered to shoot five horses.'

'W-why?' Billy had asked in a strangled voice.

'The poor buggers were too worn out to help in the war effort anymore. The army wouldn't ship 'em back to England, nor carry on feeding them.'

Tom saw tears in the old man's eyes.

'Why did animals have to suffer?' Wilbur continued. 'The war wasn't of their making. I'll never forgive myself for shooting those horses, one after the other. Even though I had no choice.'

This story shocked Tom and Billy; they were unusually quiet for the rest of the evening. Wilbur spoke less of the war after that, mainly talking about his childhood; often making the boys laugh.

One night around the fire the wind whipped up, branches bending to the breeze, leaves rustling.

'What does that sound like to you, Billy?' asked Wilbur.

Billy hesitated. 'The w-wind?'

'Yes,' smiled Wilbur. 'But does it sound like anything else? Close your eyes for a moment.'

The two boys closed their eyes, the fire warm on their faces like the sun was during the day.

'The sea,' whispered Tom.

'Y-yeah,' said Billy. 'Waves on a stony beach.'

'We're a long way from a beach,' said Wilbur. 'But inside our heads, we can be anywhere we want to be, if only we use our imagination. That might be useful to remember.' Billy knew it would be – as soon as he had to go back to school.

* * *

Billy still climbed trees and looked for snakes and mice, but Tom did this less often, content to sit and watch his friend, or play with Tanner. The vision of Keziah dancing was never far from his mind.

Sometimes, Lisa joined them in the woods, but when she did, Tom noticed Billy acted differently and became quieter, looking at Lisa in a strange way. Tom also felt a bit uneasy when Lisa joined them – for some reason he didn't want Lisa to meet Wilbur. He had no idea why.

Before they knew it, their mums were moaning about how much they'd grown and talking about getting new shirts and trousers for the start of school.

September came and Tom and Billy fell back into meeting at the conker tree after school. The leaves started to gain patches of yellow and brown, but the fair – and Keziah – still hadn't come back to Tyneford.

Meeting Billy one afternoon, Tom asked him the question he was desperate for an answer to. Leaning against the trunk with his legs astride a branch, he looked casually at his friend. 'When do you reckon the end of the summer is?'

Billy didn't answer straight away. He looked at Tom, who'd started carving a piece of wood with his penknife. Although Tom looked as if he wouldn't care about Billy's reply, Billy sensed he cared very much. Looking around him, he saw the bright green conker cases hanging amongst the leaves, protecting the mahogany treasure growing within.

'When the first conker f-falls,' he said.

Three weeks later, it did.

* * *

Neither Tom nor Billy saw that first conker fall. It happened in the early morning, just as the fair was making its way to Tyneford.

Joe Cooper brought up the rear of the cavalcade in his mother's cart with a piebald cob in the shafts. The roads were quiet and to amuse himself, he whipped the cob on, then pulled it viciously to a standstill. He did it over and over, until the cobs flanks were lathered in sweat, its head jittering.

When the fair finally arrived at the field beside the school, the men set about constructing the rides and stalls, whilst the women cooked breakfast. Keziah unharnessed the horses and led them to the back of the field, tying them on long ropes to the oak in the corner. She fetched them water and brushed each one down as they grazed on the lush grass. Reaching the piebald that Joe had driven, she saw the sweat and pink froth round its mouth, and understood instantly why it shied away from her hand. 'I'm sorry, Patch,' she whispered in the horse's ear, 'I'm sorry it was you that had to put up with him today.' She went to the caravan to fetch a damp sponge. Cutting up some apples and carrots and putting them in her pocket, she returned to the horses, gently wiping the piebald's flanks. When she fed them, she gave Patch the most treats.

By first break, the entire school knew the fair was back. And it was Friday. Until home time, the heavy, humid air hummed with excitement.

When Billy joined Tom at the conker tree, Tom wondered if his friend could notice the change in him. Even though he hadn't seen her yet, the thought that Keziah was here, close by, set his body alight. His mind frantically worked on the how and when he'd be able to meet her.

'So, w-what do you think?' said Billy.

Tom looked at his friend. 'What do I think about what?'

'B-blimey Tom! You n-never listen to me anymore!' His friend's voice broke and rose, not yet secure in manhood.

'Er, I'm sorry Billy. I was miles away.'

Billy looked in the distance. 'You always are l-lately.'

'Yeah. Sorry. C'mon. Let's get Tanner.'

As they walked down Budds Lane, Tom wondered when he could see Keziah. He wouldn't mention going to the fair to Billy; he knew his friend would try to stop him, thinking he'd want to fight Joe Cooper. But Tom, even though he didn't accept Cooper was his brother, had tried to forget Cooper's cruelty towards Tanner. He wouldn't fight him, not now. Not unless Cooper started it. He just wanted to see Keziah. He couldn't wait. He'd go tonight.

They collected Tanner and took him to Stickleback Brook for a swim. Throwing sticks for him to fetch, they sat on the bank. 'I feel like a swim myself, it's so hot,' said Tom.

'M-mum said it's an Indian s-summer.'

'Yeah. My mum called it that too, because it's hot for longer than usual. I think it's always hot in India.'

'My dad was st-stationed there after the war.'

'Oh? Did he say what it was like?'

'Y-yeah,' grinned Billy. 'He said it was bloody hot.'

Tom jumped on his friend playfully and grappled with him, trying to push him into the brook. But Billy held on and pulled Tom in with him. Their socks and shoes soaking, and most of their clothes, the two boys collapsed on the bank, laughing so hard their sides hurt.

\* \* \*

Slipping some clothes under the blankets, Tom put his torch in his jacket pocket. He could've told his parents he was going out, but not knowing when he'd be back, it was easier to pretend he was having an early night.

Tanner was on the bed. 'You coming, boy?' he whispered. It was dodgy taking Tanner with him. If his parents did check on him, they'd probably notice Tanner wasn't there. But Keziah had wanted to see the dog, and jumping from the bed, Tanner waited eagerly by the door to follow Tom. 'C'mon then boy, but be quiet.' Tom led the way down the stairs and out the back door, his dog right behind him. Jogging there, Tom cut through the school grounds to go to the back of the field where the caravans would be. He could see the horses grazing there, but most of the caravans were in darkness.

The fair bustled with people and noise and there were more stalls than Tom remembered. The air smelt sickly sweet with candy floss and toffee apples, but diesel fumes still caught the back of his throat. He hoped to see Keziah working at one of the stalls, but he'd have to wander around. He passed the ghost train, sirens and screams punctuating the night, a queue of excited teenagers waiting to get on. Raucous laughter and tinny music came from the dodgems. Then he spotted her.

She manned the stall where children hooked yellow plastic ducks that bobbed around in the water. If there was a number on the bottom, they'd won a prize. Tom watched as Keziah chatted and laughed with the children. A smaller child, a little girl with wild blonde hair, wasn't able to hook a duck. Eventually, Tom saw Keziah quickly loop the wire around a hook when the girl wasn't watching. Then Keziah reached behind her, giving a small teddy to the girl, who beamed with delight.

Smiling, Tom started to walk towards her. But he nearly lost his balance as someone barged into him.

'I thought it was you, yer scumbag.' Joe Cooper loomed in front of him, a cigarette in his mouth. 'I see you found my feckin' mongrel.'

Tanner stood at Tom's feet growling, his lips pulled back, his teeth, catching some fluorescent light, glowed white.

'If he is your dog, he doesn't like you much, does he?' said Tom, holding Joe's stare.

'I don't give a feckin' shit!' screamed Joe, losing any semblance of control. Flicking his cigarette in Tanner's direction, he drew his arm back, slamming his fist into Tom's stomach. Tom doubled over, gasping for air. Sneering, Cooper grabbed Tom's arms and jerked up a knee hard between his legs. Tom slipped to the ground groaning. Cooper aimed a kick at Tanner to try and block him, but the dog was too quick. Launching for his throat, Tanner sank his teeth in Cooper's sallow flesh.

# Chapter 23

## September 1969

'Come here, boy.' A tall, heavy-built man grabbed Tanner's collar, pulling him off Cooper. Tom started to get up. A small crowd had formed a circle, watching.

Cooper clasped his bloodied neck with both hands. 'Get that feckin' dog away before I kick it to death!'

'Leave the dog alone,' said the big man, holding Tanner back as he strained to get at Cooper. 'You deserved what you got. I saw you hit this boy here for no reason. The dog was just protecting him.'

Cooper sized the man up, then turned to face Tom. 'I'll 'ave you soon, scum. You'd better watch yer back,' he said, spitting on the ground at Tom's feet before pushing and elbowing his way through the crowd.

'Thanks,' said Tom, looking up at the man as he let go of Tanner. The dog ran to Tom, licking his hand.

'What was that all about?' asked the man.

The people around them dispersed, the excitement over.

'He doesn't like that I rescued this dog from him. He beat him, tied him up and left him for dead.'

'No wonder it bit him then,' said the man. 'You ok?'

'Yeah, I – '

'Tom!' Keziah ran over to him. 'What happened? I heard Tanner growling but there were too many people, I didn't see – '

'I'll leave you to it then,' said the man, who nodded at Tom before turning to walk away.

'Wait, what's your name?' Tom asked.

The big man looked over his shoulder and smiled at him. 'Albert.'

'Thanks again, Albert.' Tom had wanted to shake his hand, but the man was already walking away, disappearing behind the stalls. He turned to Keziah. Lifting his arm to put it round her shoulder, he grimaced in pain.

Keziah looked worried. 'Are you hurt?'

'Did you see Joe Cooper?' asked Tom.

'No, was he here? Have you had a fight? You look really pale, Tom.'

'Well, I don't think you'd really call it a fight. He saw I had Tanner – realised he'd been found. Cooper thumped me in the stomach and winded me. Tanner went for him, but that man who just left – pulled Tanner off him.'

'And Joe went?'

'Yeah. Didn't you see the size of that guy?'

Keziah grinned. 'So, how's your stomach?'

'I'll live,' smiled Tom, 'but I could do with sitting down for a bit.'

'I'll shut the stall. You can come to the caravan and rest for a while.' Keziah stood on tiptoe and kissed Tom's cheek before pulling down the shutters and locking up. She took his hand, leading him to the back of the field. Pulling a key from her pocket she unlocked one of the caravan doors, going in and lighting a small oil lamp on the table. Tom followed her up the steps. It felt cosy inside with warm honey walls and brightly-coloured rugs. A small table and chairs were in front of the sink and tiny kitchenette. To his left were two beds, partly obscured by a velvet curtain, and on the other side, a small sofa and coffee table.

'Sit down, Tom,' Keziah smiled. 'Would you like a drink? Shandy? A cup of tea?'

Tom sat down heavily on the sofa. Keziah stroked Tanner as he stood by her side, tail wagging.

'Yes, a shandy will be great.' Tom paused. 'I've missed you so much,' he said quietly.

'I've missed you too,' whispered Keziah. She put a bowl of water on the floor for Tanner who was panting, the evening still warm despite the darkness. Pouring Tom's drink and one for herself, she joined him on the sofa, putting the glasses down on the coffee table. Tom reached for her, kissing her properly. Tanner came and lay at their feet.

Taking a gulp of cool shandy, Tom started to feel better. 'I hope we can spend a lot of time together over the next two weeks,' he whispered.

215

Keziah's face clouded. 'I hope so, Tom. But Ma, she's been a bit strange, ever since I told her about you. She says she doesn't want me to see you. I don't know why. She normally trusts me, and is so sweet. Maybe it's because you're not part of the fair? I don't know, but we'll have to meet up away from here, in secret.'

'What did you say about me?'

'Nothing much. Only that you saved Tanner and seemed nice. I mentioned that you'd been one of twins born in a barn, and that the other baby was taken before your mother could get it to safety. I didn't mention what Wilbur had said – about your twin being Joe. So, I really don't know – '

The door opened. Tanner sat up. A slight, blonde-haired woman walked in.

'Ma!' exclaimed Keziah.

'Who's this?' The woman looked at Tom. Her eyes narrowed.

'Hello, I'm Tom,' he said, standing up and offering his hand.

The woman ignored him and turned to Keziah. 'I told you not to see this boy!'

Keziah jumped up. 'But Ma! Joe Cooper thumped him in the stomach. He needed to rest. Anyway, why can't I see him?'

'I've told you. No good will come of it.' She faced Tom. 'Get out! Get out of my caravan and leave my daughter alone.'

'Ma! I can't believe you're being so mean. Tom hasn't done anything wrong.'

216

Keziah's mother faced the sink, grabbing hold of the worktop edge, her knuckles white. 'Get out Tom,' she said in a low voice. 'Now.'

Tom looked at Keziah and headed to the door, Tanner at his heels. She followed him outside to the edge of the field. 'I'm sorry Tom, I didn't know she'd come back this early, I don't understand why she's being like this – '

'Sshhh,' said Tom, reassuringly. 'Don't worry, it's not your fault. We can still meet, but away from the fair. That's probably best, anyway.'

'Shall I come round to see you tomorrow? I remember where you live.'

'It's Saturday tomorrow,' Tom said, 'are you free during the day?'

'Yes.'

'Come round in the morning, about ten? We'll spend the day together. What will you tell your mum?'

'I'll think of something.' She squeezed his hand. 'See you tomorrow.'

Tom's eyes followed Keziah as she walked back to the caravan. He was shocked to see her mother leaning against the door frame, staring at him. Despite the humid night, he shivered.

# Chapter 24

## October 1915

Fishing the raw slices of carrot from the soup in his billy-can, Wilbur shoved them in his pocket for Molly. He'd become fond of the little brown mule, and she'd be here soon. He fancied he saw hope in the one eye she had left; something that he didn't see in the eyes of the soldiers stood beside him in the trench. Maybe it wasn't hope he saw in Molly's eye; just thankfulness for the small pieces of carrot. The fodder she had each day wasn't enough to keep a goat alive, let alone an ammunitions mule, pulling heavy loads of shells and artillery in a wooden cart through thick mud, day in, day out.

Albert nudged him; his dark eyes sunken in his pale face. 'The ammo's arrived. Rumour is we're going over the top in a couple of hours.' Albert reached inside his uniform for a cigarette, lighting it with shaking hands. A mountain of a man, Wilbur knew him to be brave and strong. Seeing him like this chilled him to the bone.

Making his way to the back of the trench, Wilbur went to find Molly. When he saw the ammunitions cart being unloaded, it wasn't Molly in the stays, but a black and white cob. He helped the two men unload. 'You've a new horse,' said Wilbur, 'where's the mule?'

'Poor wee thing got mired in the bloody mud. Didn't have the strength to get herself out. She was exhausted when I had to put a bullet in her and go back for this one.'

Wilbur felt the back of his eyes pricking as his vision blurred. Giving the carrots to the cob, he rested his face on the warm fur of its neck. 'How long will you last?' he whispered.

Back in the trench, Albert was slumped against the side, his hands still shaking as he clutched his empty billy-can. 'I'll not be back from this one,' he said, his voice cracking. 'I can feel it.'

Wilbur reached out and squeezed his shoulder. There was nothing he could say.

When the whistle went, the regiment ran into the machine gun fire. Within minutes three-quarters of the men were down. Those still alive eventually headed back to the trench. Wilbur passed a piper in a tartan kilt. Hit by shrapnel he lay in the mud with blood covering his face, his body twisted and bent, his bagpipes a giant spider askew across his chest.

Then he saw Albert, his legs mangled in barbed wire, half his broad chest blown away. Swallowing down a scream, Wilbur crawled in the mud across no man's land, a cold clammy sweat on his skin.

Back home, unnoticed, the first conker fell amongst leaves on the empty station platform.

# Chapter 25

## September 1969

Wearing his new trousers and favourite striped cotton shirt with the sleeves rolled up, Tom watched out of his bedroom window for Keziah.

Lisa popped her head round the door. 'What are – ' she stopped, staring at Tom. 'Oh! Who are you seeing? Dressed like that it can't be Billy.'

Tom winked at her. 'No one you know, Lis. Do I look alright?'

Lisa opened the door wide and took a step forward, looking him up and down. His hair was getting long. 'Yeah, I guess. You look a bit like that singer. The one Mum likes. Elvis the Pelvis.' She giggled.

'Wish I could sing like him,' grinned Tom, secretly pleased. He knew Elvis was considered sexy and good-looking and girls flocked around him.

Lisa heard horse's hooves clattering down the lane. She ran to the window on the landing. 'Wow! What a beautiful horse.' She watched as Keziah pulled Beauty to a stop. 'Who's she? Is that who you're seeing, Tom? The girl riding the black horse bareback?'

Tom joined her at the window. 'Yes,' he said, smiling down at Keziah. 'Lis, tell Mum I won't be back for lunch, will you?' Rushing downstairs with Tanner at his feet, he closed the front door behind him.

Lisa couldn't hear what they said, but they were smiling at each other. The pretty girl took the horse to the low wall in front of the Bannons' garden. She held out her hand to help Tom up. They laughed as he scrambled awkwardly onto the horse's back behind her, slipping his arms around her waist. Lisa watched as they rode towards Jackdaw Woods and out of sight.

* * *

The flowery scent of Keziah's hair reminded Tom of the night he first met her, riding like this along the old train tracks, searching for Tanner. He glanced round to make sure Tanner was following them. The dog trotted happily behind.

Tom whispered in Keziah's ear. 'So, what did you tell your mum?'

'Just that I was taking Beauty out for a ride. I often do if I'm not working at the fair. I don't think she suspected anything. But I have to take over running the stall at seven tonight, so I'll need to be back by then.'

'Great,' replied Tom, 'we've got all day.' He put on a posh voice. 'So where are you taking me, my fair lady, on such a fine steed?'

'Over the hills and far away, my handsome knight.' Keziah replied. They both laughed.

'No, really,' Keziah said, 'since it's still warm, I thought we could go to the pool off Stickleback Brook and have a swim?'

'The pool?'

'Yes, it's in the opposite direction to the old station. Haven't you been there? It's a bit of a way, but deep enough for a proper swim.'

'Sounds good,' said Tom, 'Tanner will love it.'

'He'll need a swim to cool off, by the time we get there,' laughed Keziah.

Tom held her waist tenderly. He could have stayed this close to her forever.

'Did – did you talk to your mum after I left last night? Do you know why she doesn't like me?'

'I did ask her why she doesn't want me to see you. But she wouldn't explain. Just told me again that I mustn't – that I didn't know you. I think it's because you're not part of the fair. She's got strange ideas about who I should go out with. She tried to get me to like Joe in the past. As if I'd ever like him!' She tossed her head, her derision for Cooper clear.

Tom smiled. 'I haven't got him as competition then?'

'No Tom,' she replied quietly, 'you haven't any competition.'

He squeezed her waist gently. 'I'm glad to hear that,' he murmured.

Reaching the woods, they rode the rest of the way in silence. Tom was content to be close to her, listening to the birds singing in the late summer sunshine, enjoying the rhythmic gait of the horse. Occasionally Keziah clicked her tongue at Beauty or spoke in a reassuring voice when she shied at a rustle in the undergrowth or a squawking pheasant.

The sun, still sultry, tripped and glinted on the water as they reached the pool. They both pushed damp strands of hair from their foreheads. Tanner ran ahead, jumping straight in. His tail a rudder, they smiled as they watched him drink as he swam.

The crescent shaped expanse of water flowed into the brook, which continued its way on the other side. Clear and inviting, the pool revealed its glistening chalk bottom like a prize. At the edge, bees hummed amongst wild flowers – from purple loosestrife, to white angelica, to blue devil's-bit, to yellow toadflax. Late September wearing June's best dress.

'What a beautiful place,' said Tom. 'I want a swim, but I haven't got any trunks.'

'I want a swim, but haven't a swimming costume,' smiled Keziah.

'I guess we'll have to swim in our underwear then,' grinned Tom.

Lifting one leg over the horse's neck, Keziah slipped down first, then Tom jumped to the ground. Leaving Beauty to have a drink and graze, Keziah took

Tom's out-stretched hand. He led her to the edge of the bank. Hesitant at first, he faced her, searching her eyes for an answer. Keziah took a step closer and he reached out, roughly pulling her to him, folding her in his arms. And in the shade of a stately weeping-willow, he whispered that he loved her.

* * *

Lisa had waited until lunch to broach the subject. Her friend had asked at school yesterday if she wanted to go to the fair on Saturday night. Well, of course she did. The whole school did. She'd been a couple of years before with her mum and dad – but wanted to go now with Judy. It'd be exciting – there wasn't much of that in Tyneford. She'd have liked Billy to have asked her, but she hadn't seen him for a few days.

Sensing her parents might not want her going to the fair, she trod carefully.

'I've managed to save quite a lot of pocket money lately,' she said, watching from the table as her mum made cheese and pickle sandwiches on the bread board next to the sink. Her dad sat opposite her reading the paper, a picture of The Beatles walking across a zebra crossing on the front.

'That's good,' said her dad, from behind the paper.

'With the money I got from Mr. Bannon for looking after Woolfy and my birthday money, it's adding up.'

'Are you saving for anything in particular?' asked her mum, bringing the sandwiches and a pitcher of iced lemonade to the table.

'Not really,' said Lisa, picking up the sandwich nearest to her. 'Just trying to be sensible, you know, in case I need something in the future.'

'Well, that is good, Lisa. You're growing up, not spending it all on sweets.'

Lisa finished her sandwich and picked up a piece of tomato.

'You don't normally like tomatoes,' observed her dad, putting the paper down and placing three sandwiches on his plate.

'Like Mum said, I'm growing up, trying different things.'

Bemused, Reg smiled to himself. 'Is there something you want Lisa, by any chance?'

Lisa coloured slightly. 'No. Well. Not exactly. I don't want anything as such. But I'd like to go to the fair tonight with Judy. I think I'm old enough to go with a friend now.'

Her dad had stopped smiling. 'Do you?' He looked at her from over his glasses. 'Well, I don't.'

'I'm not a kid anymore Dad, I'm thirteen!'

'That's why I'm worried,' he said quietly.

Her mum, seeing her daughter's disappointment, turned to her husband. 'Maybe if she promised to get back by ten? We've got to start trusting her, Reg.'

'It's not that I don't trust Lisa,' he said, 'it's because I don't trust boys.'

'Yes. But we can't be with her all the time, can we? She's growing up, Reg. At least she'll be with a friend.' She looked at her daughter. 'You'll stay with Judy all evening?'

'Yes. I'll walk home with her. She said I can stay the night if I want.'

'She lives near Billy, doesn't she?

'Yes.'

'Well, that sounds alright to me.'

Reg glowered. 'Looks like you two have decided the matter,' he said, getting up noisily from the table and leaving the room.

Lisa's mum looked at her. 'Don't worry, he'll calm down later. It's only because he worries about you.' She poured herself a drink. 'I think there'll be a thunderstorm tonight, the air's so heavy. Just be sensible and make sure you're back to Judy's no later than ten. Promise?'

'I promise. Thanks Mum.'

# Chapter 26

Listening to Radio Caroline on her tiny transistor radio, Lisa applied a little eye-shadow, mascara and lip gloss in her bedroom mirror. She was looking forward to the rides at the fair; to some excitement. But she didn't want a row with her dad on the way out, he didn't like her wearing make-up. Creeping downstairs, she opened the front door before calling out 'Bye!'

'Bye love, have a nice time,' replied her mum before Lisa closed the door behind her. She heard nothing from her dad – until she stepped into the front garden, where he stood pruning shrubs by the side of the path. It took Lisa by surprise, as it was nearly quarter to seven and beginning to get dark.

Reg looked at his pretty daughter, the sick feeling of unease he'd had since lunch time intensifying. 'Be careful Lisa,' he said, his voice gruff. 'Come straight home if there's any trouble.'

'I will dad, don't worry.' She smiled at him.

'Are you sure you don't want me to come and collect you at ten?'

'Don't be daft dad, I'll be fine. See you later.'

He watched her as she walked up Sandy Lane, still unable to shake off a feeling of dread. For God's sake Reg, get a grip, he said to himself. Wiping the sweat from his forehead, he returned the secateurs to the shed.

\* \* \*

'Come in Lisa, she won't be long.' Judy's mum called up the stairs, 'Judy, hurry up, Lisa's here!' She started to ask about school, but then Judy clomped down to the hall. Lisa hardly recognised her. She wore three-quarter length pedal-pushers and white block-heeled sandals. With heavy black mascara and bright pink lipstick she looked sixteen, not thirteen. Lisa expected Judy's mum to say something, but she didn't – she just waved them good-bye from the door.

They didn't take the short-cut through Budds Lane as Judy didn't want mud on her shoes. Not that there would have been any – it hadn't rained for ages. Lisa remembered what her mum had said and wondered if it'd rain tonight. If it did, Judy wouldn't be able to run home – not in those heels. Lisa was glad she'd worn her bumper boots.

On the way there, her friend talked non-stop about boys and music. When she paused for breath, Lisa told her about the girl on the horse calling for Tom that morning. Unlike Lisa, Judy wasn't much interested in horses. But she fancied Tom.

'Did she bring him back home?' asked Judy, 'only I wondered if Tom might be coming to the fair tonight?'

'She dropped him off about an hour ago. But I don't think he's any plans to come. He was carving a piece of wood in his bedroom when I left. He said it was going to be of a horse – to give to that girl.'

'Oh. That's a shame.' Judy giggled. 'He's quite good-looking, your brother.'

Lisa hadn't told any of her friends that Tom wasn't really her brother. She wondered whether she ever would.

'I think they're going out together,' Lisa said. 'I saw him kiss her.'

'What – the girl on the horse?'

Lisa nodded.

'Where's she from? Does she go to our school?'

'I don't think so,' replied Lisa. 'Tom didn't say. I've never seen her before.'

'Oh, well. There'll be plenty of boys at the fair,' grinned Judy.

They heard the music and screams before they reached the school. Dark now, flickering bright lights pulsed excitement into the sultry warm air and the veins of every teenager.

'Let's go on the dodgems first!' Judy shouted as everyone swarmed onto the ride, trying to grab an empty car. 'I'm driving!' She jumped behind the steering wheel of a bright red dodgem, just before a father and his son tried to get in. The man turned away, looking for another empty car.

'I'm driving next time,' smiled Lisa, scrambling in beside her.

A siren sounded to signal the start of the ride, then "Ob-La-Di, Ob-La-Da" blasted through the speakers. Lisa sang along as Judy slammed the pedal to the floor. The dodgem lurched forward, jolting Lisa's head back. She saw the white sparks fizzing from the curved top of the pole as it rasped across the metal mesh above. Within seconds, they were stuck in a jam at the corner, five dodgems going nowhere. A boy about sixteen jumped on the back of their car, a leather money pouch slung around his hips, his shirt undone nearly to his waist. Pushing their car away from the jam, he held on casually to the pole. Judy's cheeks flushed as she drove the car fast round the outside.

'Evenin' girls,' said the boy, ogling Judy's chest. 'That'll be two shillings fer the car.'

Lisa pulled a shilling from her pocket, giving it to Judy, who threw it in her bag and handed the boy a two-bob bit.

'Come back later girls,' sniggered the boy, 'an' you can have a free ride on me.' He jumped to the next car.

'He's a bit of alright,' said Judy, looking him up and down as he held the pole of the other car. She crashed into another dodgem at full speed, laughing.

'I dunno. He was leering down your top.' said Lisa. 'You didn't really like him, did you?'

Judy yanked the steering wheel to the left and they were off again. 'Well, he said we could have a free ride later. It'll be worth coming back for that.'

Lisa didn't answer her. She didn't want to see the boy again – even for a free ride. He made her flesh creep.

After the dodgems they went on the ghost train, Lisa's favourite. They knew the scary things that brushed against their faces in the dark were only string or cotton wool, and that the skeletons that lit up as the train lurched around a corner were only made of plaster; but it didn't stop them grabbing each other and screaming. Uncontrollable shrieking laughter played as the train pushed through the swing doors to the outside and jerked to a stop.

It'd been musty and stale inside, but a slight breeze had picked up now, cooling the night air. Giggling, Lisa and Judy moved on to the rifle range, and despite the sights being out of line, Judy won a small toy rabbit on a keyring. They went on every ride and visited nearly every stall, saving the switchbacks for last.

Exhilarated after the ride, they sat on the steps eating pink and white candy floss, listening to "The Israelites." Lisa looked at her watch. 'We'd better get going. It's twenty to ten.'

Judy scowled at her. 'For goodness sake, Lisa, how often do we get to go out? It's not late.'

'I promised I'd be back by ten. Dad'll kill me if I'm not.' A large raindrop plopped on her hand. 'Anyway, it's starting to rain.' As if on cue, a loud clap of thunder ripped through the air, just as the music changed to Lulu belting out "Boom bang-a-bang."

'C'mon,' said Judy, 'let's have one last go on the dodgems, then we'll go home.'

Lisa looked over to the ride. The cars were stationary, the people climbing out. 'Beat you there then!' she laughed, running over and jumping in the driver's seat of a yellow car. Judy got in just before Lisa put her foot to the floor, steering the dodgem to the centre to avoid the pile ups. They managed to circle a few times without a collision.

'Oh, look who it is!' giggled Judy, as the boy they'd seen earlier hopped on the back again.

'Two shillings girls,' he demanded, holding out his hand.

'But you said we could have a free ride if we came back.' Judy looked up at him through her eyelashes.

'Here,' said Lisa, pulling her last shilling from her pocket and slapping it in the palm of his hand.

Joe Cooper grinned at her. 'I like a girl who pays 'er way.'

Lisa looked straight ahead, ignoring him.

'Do I have to pay?' Judy looked up at him, pouting.

'Depends.' He looked the girls up and down suggestively.

'On what?'

But he wasn't listening to Judy. He was too busy ogling Lisa.

The music stopped and the car lost its power, grinding to a halt. Lisa jumped out, but Judy stayed in the car looking up at her. 'C'mon, one last go?'

Lisa felt Joe Cooper's eyes on her and shuddered. 'No. We've got to leave. It's nearly ten.'

'Well, I'm not going,' said Judy, admiring Joe's biceps as he tightened his grip on the pole, the car moving away again.

Lisa sighed, exasperated. She'd have to walk home alone. She shouted at the receding bumper car. 'I'm going Judy!' Judy put one arm in the air without looking around, and waved. The dodgem merged with the others.

Untying the arms of her jacket from around her waist, Lisa walked down the steps, heading towards the road. She held the jacket over her head as the rain began pounding down, massive drops bouncing back up from the ground. Fine friend she isn't, thought Lisa.

Seconds later, Cooper jumped off the yellow bumper car and swaggered over to his mate, who lounged against the rail at the edge.

'Take over 'ere will yer? I've a bit of business to see to.' Cooper unbuckled the money pouch and held it out to Jake.

'Yeah, alright Joe,' Jake replied, throwing his roll-up to the ground and taking the belt.

Turning around, Joe Cooper set off after Lisa.

# Chapter 27

Tom was in his bedroom carving the horse for Keziah. That afternoon, when he'd told her he loved her, she'd said she loved him, too. He'd never felt this way before, so engrossed in another human being; so happy to be alive. He pictured her face as he'd kissed her, tanned and flushed; so beautiful. They'd swam and kissed and played with Tanner – and swam and kissed some more. Resting, he'd cuddled her in the shade of the willow, Tanner asleep at their feet. He'd never forget this afternoon. Not as long as he lived.

When he finished the horses face, he looked around for Tanner. He wasn't there. 'Hey boy, where are you?' he called out, placing the carving on his bedside table. Slipping the penknife in his pocket, he went downstairs. His parents were in the front room watching the telly. Because it was still so warm, his mum had propped open both the front and back doors. Tom walked out to the garden and found Tanner laying on the front lawn, panting. 'You trying to cool off, boy?' Tanner thumped his tail on the grass. 'Ok. I don't suppose it'll hurt for you to stay out a bit longer.' Tom returned to the house, getting himself a glass of Tizer. Checking that Tanner had plenty of water in his bowl, he joined his mum and dad in the front room as The Avengers theme tune began.

**\* \* \***

Lisa knew Budds Lane would be dark, but the time she'd save getting home would be worth it. She'd be in serious trouble if she was late, especially with her dad. She wished she'd realised Judy might be difficult. She wouldn't be going anywhere with her again, that was for sure.

Walking quickly, she tried to avoid the puddles that had formed already. Her bumper boots were comfortable but they weren't waterproof, and her jacket was soaked. The rain had eased a little but the drops were still large, pitter-pattering on the leaves and ground. A streak of lightening silently lit the sky, silhouetting the twisted tree branches above. Thunder rumbled a few seconds later; the storm right overhead.

If she'd looked behind her, she'd probably have seen Cooper skulking in the shadows, running from one tree to another, getting closer. But she didn't. She was wondering what it was like to ride that gorgeous black horse, and where it was now. How had Tom met that girl, and learned to ride? She smiled as she remembered how awkwardly he'd got on the back of the horse. But she supposed it couldn't be easy without a saddle to hold, or stirrups to put your feet in.

'Well, well, looky 'ere sexy, fancy bumpin' into you.'

Lisa jumped, then turned around. It was that creep from the fair.

'Are you following me?' Her eyes flashed with annoyance.

'C'mon darlin', you know yer like me.'

'No, I don't!' It came out louder than she intended, but she was glad. He's full of himself, she thought.

'Playin' hard to get, are we?' he leered. He came behind her and jumped forward, grabbing her hair at the roots. Lisa couldn't move. He pulled her head back.

'Get off of me!' she screamed, anger powering her elbows into his stomach. He loosened his grip long enough for Lisa to get away. She started to run. The wind picked up, buffeting her from behind, aiding her escape. Fear kicked in and gave her extra speed, pumping her legs, giving her wings. She thought she'd got away. But she didn't see the deep hole filled with water. Her right foot sank down, her ankle twisting. She went sprawling, her hands muddied and stinging, her knees cut, her foot pulsating with pain.

Joe Cooper laughed and straddled her back. He pinned her arms to her side before she had chance to get up, forcing her face into dirt and wet leaves. It was then she started to scream, tears clouding her eyes, terror pounding in her heart. Joe Cooper clamped a cold, smoky hand over her mouth.

'No one's gonna hear yer darlin',' he whispered in her ear. As if to confirm the truth of what he'd said, a loud crack of thunder shook the sky, its deep rumble reverberating down the trees into the ground. Leaning his weight on her, Cooper threw her jacket aside. Lisa couldn't move; she could hardly breathe. She felt the yank as he tore at her blouse; heard the rip as the material gave way. *Please God*, she thought, *not here, not now. Not him. Please. No.*

* * *

Reg looked at the clock again. Almost ten o'clock. He glanced across at his wife. 'Lisa was supposed to be back by now.'

Elsie stopped sewing as the clock began striking the hour. 'Well, yes. She promised to be back by ten, but she might have meant back to Judy's by ten.'

'But she said she wasn't staying at Judy's. She said she'd come home.'

'Yes, I know dear. But she'll walk with Judy back to her house first. Give her another few minutes before you start worrying. I'm sure she'll be here any minute now.'

Reg stood up, restless. 'Do you want a cup of tea?'

Elsie nodded. 'That'd be nice.' She looked across at Tom. He seemed half asleep. 'Where's Tanner, Tom?'

Tom opened his eyes. 'He went outside to lie on the grass, I think he was hot.'

'Well, you'd better call him in and close the doors. It's starting to rain – there's a thunder-storm.'

Tom stood up slowly, muscles aching that he hadn't known he had. This riding malarky was harder than it looked. Walking to the front porch, he called Tanner's name, but he didn't come. Tom pulled his jacket from the peg and put it on. It was tipping down.

'Tanner? Here boy!' Tom walked to the spot where he'd been earlier, but there was no sign of him. 'Tanner!' He ran in for a torch and then to the back garden, sweeping the light around. Nothing. A sick feeling rose in his throat and he swallowed it down. Where was he? Running back to the door he shouted inside. 'Tanner's gone. I'm going up the road to look for him!'

Reg dropped the spoon and it clattered in the kitchen sink. His head spun like the tea-leaves in the teapot, the feeling of unease a tight knot in his chest. He looked at the clock on the wall. Five past ten. Thunder clapped outside and he closed the back door. Grasping for normality, he poured out the tea and took it through to Elsie.

**\* \* \***

As wind shrieked down Budds Lane, a crack of thunder masked the sound of the branch splintering above Joe Cooper. In slow motion, it fell on his shoulders, spindly sticks whipping his head and face. He jumped up, pushing the branch aside, and Lisa took her chance. Even with the pain shooting up her leg, she managed to evade his grasp, staggering in the mud. For a few seconds, she dared to hope; but he was too fast for her. 'Oh no you don't,' he hissed, grabbing her arm and pulling her to the ground again, the jolt almost knocking her out. 'Not when I've gone to all this feckin' trouble.'

He straddled Lisa's stomach and pinned down both her wrists with one hand. With the other he began to undo his belt.

Cooper didn't even see Tanner coming. A flying bundle of fur, snarling with his lips pulled back, the dog sank his teeth into Cooper's thigh, ripping at skin and muscle. Cooper yelled out, flailing his arms, struggling to get to his feet. Tanner held on, his jaw locked, his grip an iron vice. Lisa scrambled to her knees.

Warm blood seeped from Cooper's thigh, the pain bringing tears to his eyes. 'Feckin' get off of me!' he screamed, trying to kick Tanner with his other leg. 'Get off, you bloody dog!' Reaching to his back pocket, he clasped the handle of his knife, pulling it out and raising it above his head. The blade glinted silver in a flash of lightening. He brought it down viciously, stabbing through Tanner's ribs.

Lisa screamed. 'Nnoooooooo!'

Yelping, Tanner collapsed on the ground. Cooper turned, running back the way he'd come, one hand clasping his thigh. Lisa rushed to Tanner, putting her arms around his neck.

'Oh my God, hold on boy, I'll get Tom, you'll be alright, hold on boy.' Lisa sobbed. She felt Tanner's warm tongue lick her hand. 'I won't be long boy, hold on.' Lisa started towards the end of Budds Lane. Dragging her bad ankle, she moved as fast as she could, panic hammering her heart.

'Lisa?'

Tom's voice. She saw him, a dark shadow in front of her. 'Thank goodness! Quick, Tom! Tanner's been stabbed, he's on the ground back there.' She grabbed his arm, pulling him to the wet and bloodied dog.

Tom knelt in the mud by his side. Tanner whimpered. 'God, Lisa, what happened?'

'A-a boy from the fair. He-he followed me. Attacked me,' Lisa wept. 'Tanner ran up and bit him in the leg. The boy had a knife. He stabbed Tanner! Oh, my God Tom, Tanner saved me! He-he won't die, will he?'

'I don't know. I'll carry him home, get him to the vet. Are you alright? Did the boy hurt you?'

'I'm-I'm ok, apart from my foot. When I was running away from him, I twisted it and fell.'

'Will you be able to walk back?'

'Yeah, just about.'

Tom picked up Tanner, cradling him in his arms, holding him gently against his chest. He whispered to him. 'It's alright, boy. We'll get you fixed up. Everything'll be ok.' They began the walk home.

Tom glanced at Lisa. Her face was muddy; her clothes ripped and filthy. *He tried to rape her,* he thought.

'What happened to your friend you went to the fair with?'

'She-she stayed there. When it was time to come home, she didn't want to. So, I had to – ' Lisa sobbed again. She had trouble catching her breath.

'Hey, Lis, it'll all be ok. Don't cry. This boy from the fair – what did he look like?'

241

Lisa looked at him, then looked away.

'Lis?'

'Well, I hate to say this, but he looked – sort of – a bit like you.'

Fury exploded in Tom's chest. 'I know who it was. I know who he – '

Tanner whined in his arms. Tom looked down at him, trying to calm himself. 'Hold on boy. You'll be ok. We're nearly home.'

But Tanner wasn't ok. He looked up at Tom, then closed his eyes, his body shuddering as he took a deep breath.

It was his last.

**\* \* \***

Tom took a few more steps before he realised Tanner was dead – his body now limp and heavy, his life-force gone. Tom sank to the ground, his unearthly scream slicing through the night. The sound would haunt Lisa's dreams for years to come. Holding his beloved dog in his lap, Tom rocked back and forth, his face in Tanner's fur.

Realising Tanner was dead, Lisa kneeled next to Tom, sobbing as she put her arms around him, rocking with him in the rain.

Eventually, Tom stood up, still carrying Tanner. Lisa followed him. Tom walked to their front garden, putting Tanner's body down gently just inside at the corner. He looked at Lisa. 'Go in, there's nothing you can do. I'll be back later.'

Tom headed back down the road. Lisa shouted after him. 'Where are you going? Tom!' He didn't answer her, but broke into a jog. Seconds later he was gone. Panic seized Lisa, her heartbeat pounding in her chest, her hands shaking. She knew Tom was headed for the fair – to find the boy who'd killed Tanner.

She didn't go indoors – she went back the way she'd come. Half running, half hobbling, she got to Daffodil Crescent. Thankful lights were on in the house, she hammered on the door with her fists.

'B-bloody hell, Lisa, what's h-happened?' Billy stood in the doorway staring, her muddy clothes ripped and torn; soaking wet.

'It's Tanner. He's dead Billy! A boy from the fair, he – he killed him! And Tom – Tom's gone after him.'

Billy caught her in his arms as she crumpled in a faint.

# Chapter 28

Billy knew it was Joe Cooper. He knew it even before Lisa recovered enough to describe him. And he knew what he had to do.

His mum had come into the hall to find out what all the fuss was about. She gasped when she saw the state of Lisa's clothes. 'You poor lass, what on earth's happened?'

'We h-haven't got time to explain Mum. I'm taking her home. I might be g-gone a while.'

Billy's mum nodded, looking concerned as her son put one arm around Lisa's waist, helping her back down the path.

Hiccupping, Lisa tried to catch her breath. 'What shall we – what shall we do, Billy?'

Billy tried to sound decisive. 'First, I'll take you home. Then I'll go and f-find Tom.'

'I want to come,' she said, leaning on Billy, still limping. 'I want to come with you.'

'Not this t-time, Lis. You're in no state to walk, l-let alone run.' Knowing Lisa wouldn't easily be persuaded to stay at home he added, 'You'll slow me down.'

Lisa sighed. 'Ok. But be careful.'

'Don't worry,' he squeezed her arm. 'I know someone who can h-help.'

'Who? A policeman?'

'N-Not exactly. But he'll know what to do.' Billy faced her. 'D-don't say much to your m-mum and dad. L- leave things to me.'

Lisa nodded. Nearing her front door, her dad rushed out. He must've been watching for her, thought Billy.

'What time do – ' he started, but seeing his daughter saturated and covered in mud, he folded her in his arms. 'Are you alright? My God Lisa, what's happened?' He looked at Billy for answers as Lisa sobbed against his chest.

'She's f-fallen and h-hurt her foot, but she's ok,' said Billy. 'Sorry Mr. Grant, but I've g-got to go.' Billy turned and ran back down the path. Only then did he see the dark hump of Tanner's body amongst the battered flowers by the gate. He swallowed his heartache. He couldn't deal with it right now. Feeling guilty at leaving Lisa, he hoped she wouldn't say too much. He didn't want the police involved. There was only one person who could protect Tom – and make Cooper pay for what he'd done.

'Billy! Where's Tom? Where's he gone?' shouted Lisa's dad, competing with the rising howls of the wind.

Billy hesitated. 'I'm going to l-look for him. P-please don't worry.' He shot down Sandy Lane towards the woods before her dad could ask any more questions.

He had to find Wilbur.

* * *

Standing across the road from the fairground, Tom caught his breath. As he'd ran, he'd imagined Joe Cooper following Lisa home; creeping behind her; terrifying her. He remembered Tanner on the front lawn earlier, trying to cool down. Had he heard Lisa scream? No, that was unlikely in the noise of the thunderstorm. He must have sensed Lisa was in trouble. Tom knew that Tanner had a sixth sense; somehow, he understood when something was wrong. Without hesitation the dog had given his life to save Lisa. Cooper, like the monster he was, had left him for dead a second time.

Fury consumed Tom; stoking him like fuel stokes a fire. In his mind, Tom justified his burning desire to kill Cooper. There was no doubt of his guilt. And although Tom knew the law said he shouldn't take someone's life – his heart told him otherwise. Didn't it say so somewhere in the Bible? An eye for an eye? That seemed right and fair. To Tom, it made no difference that Tanner was a dog and Cooper a person. Tanner had been good and didn't deserve to die. Cooper was evil and didn't deserve to live – even if he *was* his brother. Even, maybe, *because* he was.

Crossing the road he could see most people had gone home, the weather closing the fair for the night. A few men still pulled down shutters, but most of the rides and stalls were in darkness, everyone having sought shelter from the storm. Tom glanced at the few still working, but Cooper wasn't among them. He made his way to the back of the field. He didn't know which caravan Cooper lived in. None of them looked homely tonight. Instead, they were harbingers of evil; grimy and flimsy, rocking in the wind. He hammered on the door of Keziah's, recognising the flowered curtains in the window. Her mum opened the door.

She stared coldly at him. 'I told you not to come here,' she hissed.

Tom ignored her. 'Keziah!' he shouted.

'Tom!' Keziah pushed past her mother to stand with Tom outside. 'What is it?'

Tom took her arm and led her away out of earshot. 'Joe Cooper tried to rape my sister tonight. And he's killed Tanner.'

'Oh my God!' She raised a hand to her mouth, her body listing before she steadied herself.

'Which caravan is his?' demanded Tom.

'He's not here, I saw him take the white van out about quarter of an hour ago. Him and Jake. I wondered why they were in so much of a hurry. Neither of them can drive – well, not legally – but they've taken the van off-road before.'

'Which way did they go?'

'Call the police Tom. Let them deal with it. Please don't – '

'Keziah, which way did they go?' Tom's eyes were wild. Black.

'They turned left out of the gate, I – '

Tom was already running back towards the entrance.

Wiping a mix of tears and rain from her face, Keziah ran to the corner of the field. The horses were huddled together, their flanks heaving. Beauty snorted and pawed the ground as thunder crashed. Keziah murmured to her as she untied the rope with shaking hands.

* * *

Billy ran round the Nissen huts, desperation making him feel sick. *Where the hell is he?* If he didn't find Wilbur soon, it would be too late. Tom would fight Cooper and Cooper would kill him. Just like he'd killed Tanner.

The tree branches swayed furiously, twigs and leaves twirling and spinning in a dance of their own. A piece of corrugated iron from one of the huts banged relentlessly, lifted then discarded by the wind. The raw sound of scraping metal set Billy's teeth on edge. As the thunder crackled, he wondered about running to the air-raid shelter. Perhaps Wilbur would be down there, away from the storm. But even if he was there, it might be too late.

He checked inside the huts, but they were empty. Going round the side he noticed their catapult target had been torn away; snatched by the greedy fingers of the storm.

Billy scanned the woods, frantically trying to think of what to do. Then he cupped his hands round his mouth, took a deep breath and shouted as loud as he could.

'Wiillllbbuurrr!'

Despite the squalling wind and rain, the ferocity of his call surprised him; echoing around the huts, it rose above the storm. Wiping his wet fringe from his eyes, he saw a dark shape emerge from the trees, coat tails flying.

'No need to shout, Billy lad. I'm right here.'

\* \* \*

Adrenaline powering her, Keziah galloped Beauty along the verge after Tom. She guided the horse with the lightest of touches, holding on to her mane and gripping tightly with her legs as they jumped fallen branches. She had to get to Tom to try and persuade him to leave things to the police. She didn't doubt Tom's courage or fighting ability – he'd be able to hold his own in a fair fight with anyone – but Joe didn't fight fair.

There was a sharp bend ahead and Keziah slowed the mare, but still felt her slip. She steadied her; then came to an abrupt halt. A large oak had fallen across the road, blocking it completely. The white van Joe had taken lay on its side, crumpled and useless. It must have crashed into the tree and turned over; the front was smashed in, the driver's door wide open. Tom, bent double with his hands on his knees, stood next to it. Keziah jumped down from Beauty and ran to him.

'Are you alright?' Keziah looked from Tom to the van.

'Yeah. Just catching my breath. I've only just got here. I think Joe's managed to get out. Looks like he's legged it.'

Keziah peered through the broken glass. The driver's seat was empty, but there was a dark shape in the passenger side, slumped down against the door wedged shut by a tangle of branches on the road.

'Tom! I think Jake's still in there!'

Tom shone his torch inside. Jake lay still, his face covered in blood. He looked dead.

'Bloody hell! Hold the torch while I get in and have a look.' Tom scrambled over the side of the van to get his top half inside and reach down towards Jake's arm. He managed to get a couple of fingers on his wrist. He felt a faint pulse. Sliding back down to the road he looked at Keziah. 'I think he's alive, but we won't be able to get him out, the dash has caved in on him. He's unconscious and his head's badly cut. Do you think Joe might have gone to call for an ambulance?'

'Not a chance,' replied Keziah. 'He only cares about himself.'

'You'd better ride back to the phone box in the village and call 999.'

'What about you?'

'I'll wait until the ambulance gets here. They might need to cut him out – tell them to send a fire engine as well.'

'Ok. I'll come back as soon as I've made the call.'

'No! Go home afterwards Kez. It's too dangerous to keep riding in this storm. I'll come and see you tomorrow.'

Keziah didn't listen. She knew Tom would go off looking for Joe. She'd have to call an ambulance for Jake, but she'd be coming straight back. Jumping on Beauty she turned and galloped towards the village green.

Tom watched her go then looked around the wreck and on the other side of the fallen tree. There was no sign of Cooper. Where would he have gone? Perhaps he'd head back to the fair now he'd crashed the van – there wasn't really anywhere else he could get to on foot. Across the field would be the quickest way – a short-cut. Tom walked to the hedge, trying to see into the blackness beyond. He flashed the torch across the field but saw nothing except the stubby stalks of harvested wheat. As he stood there, still breathing heavily and coiled like a spring, a flash of lightening lit the horizon. For a fraction of a second, movement snagged his eye. A figure, moving along the brow of the hill.

He sprinted after it.

* * *

251

Billy ran towards Wilbur. 'T-Tom's gone after-Joe Cooper! He hurt L-Lisa and he's k-k-k. K-k-killed Tanner!'

'Calm down, Billy. Cooper's killed Tanner?' Wilbur held the boy's arms. He looked like he might collapse.

'W-with a knife. He st-stabbed him.'

'And Tom's gone after him? To the fair?'

Billy nodded.

'You go home, lad. I'll go to the fair and sort things out.'

'I-I'm c-coming with you.'

There was no time to waste arguing. 'Ok. But stay out of harm's way. Don't go near Cooper.'

'O-o – ' Wilbur had already gone. Billy had never seen him run before. Despite his age, Wilbur was fast; wiry and sure-footed, he knew every inch of the woods and common. Billy struggled to keep up, his heart hammering. Wilbur didn't even stop at the road opposite the fair; he just ran straight across into the entrance. Everything was in darkness and there was no one around; only the howling wind and rain attended the shuttered rides and stalls.

Billy followed Wilbur to the back of the field. One of the caravans had a light on. Wilbur banged at the door with his fist. 'Keziah! Betty!'

Keziah's mother opened the door.

'Betty! Where's Keziah?' asked Wilbur. He wasn't even puffing.

'She went off after that boy – Tom. I don't know where they've gone. What's going on Wilbur?'

'Don't worry. I'll find them.'

Wilbur turned and headed back to the entrance; Billy close behind.

* * *

Keziah pulled up at the phone box, looping the reins over a wooden bench. As she pulled open the heavy door and stepped inside, it swung closed behind her. The glass steamed up; rain lashing the little square windows. She picked up the black receiver and dialled 999. They'd send an ambulance, the woman said, her voice high-pitched and tinny. And yes, they'd send a fire engine too. They were busy tonight, but they'd be there just as soon as they could. Leaving the box, Keziah jumped back on Beauty. Two figures ran from the entrance to the fair. She wiped her arm across her eyes and squinted. Wilbur.

'Keziah!' Wilbur ran towards her and stood by Beauty, laying one hand softly on the horse's neck. The mare nuzzled him. 'Where's Tom?'

'He's a couple of miles up the road with the van. You know Joe attacked his sister and killed Tanner?'

Wilbur nodded.

'Joe took the van out with Jake, but they crashed into a tree. Joe's disappeared, but Jake's badly injured in the van. I've just called an ambulance for him. Tom said he'd wait there, but he won't – I know he'll go after Joe

– and if he finds him, Joe will – Joe will – ' she stopped, a sob escaping her. 'Oh God, oh my God…'

'It's alright Keziah. Hold on – let me get on the back of Beauty. We'll find him.'

Wilbur's voice had a calming effect. Taking a deep breath, Keziah moved Beauty next to the bench. Wilbur stood on it, then jumped up behind her.

He looked down at Billy. 'Get off home, Lad. We'll find Tom, I promise you.'

'Hold on tight Wilbur,' Keziah said over her shoulder. 'C'mon girl.' Clicking her tongue she kicked Beauty into a gallop. Thunder crashed as the horse's hooves pounded the road. They disappeared into the darkness.

Wiping the rain from his eyes, Billy tore after them.

# Chapter 29

Tom thought he'd gained ground. The figure seemed closer, but he couldn't be sure. The only time he caught sight of it was in the brief flashes of lightening. He slipped and skidded along the muddy path, chasing the figure over the ridge of the hill and down the other side. It had to be Cooper – who else would be out here?

A line of trees loomed ahead, marking the top of the old railway cutting. Cooper would go left and run down the train track, taking him back towards the fair. Tom half-ran, half-slid down the cutting, grabbing at a couple of bushes to slow himself. Reaching the bottom, he started down the track. Fifty yards on and without warning, he sprawled head first, his feet taken from under him.

'What the hell – feckin' piss off!' screamed the figure sat on the track behind him, tying his shoelace, one leg out in front of him.

Tom stood up. He knew it was Cooper. He pulled his torch from his pocket and flicked it on.

'Turn that bloody thing off! It's blindin' me!' Cooper jumped up, knocking the torch from Tom's hand. It soared in the air before hitting the ground and going out. 'Why are yer following me? Piss off before I put your lights out, too.'

'No.' Tom's voice was low; menacing. 'Not until you've paid for trying to rape my sister. And for killing my dog.'

'He's dead, is he?' Cooper sniggered, swaggering closer. 'So bloody what! And as fer that girl, she was gaggin' fer it.' He put on a high-pitched voice. ' "Give it to me, Joe, give it to me!" I can hear 'er beggin' me now!'

Tom stared at the boy in front of him, ashamed that he even looked like him.

'You left your own friend for dead in the van – you don't care about anybody or anything, do you? You're not sorry for any of it!'

'Sorry fer what?' spat Cooper, pushing his face forward into Tom's, eyeballing him. 'The dog an' girl 'ad it coming.'

Tom saw through Cooper's eyes to the horror behind. Without morals or empathy, only evil writhed there. Shocked, Tom realised a terrifying fact – Joe Cooper had no soul.

Ferocity towards this monster burned in him, consuming every last cell of his being with painful intensity. The thought that this excuse for a human being could be his twin, sickened him to the core. Unbidden, a thought struck Tom. Strong as a spear of steel – clear as the water he'd swam in that afternoon – a life-time away.

Cooper must die.

* * *

After Billy had run a mile, he stopped, a stitch in his side. Leaning against the wall of the bridge, he sucked in the night air. He was going to be too late to help, to do any good. He hoped Wilbur would get to Tom before Tom got to Cooper. Billy had faith in Wilbur. He knew he'd protect Tom – providing he got there in time. He didn't know how, exactly. Just that he would.

Billy massaged the stitch, listening to the wind. Still wild, it whipped his hair and face, but now the air smelt fresh; washed. The rain had virtually stopped, but there was still the odd flash of lightning and some grumbling thunder in the distance, the storm reluctant to leave.

Looking over the wall into the darkness, Billy tried to remember what was under this road bridge. Then it came to him. The bridge spanned the old railway cutting. A little way down the line, a sudden light arced in the air like a fire-fly, then went out. Billy caught the faint sound of raised voices, carried on the wind. Tom's voice. Then Cooper's.

Sliding in the mud down the side of the bridge, Billy steamed up the track, like the trains that used to run there.

* * *

Keziah stopped Beauty by the fallen tree as she and Wilbur slid to the ground.

'He's not here!' she shouted, looking around wildly.

Wilbur went to the van and looked inside. The ambulance hadn't arrived. If it didn't come soon, it'd be too late for Jake. He leant on the tree and closed his eyes, chanting softly to himself.

'Wilbur! What shall we do?'

'Hush Keziah. I'm calling up a friend. He'll be able to find Tom.'

A minute later, from the woods behind the van, a wolf-like dog appeared, his fur a pale grey.

'Hello boy,' murmured Wilbur, stroking the dog's ears. He turned to Keziah. 'Have you got anything that might have Tom's scent on?'

Keziah thought for a moment, then fished in her pocket, pulling out a white cotton handkerchief. 'Is this any good? He gave it to me today to dry my face.'

'We'll soon find out.' Wilbur took the hanky from her and held it to the dog's nose, who immediately turned and ran through the hedge. 'That's the way we need to go,' said Wilbur, 'but I don't know how we'll get Beauty through.'

'She'll easily jump it,' said Keziah, getting on the horse's back and taking her to the far side of the road. Giving her a run up, Keziah and Beauty flew over the hedge with a foot to spare. Wilbur climbed the locked gate into the field, Keziah helping him back up behind her.

Some of the storm clouds passed and the moon emerged, it's watery light reflecting on the dog's coat as he ran up the hill, then shot down towards the trees and railway cutting beyond. Throwing up great clods of earth, the black horse galloped behind.

* * *

Tom pulled back his right arm with every last piece of strength he had, powering his fist into Joe's stomach. He heard the sudden exhalation of air; felt the slump of his body; saw the glistening spittle fly from his mouth.

But he didn't see him reach to his back pocket for the bloodied handle of his knife.

Billy did.

'Tom, watch out!' he screamed, flying down the track. 'He's got a knife!' Cooper turned to face Billy, just as the smaller boy barged into him. They both fell to the ground; but Cooper didn't drop the knife. Tom saw it glint in the moonlight as he brought it up above his head. Tom kicked hard at Cooper's arm, his boot making contact. Cooper cried out.

'Feckin' get off me! I'll 'ave the both of yous.' He jumped up, flailing the knife around like a madman. Billy scrambled to his feet and stood by Tom. Warily they watched Cooper, not sure what to do.

'Tom! Get back!' Keziah's voice. A large grey dog ran towards them, growling at Cooper.

Tom turned to see Keziah and Wilbur riding down the cutting.

'Joe, drop the knife!' Wilbur jumped from Beauty to stand in front of Tom and Billy. 'Or you'll have to kill me first.'

'If that's what yer want,' Joe sneered. He sprang forward, thrusting the knife out in front of him. Keziah screamed. And that's when they came. From nowhere.

A pack of dogs, all breeds and sizes, materialized in front of their eyes. The grey dog joined them as they surrounded Cooper, hemming him in. Howling like coyotes they rushed at him, ripping and tearing his flesh. Too numerous for Cooper to fight off, they forced him to the ground. Staring in disbelief, Tom and Billy watched as he disappeared under the mass of heaving dogs, their forms ebbing and flowing like tides of fog. Their shapes faded; became transparent, then opaque again. They throbbed and attacked as one entity; their snarls surging then abating on the wind. For a split second, Tom thought he saw Tanner amongst them. Cooper must have screamed as they ripped him to pieces; but if he did, nobody heard him.

Their job done; the dogs disappeared. Wilbur went with them.

Tom and Billy couldn't see anything on the ground to show that Cooper had ever been there. Only Tom's broken torch remained, half-buried in the mud.

The storm stopped and the wind died; the night finally calm. Keziah slipped down from Beauty to stand by Tom. He put his arm around her and the three of them stood in silence; stunned.

Eventually, still staring reverently at the spot where the dogs had been, Billy spoke.

'The Essences,' he whispered. 'Those dogs... just like Wilbur told us. Ghosts. They came to help.'

Tom, who'd been staring at the same spot as Billy, turned to look at his friend.

Slowly, he nodded.

# Chapter 30

Tom and Billy walked either side of Beauty as Keziah rode her back to the fair. Everything was dark and silent when they got there. Keziah slipped down from the horse, tying her up with the others. Tom walked round the back of the caravans with her as she fetched a bucket of water and some hay.

'What about Cooper's mother?' whispered Tom. 'Should we tell her what's happened?'

'Yes, but not tonight, it's late. We'll tell her tomorrow.'

'Won't she be worrying about him?'

'I don't think so. She's used to him being out at all hours. And – well, they have lots of rows. They're not very close.'

'Ok. I'll come round in the morning. We can tell her together. I wonder if Jake's ok.'

'I'll find out. But to be honest, Tom – I don't really care. He's a lot like Joe.'

He kissed her softly on the cheek. 'Sleep well. And thanks for everything you did tonight.'

Keziah watched from the step of her mum's caravan until Tom and Billy disappeared from sight.

When they reached Billy's house, Tom touched his friend's arm. 'Thanks Billy,' he whispered. 'You saved my life tonight.'

A flutter of a smile touched Billy's lips but then it had gone. 'Yeah. Maybe. But I wish I'd been around to help Lisa and save Tanner.'

'Me too. But… did you see him, Billy? In amongst the other dogs that attacked Cooper? His spirit? I'm sure he was there.'

Billy nodded. 'I didn't want to say in case you hadn't seen him. His essence – I saw it. In a way, he's still alive.'

'It makes me feel a bit better,' Tom said quietly. 'But I'd rather have him back here with us.'

'Yeah. I'm really going to miss him.' Billy's voice cracked. 'Will we bury him tomorrow?'

Tom nodded. 'I'll call for you with Keziah after I've seen Cooper's mother.'

'Tom – d'you think – that Joe Cooper had an essence? That he might come back as a ghost?'

'No. There's no chance.' Tom shuddered, remembering what he'd seen in Cooper's eyes. 'He didn't have a soul.'

Tom turned to walk on, but Billy caught his sleeve. 'I nearly forgot to mention – I told Lisa not to say much to your mum and dad as I didn't want them phoning the police.'

'Oh. Ok, thanks. Night, Billy.'

When Tom got home, the downstairs lights were blazing. As he walked into the kitchen his mum and dad rushed out from the front room.

'You haven't found him then, son?' asked his dad.

For one weird moment, Tom thought he was referring to Cooper. But then realised he meant Tanner. *Lisa hasn't told them he's dead.*

'Where's Lisa?' asked Tom. 'Is she ok?'

'She's finally fallen asleep,' his mum said. 'She was really upset about her friend not coming home with her, and then falling over in the mud. She cried a lot. I think she hurt herself more than she let on. She felt a bit better after having a bath.'

Tom sat heavily on the sofa. Lisa hasn't told them anything about Cooper, either. Best to keep it like that as they wouldn't believe it, anyway. He thought quickly. 'Tanner's been hit by a car. He's – he's dead.'

'Oh my God!' His mum rushed to him, sitting by his side. He put his arm around her. His dad stood behind the sofa. Tentatively, he put a hand on Tom's shoulder, giving it a brief squeeze.

'I'm so sorry, Tom,' he said. 'He was such a great dog.'

Finally, Tom let them come. Great wracking sobs that made it hard to breathe and tore his aching chest apart.

He didn't cry alone.

* * *

In the morning, Tom spoke to Lisa in her bedroom. He told her what happened the night before. She listened wide-eyed.

'I still can't believe Tanner's gone. I probably shouldn't say this Tom, but I'm glad Cooper's dead. He deserved it.'

'You can say it to me. I'm glad he's dead too.'

'And you saw Tanner's ghost – his spirit?'

Tom nodded. 'Billy saw it as well.'

'Good. I probably shouldn't say this either, but I'm glad Tanner got his own back.'

'Yeah. I guess he did, didn't he?' He paused, fighting to hold back the tears. 'We're burying his body later, at the graves.'

'I'll come. I'll bring that old ball he loved.' A smile trembled on her face. 'Tom – you and Billy – you're both really brave.'

He winked at her as he left, closing the door gently behind him.

**\* \* \***

As Tom walked down Budds Lane, he wondered what to say to Cooper's mother. Should they tell her the truth? No, she wouldn't believe it. Perhaps it'd be better to tell her Joe left the crashed car, but they couldn't find him. But then she might want him looked for – or might hope he'd come back. He sighed. He'd ask Keziah what she thought.

When he knocked on her door, she came straight out. 'The police were here early this morning, Tom. Jake died. They got him to the hospital, but it was too late.'

'I'm not surprised. Did they know Cooper was driving?'

'Yes. They were asking lots of questions. I told them I saw them leave in the van, but nothing else.'

'Yeah. Well, even if we told them the truth they wouldn't believe us, would they?'

'No,' agreed Keziah. 'What do you think the police will do?'

'Well, they'll look for him I guess. But when they don't find him, he'll get put down as missing. They'll probably think he scarpered because of the crash.'

'What if they find his blood – where it happened?'

'I didn't see any. But if they did, they'd probably assume it was from an injury he got in the crash. There's no evidence he's dead.'

'No,' Keziah replied. 'No, there isn't.'

They walked towards Cooper's caravan hand in hand. 'Kez – what are we going to tell Cooper's mother?'

'The truth.'

'But she won't believe it.'

'She will. Bessie knows what Wilbur can do. She warned Joe often enough. Tom – ' Keziah hesitated. 'Don't be surprised if she isn't upset by his death.'

Tom's eyes flashed. 'Maybe that'd be because he wasn't hers in the first place?'

'No. I don't think so. It's because of the way he was.' Keziah glanced at him. 'I'll talk to her Tom. Leave it to me.'

She went to knock on the door, but Tom reached for her arm. 'If you tell her the truth, will she go to the police?'

Keziah shook her head. 'No. I know she won't.'

The woman who opened the door was dark-haired and worn-looking, but Tom thought she'd probably been pretty in her youth.

'Hello Bessie,' said Keziah. 'I'm sorry to tell you this, but Joe won't be coming home. Wilbur was involved. I think Joe's dead.'

The woman leant listlessly against the door frame and sighed. 'I knew it wouldn't be long before it 'appened. The police have been askin' where he is. Was 'e cruel to an animal again? Wilbur saw 'im?'

'Something like that. You know he was driving the van? He got out after the crash, but he didn't call an ambulance for Jake. Earlier he'd attacked a girl and killed a dog. I think that's why he took the van out.'

Bessie looked resigned. 'Tore up by a pack of dogs, was 'e?'

Tom's jaw dropped. 'How did you know that?'

'I saw it. His future. In the crystal ball, a couple of years back. Jus' didn't know when it'd 'appen. Thought it'd be sooner rather than later – an' so it 'as been.' She looked at Keziah. 'He was jus' bad, Kez, I'm sorry to say. Bad to the bone. T'was nothin' I could do to change 'im.'

'Maybe,' Tom interrupted, 'Maybe if you hadn't stolen him from the barn, he wouldn't have turned out so bad! He was my twin brother.'

The woman looked at him, a puzzled expression on her face. 'I ne'er took Joe from no barn! What d'yer mean? He ain't your brother! He was my own son, more's the pity. A bad seed, jus' like his bloody father.'

'But Wilbur said he saw you take a baby from the barn!' Tom shouted. 'When my mum went back the baby had gone – you stole it!'

The woman's face changed; softening with realisation. She didn't look so old. But as she looked at Keziah, she frowned again. 'Your Ma should 'ave told you. I did take a baby from the old barn. Near on sixteen year ago, now. But the baby I took wasn't Joe. I'd already had 'im. His dad was still 'ere so 'e was only a few months old.'

'So why did you take the baby?' Tom demanded. 'And what did you do with it?'

'I 'eard it crying. I thought someone had abandoned the poor wee thing, left there in the dark. That's why I took it. I gave the baby to your Ma Keziah, because she didn't have none of her own.'

The blood drained from Keziah's face.

'I'm sorry if it's a shock lass,' Cooper's mother continued. 'She should 'ave told you she wasn't your real Ma. I thought you'd been left there; I didn't know anyone was comin' back for you, or that you had a twin. I'd never 'ave taken you if I'd known.'

Tom turned and looked incredulously at Keziah. 'You're my twin?' But as he took in her dark hair and blue eyes, so much like his own, he knew it was true.

As Keziah's legs buckled, Tom reached out to catch her.

# Chapter 31

'Bring her in an' sit 'er down lad,' Bessie said, 'I'll make a cup o' tea.'

Tom helped Keziah to the chairs around the little clover-leaf table, a fortune teller's crystal ball in the centre. She avoided his eyes as he sat beside her.

'Drink this love,' Bessie said, placing a mug of strong tea in front of Keziah, 'it'll help with the shock.'

She put two more mugs of tea on the table before sitting down.

'Don't blame your Ma, Kez. She should 'ave told yer, but prob'ly worried you'd be upset. She loves you like her own, yer know.'

Keziah stared at the green velvet table top, nodding slowly. She picked up the mug in front of her and took a sip of the sweet dark tea.

'I know Ma loves me,' she said quietly. 'And I don't blame her. Or you, Bessie. You were only doing what you thought best for the baby – for me. But… it's just the shock I think. Everything I took for granted – ' A tear slid down her cheek.

'Now love, don't go upsettin' yerself.' Bessie passed her a tissue.

Tom knew exactly how she felt; he ached to hold her. But he couldn't – not in the way he had before, anyway. Now he knew she was his sister; she couldn't be his girl-friend. He felt confused; unsure how to feel. Should he be pleased? It meant that Cooper hadn't been his brother, after all. But how could he stop loving Keziah in the way that he did?

Bessie looked at him. 'Is yer Ma in the village, lad?'

'No,' Tom said, looking down at his hands. 'She died when I was four.'

'Oh. I'm sorry 'bout that,' Bessie said. 'What about your Pa?'

'I don't know who he was.'

'So, who are yer livin' with?'

'A couple that adopted me – well, sort of. Friends of my mum's sister.'

Bessie nodded. 'I see. An' do they look after yer well? Do they love yer?'

'Yes,' Tom said. 'Very much.'

'Well, there y'are then!' Bessie reached for Keziah's hand. 'There's no need to cry, lass. You've both been brought up by other people that love yer. An' now you've found each other. An' what hansom' twins yer be! Now get that tea down yer afore it's cold.'

Despite her tears, Keziah managed a tremulous smile. She looked at Tom.

'Hello, my handsome twin brother,' she said.

**\* \* \***

271

Half an hour later, Tom called for Billy.

'Where's Keziah?' Billy asked.

'She needed to talk with her mum. She'll meet us at the graves around one o'clock. That'll give us time to dig the hole. C'mon, we'll get a fork and spade from Dad's shed.'

Carrying one each on their shoulders through Jackdaw Woods, Billy glanced at Tom. 'Do you think Wilbur will come when we bury Tanner?'

'I'm not sure. But I don't think so. I've a strange feeling that we may never see Wilbur again.'

'I felt that too,' replied Billy. 'Last night, when he disappeared with the dogs. I don't know why, but it felt like he'd gone for good.'

They walked on in silence for a while but as they passed close to the air-raid shelter, Tom spoke.

'I've found out that Joe wasn't my twin.'

'Oh? How do you know?'

'When we talked to his mother this morning – she admitted she'd taken a baby from the barn. Only the baby wasn't Joe.'

Billy frowned. 'Who was it then?'

'Keziah.'

Billy let out a long low whistle. 'Well, I never.'

'Joe's mum thought the baby had been abandoned, that's why she took it. But she already had Joe, he was a few months old. She gave the baby to Keziah's mother who couldn't have children of her own.'

'Keziah's nice. I'm glad Joe wasn't your twin – I never thought he was, anyway.'

'You liar, Billy!'

Billy grinned. 'Yeah, well. You've got two spunky sisters now.'

They'd reached the bramble-covered bank which led through the bracken to the graves.

'Looks like we're not going to need these tools, after all.' Tom was looking to the far side of the clearing, at a freshly dug hole big enough for a dog. As they walked over to it, Tom could see a wooden cross in the ground at one end. When he got close enough, he read the carved words on the cross. "Tanner. A good dog. R.I.P."

'Wilbur,' Tom said quietly. 'Wilbur's done this.'

Billy didn't doubt it.

* * *

They walked back slowly, knowing they'd be carrying Tanner's body along here soon. Lisa met them in the lane outside the house. 'Mum's got you both some lunch.'

Neither boy was hungry, but they went in the kitchen and sat at the table. Elsie brought over bacon sandwiches. They managed a few bites, but neither boy tasted anything. Tom got them both a glass of Tizer and looked at the clock.

'It's quarter past twelve. We need to go soon.'

Gulping down their drinks, they went to the shed for an old sheet to carry Tanner in. When they reached his body, he'd already been wrapped in a dark grey blanket. Tom thought his dad must have done it last night before going to bed.

Lisa joined them, carrying Tanner's ball and some yellow daisy-type flowers she'd picked from the back garden. 'I've told Mum and Dad that we're burying Tanner at the graves.'

Tom nodded. He lifted one end of the blanket and Billy got the other. Putting the wrapped body on the sheet, they carried it between them, Lisa walking beside Billy. None of them noticed Elsie and Reg watching from the kitchen window.

They were nearly there when Billy said, 'I'd like to read something out. For Tanner.'

'Yeah,' Tom said. 'Of course.'

They placed Tanner's body down gently at the side of the grave as Keziah arrived on Beauty. Jumping down and looping the reins over a branch, she stood at Tom's side, briefly giving a half-smile to Billy and Lisa.

'Let's put Tanner in the grave first,' Tom said, 'then you can do your reading before we fill it in.' The two boys lowered him into the hole. Billy pulled a folded piece of paper from his pocket and opened it up, smoothing it against his trousers.

'We're here to say goodbye, Tanner,' started Billy, the paper shaking in his hand. 'You were the best dog I've ever known. I'm glad we found you and got to know you. You loved us very much, and we loved you very much.' Lisa started crying. Billy looked up as Tom put his arm around her. 'You were very, very brave,' Billy went on, 'and lost your life because of it. Lisa saved you from the chicken farmer, and you saved Lisa from Joe Cooper. We will never forget you, Tanner. And we know — ' Billy swallowed and took a deep breath, 'we know you live on.'

The tears rimming Billy's eyes fell down his face as he thrust his hand in his pocket again. He pulled out a sausage his mum had cooked him for breakfast, throwing it into the grave. Tom fished in his own pocket for the sixpenny piece Tanner had dug up two years ago. Never having spent it, the silver coin glimmered in the sunlight as Tom threw it in.

'We'll miss you, boy,' he whispered.

A blackbird chirruped nearby as Lisa stepped forward, dropping in Tanner's ball and scattering some of the flowers. The rest she placed by the cross.

Then Tom and Billy filled the grave, pushing in the soil and the tears.

# Chapter 32

They walked back in silence, Keziah leading Beauty instead of riding her. The rhythmic plod of her hooves was calming; a background to their thoughts.

They were nearly back before Tom spoke.

'That was a really good speech, Billy. D'you know, you didn't stutter once.'

'Thanks. I don't know how or why, but I seem to have lost my stutter over the last couple of days.'

'Well, don't go looking for it,' Tom said.

Billy grinned. 'Have you told Lisa about Cooper not being your twin?'

'What?' asked Lisa. 'What did you say, Billy?'

Tom said, 'I don't think I told you, and maybe Mum and Dad didn't say? I had a twin that was taken when I was born.'

'Really? No one said. What do you mean, it was taken?'

'My mum had us in a barn. She took me to safety, but when she went back for the other baby it had gone. Somebody took it, thinking it was abandoned.'

'Oh no! That's awful, I didn't know. And what Billy said – did you think that horrible boy Joe Cooper was your twin?'

'Yes, for a while. But he wasn't. And guess what? I found out this morning that Keziah's my twin sister.'

Lisa stopped walking and looked at Keziah, open-mouthed. 'Oh, wow! That's great! So, you're my sister too. Sort of.'

Keziah linked her arm through Lisa's and smiled at her. 'I've always wanted a sister.'

'Me too,' Lisa smiled back. 'Much better than a brother, any day.'

'Oiy!' Tom said. 'I heard that.'

Lisa giggled.

'Tom told me you like horses?' Keziah continued.

'Oh yes,' Lisa said, looking at Beauty. 'But I've never ridden one.'

'I'll teach you how to ride if you like.'

'That would be fantastic!'

Tom dropped back to walk with Billy, leaving the girls to chat. 'Thanks again Billy. For everything. You're a great friend.'

'Yeah,' Billy replied. 'So are you.'

* * *

The next day, Tom introduced Keziah to his parents, and the day after that to his Aunty Joyce, who'd been ecstatic that Tom's twin had been found. For a couple of hours, plying them with delicious home-made cake, Joyce told them about her sister – the mother they'd never known.

'I only wish Kathy was still alive to meet you,' said Joyce. 'You're so much like her, Keziah. I've got a few photos here.'

Keziah eagerly looked through the photos, and although they were in black and white, anyone would see the resemblance. 'Have you seen these, Tom?' Keziah asked.

'Yeah, Aunty Joyce showed them to me a while ago, when I first found out I was adopted. But I hadn't met you then. And when I did meet you, I didn't think for one moment that you might be my twin – I had no reason to.' Tom coloured up. 'I just thought you were beautiful.' He looked down at the carpet.

'Would you like to meet your grandparents?' Joyce asked. 'I know they'd be delighted to find out they've twin grandchildren.'

Tom looked at Keziah. 'I'm happy to, if you are?'

'Yes. I'd like that,' Keziah smiled. 'Can you arrange it before the fair moves on next week?'

'Yes, I'm sure I can. When the fair goes, you'll stay in touch until you come back?'

'Of course!' said Keziah. 'I've gained a lovely brother and aunty I never knew I had. I don't want to lose you for a second time.'

'We don't want to lose you, either,' Joyce said, hugging her.

\* \* \*

278

Their grandparents place seemed impressive to Tom, the gravel drive running through trees to the front door. The thatched cottage was like something off a box of chocolates.

Tom got out of his aunt's car and stood with Keziah, suddenly feeling nervous. He started to reach for her hand; but dropped his arm again, remembering.

'They're really looking forward to meeting you both,' Joyce said, as two figures appeared in the doorway.

'Tom? Keziah? I'm your Nan, and this is your Grandad,' the woman said, walking towards them. 'We're so very pleased to meet you.'

Seeing the glint of tears in her eyes, Tom walked forward, smelling her lavender perfume as he wrapped her in his arms, his nervousness gone. Their grandad hugged Keziah as they walked into the house.

All afternoon, Tom and Keziah talked of their lives and asked questions about their mother. Their grandparents delighted in recalling happy memories of their youngest daughter, and passing round photos of her.

'You both look so much like her,' said their grandfather as his wife made tea in the kitchen, 'and you both seem to have Kathy's sweet nature. We wish she'd told us about the pregnancy. Although we'd have been shocked to start with, we would've come round. But she was strong and feisty and made her own decisions. She had a backbone of steel.'

'I think that's the bit Keziah's inherited,' said Tom, winking at his twin.

Their grandad smiled. 'She fought so hard to stay alive – ' his voice wavered and he swallowed. 'But now – we find she's left us a glorious gift of two grandchildren.'

Their grandmother wheeled in a trolley stacked with sandwiches, cakes and fine bone china. A spiral of steam escaped from the spout of a dainty teapot painted with flowers; a jug of lemonade clinked with ice and slices of lemon.

She looked at her husband. 'Have you told Tom about the neighbour's dog?'

'I was just about to, dear. Tom – your Tanner, well, it sounds like he was a grand dog. It's just that our neighbour – their dog has recently had three pups. Two of them have got new homes, but there's one male left. When Joyce told us that you'd lost your dog – we wondered if you might like the puppy? Or is it too soon?'

Tom heard the whirring mechanism inside the grand-father clock in the corner, just before it struck the hour. He hadn't given a thought to getting another dog. How do you replace a dog like Tanner?

'You don't have to make a decision now, Tom,' said his nan. 'Have a think about it.'

Keziah turned to him. 'It wouldn't hurt to see the puppy, Tom. Like Nan says, you can decide later.'

Tom nodded. 'Would that be ok?'

'After we've eaten, we'll walk round there and find out,' smiled his grandad.

* * *

Tom and Keziah both gasped when they saw the puppy. The colour of autumn bracken and his warm brown eyes flecked with amber, he was a miniature version of Tanner. The mum dog was golden, about the same size as Tanner had been.

'He's exactly like him!' exclaimed Tom, letting the pup lick his fingers. 'Do you know who the pup's father was?'

'No, we don't,' the neighbour said. 'We didn't intend for her to have pups. It was a real surprise – we just thought she was getting a bit fat.'

Tom couldn't stop grinning. 'I'd love to have him, if that's ok?'

'Joyce has already told us you'd give him a really good home, so that's fine by us,' said the man. 'He's a lovely little dog. I think they call that colour apricot.'

His grandad squeezed his shoulder. 'Can the boy take him now, George?'

'Yes, of course. We're glad he's found a good home.'

Tom squatted down and they all laughed as the pup ran to him, jumping into his arms.

* * *

A few days later, Tom, Billy and Lisa took the pup with them to say goodbye to Keziah. The fair was getting

281

ready to move on. They all walked to the village green across the road, not wanting Keziah to go, but knowing that she had to.

'Have you decided on a name for him?' asked Keziah, bending to stroke the pup.

'Not yet,' replied Tom.

'He'll be lucky to get a name before Christmas,' grinned Billy, 'it took Tom ages to decide on a name for Tanner.'

'There's loads of names on here,' Lisa said, as they passed the old war memorial of fallen soldiers, shaped as a cross.

'Look!' Billy said. 'There's a Wilbur. Wilbur F. Garrity. Died in World War One. I've never noticed that before.'

'That's what I'll call the pup,' Tom said, picking him up. 'Wilbur.' The little dog licked his hand.

Lisa wandered round the other side of the stone cross, still looking at the inscriptions.

Billy lowered his voice. 'Great name. I miss old Wilbur. Do you think – do you think this Wilbur – this Wilbur F. Garrity – could've been – '

He didn't need to finish. Tom stopped rubbing the pup's velvety ear and looked at his friend with shining eyes.

'Non omnis moriar,' he said.

'Not all of me shall die,' Keziah whispered.


### THE END.

# Author note.

Dear reader, thank you for reading my debut novel, which took around 4 years to complete from conception to typing 'The End'! I really hope you enjoyed it. Word of mouth and reviews are crucial to any author's success, so if you enjoyed 'when the first conker falls', please leave a brief review on Amazon and tell your friends about it! If you would like to hear news about special offers, promotions and my next book, please sign up for my newsletter on my website at www.sldavisauthor.com

'Til we meet again between the pages of my next book...

Sarah.

\*\*\*

# Acknowledgements

I wouldn't have been able to write this book without the help of my critique group and fellow writers. Grateful thanks to Dai Henley, H.Noss, Di Ingram and Barbara Needham.

I also wish to thank Sue Harrap and everyone who has supported me by being a beta-reader or part of my launch team. You know who you are!

\* \* \*

## Also by the same author:

'Twists and Churns' – Thirteen dark tales from England.
(Short stories – mild horror/black humour.)
Available on Amazon .